Beth Cato

CHEDDAR LUCK NEXT TIME

T0349123

DATURA

DATURA BOOKS
An imprint of Watkins Media Ltd

Unit 11, Shepperton House
89-93 Shepperton Road
London N1 3DF
UK

daturabooks.com
twitter.com/daturabooks
Early Bird gets the cheese

A Datura Books paperback original, 2025

Edited by April Northall and Andrew Hook
Cover by Sarah O'Flaherty
Set in Meridien

ISBN 978 1 91552 347 1
Ebook ISBN 978 1 91552 348 8

Printed and bound in the United Kingdom by CPI Group (UK) Ltd, Croydon CR0 4YY

The manufacturer's authorised representative in the EU for product safety is eucomply OÜ - Pärnu mnt 139b-14, 11317 Tallinn, Estonia, hello@eucompliancepartner.com; www.eucompliancepartner.com

9 8 7 6 5 4 3 2 1

*For Grandma, who yearned to finish her own mystery novel.
I know that if I had the chance to tell her that my first cozy
mystery was about cheese, she would nod and say,
"Of course it is."*

Chapter One

For many years, I had been of the belief that a sizable hoard of delicious cheese is what makes a house a home. By that rule, my grandma's old place was going to be the best home ever.

"Oh, goodness, why do I have so much cheese?" I said aloud, groaning. The laden cardboard box in my arms groaned too. My cheese payload tested the packing tape at the bottom in a worrisome way. I kicked through the partially open door into the tiny house that Grandma had made into her Kitchen. That's 'Kitchen' with capital K, as it took up the majority of the outbuilding and was the kind of facility that most cooks could only dream about. I staggered a few more steps to slide the cardboard onto the granite-countered island alongside more boxes.

So many boxes. Stacks upon stacks everywhere. The room stank of musty cardboard.

Stress hit me like a tidal wave. I had to pause for a second to blink back tears. More than anything, I wanted to sit down and relax by mindlessly scrolling social media for hours, cooing over cheese board pictures and silly cat videos, but I knew I'd scarcely have time to check my email these next few days, let alone anything else. The Kitchen had to be sorted, pronto. I had orders that needed to be processed and delivered starting tomorrow. No days off for the self-employed businesswoman.

Overwhelmed as I was, that designation made me grin. I was a self-employed businesswoman! After years of being a night-shift grocery stocker, I could finally afford to go full-time on my cheese board business, Cheese Boards by Bird.

I hated that Grandma's death was what had made it all possible, though.

After my parents died last year, Grandma had pushed me to become a joint owner of her property and accounts just in case something happened to her as well. Her morbid foresight had spared me the usual five-year wait necessary to inherit an estate after a person vanishes. That was, legally, what she was to the state of California: a missing person, presumed drowned in the Pacific Ocean, no remains found. I still couldn't accept that she was gone. Grandma swam as if she was half fish. When I was a kid, I'd even watched her save a kid from drowning at Pismo Beach! On the day she vanished, though, witnesses on the beach said she'd been in distress, clutching her head, waving her arms. I had to wonder if she'd had some sudden health episode, like a heart attack, but she was probably in better physical condition than I was. Grandma didn't even suffer from seasonal allergies.

I could've moved onto her property right away, but I kept waiting for her body to be found. I kept waiting for that nebulous thing that people call "closure." As the six-month point neared, I had to accept that I was never going to feel right about the situation; I just needed to move forward. That's what Grandma would've wanted. So here I was, finally moving onto the acreage that she'd owned for some thirty years.

"Okay, in you go, Manchego," I said to the half-round of Spanish sheep cheese as I shoved it into the fridge. I liked to talk to myself. For me, it was a major form of 'stimming,' self-stimulation that helped me organize my thoughts and work through stress.

I shifted the rest of my stock to the fridge, quickly filling two interior shelves in the jumbo-sized cold storage unit. I'd been renting space at a commercial kitchen in San Luis Obispo for the past year as I developed my business. Meanwhile, Grandma had run her own cottage business out of the Kitchen, making preserves and jams to sell at local farmer's markets. There was still a half-full pantry of her olallieberry, fig, blueberry, and strawberry jars. I'd be using her stockpile as cheese accompaniments for months to come.

I wiped away a tear. Grandma would love to know that she was still taking care of me in lots of little ways. She had never been a stereotypical Grandma. She made fruit preserves, sure, but she also taught me how to hot-wire a car when I was seven. She didn't say "I love you" very often, but I always knew that she adored me, no matter what. I'd been very close to my parents, too, but my relationship with Grandma had been something special. "You're my living legacy," she told me in one of our final conversations. Those words meant a lot to me now.

I returned to my blue Kia Soul in the driveway, gravel and old acorns crunching under my feet. Oak trees encircled the house and flanked the drive out to the semi-paved road that wound through the rounded California hills. The Pacific Ocean met the shore mere miles away. Sometimes the scent drifted this far, all salty and fresh.

I suddenly heard music: a heavy bass, like an electronic club dance track. I faced east, looking farther up the road, wondering if I was imagining things. No one lived up that way. From what Grandma had told me, that tail end of the road was mostly used by the power company for line maintenance, though the occasional lost tourist ended up that way as well.

I carried my next box into the house. I could still hear the music.

Like most of the nearby village of Foghorn, Grandma's place – well, my place now – was built in the 1920s in an English cottage style with white-washed walls, exposed wooden beams, and a customized roof curved to mimic thatch. I'd kept most of Grandma's furniture since I barely had any of my own, but few pieces could be used right now. The living room was a labyrinth of boxes and garbage bags filled with stuff. I wormed my way to the tiny kitchen. Boxes made it feel even smaller than it was. I unpacked my personal cheese stash, plus a few condiments and other things, into Grandma's fridge. I'd moved all of my personal cold items into my commercial fridge space two days ago so that I could deep-clean my apartment.

"Ugh, I need to figure out how to arrange things in here. I might need to redo the shelves." I squatted, staring into the fridge, then shook my head as I felt my anxiety level rise. "No, no. That needs to wait."

I stood, brushing my hands on my black pants. My entire wardrobe consisted of ten pairs of yoga pants. I had a broader variety of tops, but whether they were short or long-sleeved, they were all loose-fitting and comfortable.

Really, a need for "comfortable" defined my daily existence. Little aggravations could send me into something beyond a panic attack. A scratchy tag on a shirt did more than feel itchy in one spot; it made me feel as though a cup of live spiders had been poured down my back. A sudden loud noise, like a breached emergency exit in a store, did more than hurt my ears; my whole world became that horrible sound, as if nothing else existed.

As I closed the fridge, I heard a knock from the front of the house. My first thought was that maybe this was the person who'd been playing the loud music, but as I peered out the peephole, the fish-eye view revealed a familiar scowl.

"Grizz!" I almost shouted as I flung the door open.

His scowl evaporated in an instant as his pale brown skin creased in a toothy smile. "Bird! How goes it? You get everything out of S-L-O?" Central California locals often dropped San Luis Obispo down to its initials.

Grizz had been Grandma's only neighbor on this road as long as I'd been alive. I'd sometimes pondered if he'd been more than a friend to Grandma, but the answer to that didn't matter much. Whatever the truth, he'd always been a sweet, if gruff, grandfatherly figure to me.

"Yes," I said. "My apartment inspection was done at seven this morning. After that, I cleared out my commercial kitchen space. All of my stuff is here." I gestured at the brown cardboard towers that loomed behind me. "Things are going well!" I didn't need him to worry about me any more than he already did.

He looked away, his expression darkening. "Except for *that*."

It took me a second to realize he was talking about the music. "Do you know where that's coming from?"

"The back of your property. It's a local punk kid, Chase Perkins. He might be alone or with just a couple o' people. The other night, he had a whole group out there playing music and partying and whatever. They were target shooting, aiming at some old posters as they–"

"What? Using real guns and bullets, or like paintball?" The idea of drunken people with guns on my property was horrifying. On the other hand, picturing paintball splatter on beautiful tree trunks also enraged me.

"Guns, bullets, the real deal." He sounded grim. "So I sneaked over and hid in the brush, started blasting an air horn. You never saw kids scatter so fast! It was like I dropped ants on 'em." He cackled.

"Grizz! You could've been shot!"

He shrugged. His blue-striped button-up shirt revealed the gauntness of his bony shoulders. "Woulda been more dangerous to let them be, since you're moved in now. I haven't found any bullets that've hit the house, and I have paced around to look, but it could happen. Plus, if they're goofing off and shooting this summer, they could start a fire with a ricochet. Or by being careless as they smoke cigarettes out there. Your place has a decent fire break around it." He gestured toward the tilled land that surrounded the house. The furrows held some low green weeds. "But all it takes is some sparks on the wind and these buildings could still go up. If the fire traveled a bit more, my trailer is right up against a lot of trees. I'd be toast, followed by most of Foghorn."

California had become dryer and dryer. The Central Coast hadn't experienced the massive fires that both ends of the state had suffered in recent years, but the threat was very real.

"Why didn't you tell me about this Chase Perkins guy?" I asked. "How long has this been going on?"

"Maybe a month. Not every day. Just here and there." He shrugged. "I didn't tell you because you've been under a lot of stress with the legal stuff and the move. No need to add to that."

I sighed. His silence hadn't eased my burden one bit, only delayed the onslaught. "I can call the sheriff's office right now–"

"And they'll probably show up sometime after dark, if they come at all." He spat off the side of my porch.

"Well, let's go talk to Chase." I stepped out to join Grizz, closing and locking the door behind me. The idea of relying on deputies hadn't enthused me, anyway; I'd lost a lot of faith in police and the legal system in the aftermath of my parents' car accident.

Grizz shook his head with the ferocity of a wet dog trying to dry off. "No, you stay here, I can–"

"I'm the property owner." How long would it take for that sentence to stop feeling weird? "I need to be there. Give me a moment to lock up the Kitchen." I'd need to be diligent about locking up everything if Chase and other people kept lurking about.

"Bird. Chase is not a good guy. A lot of people in town say he swished Slocombe House last year to get revenge on 'em after they accused him of vandalism."

I blinked. "Swished?"

"Yes, swished. Someone did a fake call to 9-1-1, saying a hostage situation was going on with people shot, causing all the emergency personnel on the Central Coast to come to Foghorn with guns drawn. There was a wedding going on there with five-hundred guests–"

Despite the horrible subject matter, a laugh escaped me as I realized his error. "Swatted. You're saying Chase may have swatted Slocombe House, not swished." It essentially meant someone had maliciously set up an innocent person to be targeted by a SWAT team or other law enforcement.

Grizz snorted. "Swished, swatted, I can't keep up with

the lingo these days. But, yeah. It created some ugly drama there. Ruined the wedding. A big lawsuit is still underway because the bride's family wants a refund. There's no proof that Chase did it, but everyone figures it was him."

"That kind of 9-1-1 call can be almost impossible to trace to the actual source," I muttered, shuddering. "And even if the police manage to track down a suspect, the legal system doesn't know how to handle those cases. The crime is too new."

His eyes narrowed. "You know all about this kind of thing?"

"Well, yeah. I'm very active online. I have to know about the threats that are out there."

"The way this world is going, I just don't know." Grizz heavily exhaled. "Leave Chase Perkins to me. I'm an old fart. Let me take the risk. You don't need to... You have to understand, he's *bad*." He struggled for words. "I didn't want to mention this because of what happened to your parents, but you oughta know, he's been in legal trouble because of his road rage. Last year, he lost his temper and terrorized some woman on one of those windy roads closer to Paso Robles. She ended up driving into a shallow ravine."

"How was she?" I asked, suddenly breathless.

"Banged up, but okay. Chase was arrested after that, but he was out again all too soon. I think the case is still dragging on. He's been a terror on the roads around here for years. That kind of result was bound to happen eventually."

"Grizz, the fact remains that I need to get work done here, and I can't do that with his noise in the background." The racket was already making me feel fluttery with anxiety. My ear plugs could block out the noise, but not the just-detectable reverberations of heavy bass. "I need to try to reason with him. We're all adults here, right? We can bring in the authorities after that, if necessary."

He didn't look happy. "Fine. But I'm going with you." I didn't quibble with that.

We rode to the back of the property in his big old Chevy pick-up truck. The diesel-powered hulk definitely had a more threatening aura than my boxy little Kia. Grizz parked beside a battered older-model sedan. Was Chase even driving legally? I really didn't like the idea of him zooming along my isolated stretch of road.

"There's a beaten path here," I murmured. The ground was largely bare and uneven.

"Takes a lot of feet to do that," Grizz said.

I nodded, trying to hide my shakiness. Not only was the incredibly loud music getting to me, but I was really, truly hoping this guy wasn't armed right now.

We trudged up a slight slope and into a grove of trees. At the very center stood a single man, staring at a phone in his hand. He looked to be about my age, in his mid-twenties, his brown hair cropped short. He glanced at us with dazed indifference. Smoke drifted from the cigarette held near his face – and even more arose from the fire in a makeshift pit.

I reacted with a gasp, dashing forward to knock dirt onto the fire with both of my feet. Only then did I stomp on the low fire, belatedly noticing the hot dog on a skewer that had been perched over the flames and was now mashed beneath my boots.

Chase's face distorted in fury, but whatever he yelled at me was lost against the din. He glanced down to tap his phone screen. The music stopped abruptly, my ears and brain aching in the new quiet.

"What the hell!" sputtered Chase.

"This is my property! You can't go around setting fires. We haven't had rain in weeks!" I snapped. An open beer box rested unevenly beside a fold-out camping chair. I reached into the dark interior of the box, finding one can at the bottom.

"You can't–" he began to say. His sentence ended in a horrified gasp as I popped open the can to dump the contents onto the dying fire.

"I can. And put that cigarette out, too. What, do you have a death wish? You'll either burn to death or get lung cancer – both horrible choices!"

Chase looked both angry and bewildered. "I don't know who you are, lady, but shut up! My favorite song was playing!"

That was what he fixated on? "You're on my property. Put your cigarette out, right now," I repeated as I motioned to the wet, smoldering firepit.

Chase looked at Grizz. "Can't you shut her up, old man?"

Grizz held up his hands and shook his head. "Kid, I keep hoping you'll grow a brain, but I guess today is not that day."

Often, I overthink scenarios to the point of paralysis, but his disrespect and inaction drove me into motion. I lunged forward and plucked the cigarette from his fingers, dropping it into the firepit as I backstepped.

"You– You–" Chase advanced on me, murder in his eyes. Fear sent a cold spike deep into my gut. Grizz had been right. I shouldn't have thought I could rationalize with Chase.

"Hey." Grizz dove between us, his arms outstretched. "Chase, don't you dare lay a hand on her."

"Or what?" He sneered. "You always talk big with your threats, old man, but you're full of–"

Grizz's face turned cold and impassive in a way I'd never seen before. "Do not mess with Bird Nichols." Chase seemed to be as caught off guard by Grizz's ominous shift as I was. Chase stood still, looking between us with narrowed eyes.

"Let's start over." I tried to keep my voice level. "As Grizz just mentioned, I'm Bird Nichols. You, Chase Perkins, are trespassing on my land. I want you and all of this stuff gone." I motioned to indicate the mess around us. Camping chairs, with wilted cardboard acting as tables, encircled the fire pit. Aluminum cans and snack food packaging peeked out from beneath the leaves. There were gun casings, too.

"Or what?" Chase's arms crossed his chest as he leered at me. He had the lean muscle mass of someone who worked out.

His intimidation tactic didn't increase my fear. No, it angered me. "Get this junk out of here within the next day and I won't report you to the sheriff's office," I said, glaring him down. Grizz made a small grunt of disapproval.

"The sheriff's office." Chase bleated out a laugh. "They're a joke."

"No, they're not," I said, though I didn't believe my own words. I had more belief in the Easter Bunny than I did in law enforcement. "All they need is evidence of your crimes. How many of these items here have your fingerprints and DNA on them, you think?"

His bravado faltered as he looked around, but then his scowl returned. "They can't pin nothing on me." As high tension as the moment was, I barely bit back the urge to correct his speech. "Trespassing isn't that big of a charge, anyway."

"You've done more than trespass in this town. Everyone knows that. It's just a matter of time until you're locked in jail and stay there," growled Grizz. "You keep breaking your mother's heart, again and again. I don't get how–"

"You leave my mom out of this," Chase snapped with a vehemence that took Grizz aback.

"We'd like to," I said slowly, thinking through each word. Maybe we had found a way to help Chase see reason. "Clean up my woods and we won't need to bother your mom."

If Chase had a gun on him, I just knew that this is when he'd brandish it. Instead, he seemed to deflate, shaking his head. "That's what I need to do to make you both shut up and leave her alone? Fine. I'll clean everything up. Damn. I wasn't doing no big harm out here. Just chilling."

"I expect the area to be tidy by tomorrow evening. And if you come back and trash my property again, I won't give you another warning; I'll go straight to the authorities."

"Whatever." Chase rolled his eyes.

"Treat Bird with respect," snapped Grizz, stepping toward Chase.

"Grizz," I said in a low voice. No way was Grizz going to win in a fist fight with a young, athletic guy like Chase. "We're done here. Chase knows what he needs to do."

"That's right, boomer," Chase said to Grizz as he sauntered by with purposeful slowness. "I'll be back later." His gaze shifted to me as a grin grew on his face. "If you own this property, does that mean you're living in the old lady's house now?"

I wasn't always good at picking up on subtext in conversation, but I recognized that he was threatening me with some form of assault. Maybe he was even considering swatting me, just as he might've swatted Slocombe House. My heart pounding fast, I affected nonchalance. "I do. And Grizz probably knows where your mom lives too. I wouldn't mind meeting her to say hi."

Grizz grunted and nodded.

Chase looked away, shoulders hunched. "You leave her alone, hear? I said I'd get my stuff outta here. Damn." With that, he headed down the path and out of sight.

Chase's car rattled as he backed it up and lurched away. The trees and brush blocked my view of the road, but I could hear the obnoxious rumble of his engine and the crunch of his tires on gravel as he headed past my house and out toward Highway 1.

I released a long, relieved exhalation as I turned around. "That could've gone better."

"I told you, Bird, I told you not to mess with Chase." Grizz was pale with worry.

"For a man who doesn't respect women, he was sure sensitive to mentions of his mother."

"Yeah. That was weird. I've known Belinda for years. Chase's been a source of constant grief for her. I brought her up out of desperation. I didn't expect him to get that defensive."

"Does his mom live in Foghorn?" I pulled out my phone.

"Yep, has for decades. Really sweet lady; owns the salon. What're you doing, Bird?"

"Recording evidence." I held up my phone and began to record video as I walked through the grove.

"That's smart," Grizz said, "I have a couple water bottles rolling around under the seat in my truck. Let's make sure the fire is good n' out." He attended to that as I made a lap of the party zone. After the fire was thoroughly doused, he spoke up. "You gotta know that you can't trust Chase to do what's right. If he does move the trash, he may just dump it farther back in the woods. I can come up here in a couple days, clean up this garbage. I'm sorry, but I didn't realize it'd gotten this bad. I didn't get this close when I used my air horn. You asked me to watch the house, and this–"

"You did watch the house. The buildings are fine. I didn't expect you to patrol the entire acreage. Grandma wouldn't have, either."

"Your grandma would've been here with a gun the first time he intruded blaring that godawful music." His voice held fond wistfulness.

"Yeah, probably. More than once she pestered me about getting licensed to carry a gun." Which was never going to happen. I didn't have anything against responsible gun ownership, but the best noise-canceling headphones in the world couldn't transform shooting into a tolerable hobby for me. I could only imagine how horrible the recoil of a gun would feel to my body. I shuddered.

Grizz gave me a sidelong look. "She wanted to teach you lots of things."

He didn't need to say why that didn't happen. My parents had kept me away from Grandma as much as possible for about ten years. I'd only seen her, under close supervision, at Christmas and birthdays. My one big rebellion against Mom and Dad had been my decision to attend Cal Poly in San Luis Obispo so that I was only a forty-five-minute drive from Grandma. I had craved the opportunity to get to know her as an adult, on my own terms. We'd managed a few visits a month while I was at college, and usually weekly meetups after that. In hindsight, I wished that I had worked less and squeezed in more visits, but how was I to know I'd lose her so suddenly?

I made a final circuit of the grove but couldn't find any immediate dangers to the property. I stopped recording. We both stayed quiet on the short drive back to my house.

"Thanks for your help, Grizz," I said. He kept the truck running as I leaped to the ground.

"Only right that you have someone look after you now that Lucille's gone." His voice sounded especially gruff. "You call me if anything comes up, got it?"

"Got it." I waved as he left.

I entered the house, stared at the boxes, and felt impossibly exhausted. I had so much to do here, but now that my cold goods were put away, everything else in the house had to wait. My upcoming cheese orders took priority.

That's when my stomach growled, reminding me of other priorities. I glanced at my watch to find it was nearing noon. No wonder I was getting sluggish. I'd gotten up at 4 a.m. and had gone nonstop since.

I stared into my fridge. I'd used up as much stuff as possible prior to moving. What remained was cheese, three kinds of mustard, pickles, and olives. No eggs, no salad. No easy-fix carbohydrates. I had lots of other supplies in the Kitchen, but I kept a distinct separation between my personal and work foods.

That meant I needed to do some shopping.

Foghorn had a tiny grocery store. I hadn't been there since I was a young kid. Foghorn was about a quarter mile north of the turnoff to Grandma's place. I never had cause to drive that far, and she'd dismissed my suggestions to go there in recent years too.

"A bunch of snobs in that hamlet," she'd said once, blowing a raspberry. "I stopped going there years ago." She was often oblivious to the fact that she could be quite the snob herself. Or more likely, she didn't care.

The prices in such a remote, tourist-heavy locale would be awful, but I'd be spared the hour drive to Morro Bay and back. Plus, a stop in Foghorn meant an opportunity to post my advertisement fliers on whatever bulletin boards were around. I kept a file of my ads in my car. About ninety-nine percent of my clients came through the internet, especially from the photographic foodie-heaven that was Instagram, but I'd take business wherever I could get it.

My stomach growled again. I responded by reaching into my fridge for a wrapped rectangle of aged Irish cheddar. I needed immediate fortification. After all, a person should never go food shopping if they were exceedingly hungry. That's how you end up with a meal consisting of two rubbery mozzarella sticks and half a pack of Soft Batch cookies. I knew that from experience.

Chapter Two

The pothole-laden asphalt road snaked along the curvy hills toward Highway 1. To my left was a creek, tucked among greenery down a long, gradual embankment, while to my right teetered the half-rotten wooden fence of a long-gone ranch. Behind that, a slope continued upward. The hills were currently fuzzed green thanks to rain a month ago. January was considered a pseudo-spring along the Central Coast – the days could be warmer and clearer here than they were in much of the state.

I paused at the stop sign at Highway 1. Beyond a hillock covered with low, thick ice plants, the lacy lines of incoming waves created long furrows in the blue expanse of ocean. I rolled down my window a few inches so I could get a whiff of sea breeze. Any remaining tension from the confrontation with Chase dissipated under the force of that brisk, refreshing air. A gasoline tanker truck rattled past, and I took the right turn toward Foghorn.

A wooden sign done in a corny, medieval-style font read, "The Village of Foghorn, population of 45. Stop, stay, ENJOY!" The capital letters on the last word seemed needy to me. I made the right turn to enter.

"Wow, this place hasn't grown from what I remember," I muttered. The commercial heart of Foghorn consisted of a frontage road on the eastern side of the highway. About twenty businesses, all following the requisite Tudor architectural theme, faced the water. I already knew from Grandma that there was no beach here, no access to the ocean at all. Not even the local sea lions favored this tiny, harsh segment of coast; they had a major breeding and lazing spot a few miles north, closer to Piedras Blancas Light Station.

Behind the glorified strip mall and some trees was the local landmark, dubbed the House, short for Slocombe House, a 1920s estate that was now a bed and breakfast and event venue. The corporation that managed that property owned the village, too. Back when this land had been bought up a century ago, there had been some drama and rivalry between British actor-gone-Hollywood Timothy Slocombe and powerful media magnate William Randolph Hearst, who built Hearst Castle on his massive estate just south of Foghorn. According to Grandma, Hearst had won the tourism and attention game from the get-go, but Foghorn still stubbornly existed as its own entity all these years later, so Timothy Slocombe deserved some credit for that feat. She'd actually known Mr Slocombe in his later, increasingly eccentric years. He'd died before I was born.

The shops had to be open by this time of day, but as I drove through the long parking lot the place looked mostly dead to me. There was a salon and nails shop with the matter-of-fact name of Salon & Nails; I appreciated businesses that did away with any ambiguity. Beside that was a coffee shop with its half-burned-out neon sign reading OFF. Down the way was a cannabis vendor, a barber shop, and a couple empty storefronts. Foghorn Grocery at the far end looked like it was maybe twice the size of a convenience store, which didn't instill in me much confidence in their offerings. They probably carried standard supermarket cheese. Better than nothing, I supposed, but, ugh.

Grandma had insisted that the people of Foghorn were snobs, but so was I – at least for cheese. I could barely tolerate commodity cheeses, the sort that combined the milk of thousands of cows across a broad area without a care for terroir – the unique flavors of an area – or for aging their cheese to develop any character. I'd lived paycheck to paycheck since I'd gone to college, but my one indulgence was quality cheese.

My grimace faded as I caught sight of a placard on the sidewalk with a red arrow pointing left with bold words screaming GRILLED CHEESE.

I'd been so focused on the strip mall, I hadn't even noticed the small building by itself in the parking lot. It'd been done up like a thatched hut. The tiny flat canopy in front of the ordering window clarified what the building had once been: a gas station, maybe from some bygone era like the 1950s. The sign on the wall dubbed it QUESOQUICK. Queso, meaning cheese. Quick, meaning fast. Oh, this was exactly what I needed. I'd still go to the grocery store for supplies in a bit, but I could get my lunch without worrying about digging through boxes for my dishes and forks.

I parked.

A couple with two bouncy kids stood ahead of me beneath the deep shadows of the overhang. Quesoquick didn't have a drive-through, but signs stated they had pickup and takeout, with online order-ahead available. I needed to remember that.

The family carried off their orders in two big brown paper bags. "Give me mine first! Gimme!" cried a small child as they ambled back toward their car. I waited until they were well past before I moved up to the order window. The divine odor of fresh bread filled my senses. A freckled arm leaned on the windowsill. My gaze traveled up over a green apron to a face ghostly pale enough to feature in ads for sun block.

"Hello there!" he said in a friendly tone. He had an unruly scramble of red hair, the kind of bedhead that celebrities would pay hundreds of bucks to get styled. On most people, it'd look a mess, but it somehow worked for him, maybe because his smile was so congenial. "First time to Quesoquick? I can give you a minute to look."

"Thanks." It said a lot that his good looks had distracted me from studying the cheese-based menu placard beside the window. "Where do you get your cheese?" As soon as the words escaped my mouth, I cringed. All too often, I had to make a conscious effort to be tactful, especially when it came to cheese, a topic that I could blab about until people's eyes became as glazed as a donut.

He was taken aback. "I wasn't expecting the cheese inquisition!" He sounded as friendly as ever.

I burst out laughing. "*Nobody* expects the cheese inquisition!"

"You know your classic Monty Python." By his nod, I felt like I had met some high level of approval.

"You sound like you're actually British."

"I am indeed, born and bred. Moved all around the country with my mum and dad, and my properly muddled accent has become even more muddled by over a decade here in the U-S-of-A. I'm Dale Keswick, owner and proprietor of Quesoquick. Very nice to meet you."

"Keswick. Quesoquick. It's a pun!" Leave it to my brain to be utterly tactless but ready to appreciate puns.

"I can't take credit for the wit. My business name came about because the voice-to-text function on a friend's phone mangled Keswick into 'queso' and 'quick.' At the time, I was considering starting a bakery. I realized, 'Hey, I could do more than bake bread.'" Someone unseen shuffled around in the kitchen behind him with a clatter of dishes and a gush of water.

"You should totally take credit for the wit. You took what could've been an embarrassing technological error and built an entire business on it. That's awesome."

"I like how you think." His blue eyes twinkled in a way that seemed cliché.

"My mind is pretty quirky." I had learned the hard way to never bring up my adulthood autism diagnosis with people I was meeting for the first time. Some would start to treat me as if I was incompetent, while others initiated an inquisition that was far more nosy and aggravating than any cheese inquisition. "My name is Bird Nichols. I moved to Foghorn today. I need to unpack a million and one boxes, but first I need sustenance."

I didn't think Dale's smile could get any bigger, and then it did. He'd outshine the Cheshire Cat. "A new neighbor! Well, then! Moving is a particular variety of hell. You do need urgent sustenance. What looks good to you?"

You, I thought, but at least I knew to hold back that comment. I hadn't attempted to date anyone since my parents died, and certainly had never felt the zing of instant attraction quite like this. I made myself focus on the menu. "Oh, wow, do you really make all of your bread here on site? No wonder the smell is so wonderful and strong!"

"That's right, I'm here baking every morning, bright and early. White bread and sourdough! We're only open for breakfast and lunch. On weekends in particular, we're sometimes out of loaves by noon because the breakfast crowd is as voracious as those seagulls." He motioned to the parking lot, where congregating gulls were picking at trash. "We press our sandwiches in a waffle iron. That makes the bread golden and buttery. The heat is just enough to get the cheese oozing."

I'd scanned the menu, my mouth filling with drool. "Oh, my. You do bread pudding for breakfast, too? That's one of the best foods on the planet." I laughed as I reached the lunch offerings. "Does every sandwich have a punny name? Nice. Very cheesy."

Dale leaned farther out the window. "I detect a cheese theme with you."

"Sorry, I'm probably about as subtle as a ball peen hammer. I love cheese like almost nothing else. I run a catering business called Cheese Boards by Bird."

"Those boards are popular right now," he said.

"Yes. I do mine a little differently, though. They are inspired by bento boxes." I had a hunch that he was of the right age and geekiness level to know what I was talking about.

Dale arched an eyebrow. "I know what bento boxes are, sure. How exactly do you translate that to cheese boards?"

"Wait, I don't know what a bento box is." A soft voice rang out from behind him. A thin arm nudged Dale over. "Hi, I'm the girl working the kitchen. I'm Jessie." She waved at me. She looked near my age, her skin a deep brown, thick black hair tucked up in a net.

Dale's lips parted to answer her, but I knew the definition by script and spoke up first. "Bento boxes are a Japanese thing, like a divided lunch tray or box. I keep dissimilar foods separate so people can combine them however they want right as they eat, and I set up everything in an artful way."

"You must be on Instagram, then," said Dale, nodding.

"Absolutely. That's the source of most of my business."

"I'll look you up. We're on there, too. We've had some cheese-pull pictures go viral in a major way."

I couldn't fault him for his pride in that. An ooey-gooey cheese pull was a marvel to behold. My stomach growled. His grin indicated that he had heard the rumble too.

"I guess I should heed my stomach and order some food," I said. "Let's see. I'm now a local, so let's go for the especially local sandwich. I'd love an Oh-la-la Olallieberry, please. On sourdough." Olallieberries were a major local crop, a 20th century cross of a Youngberry and a Loganberry that, to me, tasted like a milder raspberry. Grandma's olallieberry preserves were probably my favorite thing from her jam business.

"Got it!" called Jessie from the recesses of the kitchen.

"The ingredients on there won't be separated like in your boxes, you know," Dale said.

I could tell he was being mischievous, but I answered with sincerity. "It's different when cheese is *melted* with other things. That heat works magic."

"I do like to think of myself as a wizard." He nodded with utter sobriety. "Tell me, how did you end up moving out here? I didn't think there were any vacancies in the village."

"My grandma lived at the turnoff just south of here, not far from Grizz." Dale nodded in recognition. "Her name was Lucille Franklin."

"I didn't know her, sorry," said Dale. "I moved here and opened shop two years ago."

"It makes sense that you never met, then. She barely left the house over these past few years, and when she did go out, she went south to the larger towns."

"I knew your grandma!" Jessie waved as she came into view again. "She lived here, like, forever. She helped my mom change a tire one time when I was a kid, and then when I was in high school, she saved me, right in this very parking lot. We had this awesome ice cream shop here back then. I was leaving with a cone and these young guys – tourists – were trying to flirt with me, but it got creepy real quick, you know? And Lucille, she marched over, pretending to be my own grandma. She even drove me home."

"Wow," said Dale.

"Yeah," said Jessie. "Back then, I was really into gymnastics, and after that happened, I did my first self-defense course. I didn't want to feel vulnerable like that ever again, and most of all, I wanted to help other women who were in that same spot."

That brought to mind an incident that'd been buried in my memories for years: I must have been five or so, so short that I had to reach up to grip Grandma's hand as we walked toward our favorite fish and chips restaurant in Morro Bay. A man and a woman were arguing up ahead. Their actions were an angry blur to me, young as I was, but I remembered the man saying, "You're stupid," and slapping the woman across the face. Right there in public, midday, on the bustling Embarcadero.

"Bird," Grandma had said to me. "Hold onto this sign, you understand? Do not let go, do not wander." As my little fists gripped the cold metal of a signpost, Grandma stalked toward the couple. The woman was sobbing. The man didn't even glance over at Grandma as she said something to him.

A second later, he was down on both knees, and a second after that, his face was on the sidewalk.

As I inspected the memory as an adult, her actions reminded me of martial arts movies or even Star Trek's famous Vulcan neck pinch. Grandma had performed some kind of innocent-looking move that utterly disabled the jerk.

His condition attracted a lot more attention than his abuse had, but no one seemed to notice Grandma or suggest she had been involved. I suppose she seemed incapable of something like that. After all, she looked like a factory-model middle-aged white woman with a curly perm and flowery blouse. As people gathered to ask the hurt man what had happened, Grandma pulled aside the woman and offered her money, a ride, help – the exact words didn't stick in my mind, but I do remember how vigorously the woman shook her head. She refused to leave.

Grandma returned to me with an expression of sadness and disgust. If she tried to explain what happened, I don't remember, but I do recall sitting at lunch and being awed at how she'd assaulted a man in broad daylight and no one had thought she'd done anything.

How had Grandma learned to attack someone with such cool confidence? And have lunch afterward with her grandchild as if nothing had happened? *Something* had been weird about Grandma. Weird, yet awesome.

"Grandma would be honored to know that she had that effect on you," I said to Jessie, my voice thick with emotion.

"Yeah. I feel like I've really helped some women, but it never seems to be enough, you know?" Jessie's smile was sad as she ducked out of sight again. "Your sandwich is done! Gimme a sec."

I turned to Dale. "I still need to pay you!"

He shook his head. "Not today. Consider this a welcome-to-the-neighborhood gift." He passed me a foil-wrapped bundle larger than my hand.

"Well, thank you. I'll return the favor soon." And I would. A cheese-flavored debt was the best kind to repay. "By the way, are there any bulletin boards around? I have some fliers I'd like to post. I'd love to save on gas and get gigs close to home."

"There used to be a big board by the parking lot, ages ago." Jessie's voice was distant. "But it got covered with graffiti too many times and was taken down." That made me think of Chase again and the mess he'd made on my property. I really, really hoped he cleaned it up, if only to spare me from dealing with the sheriff's department.

"Talk with Rita up at Slocombe House," said Dale. "She's the manager and also acts as landlord over everything here." He gestured to the whole plaza. "She books weddings and other events at the House. Even if she doesn't know of a place for you to post your advert, she'd be the person to help you get bookings here."

I bounced on my toes a few times, thrilled by a potential connection at Slocombe House. "Thank you! I'll seek her out."

"Now go eat. That sandwich will be at its prime right now." He shooed me away with his fingers. "We'll talk more later. And Jessie, you can clock out. I'll handle everything from here."

"Hooray!" Happiness projected in Jessie's voice as I headed back to my car.

I turned on the Kia long enough to roll down my windows, then peeled back the foil envelope to dig into lunch. My lips posed over the bread, I paused. No, I couldn't eat yet. There was one thing I had to do first.

I dropped my phone into the holster on a pivoting arm affixed to my center console. I angled the camera to face the windshield and the cloud-freckled blue sky over the Pacific. With a few taps, I started recording video.

I leaned forward over the steering wheel. "Behold!" I declared in as thunderous a voice as I could muster. I held out the two diagonal halves of my olallieberry grilled cheese and slowly pulled them apart. The small gasp of joy I made was not done for the camera alone. The mix of white cheddar and provolone drew apart with thick, gooey lines tinted reddish-purple by berries. "I bought this beauty at Quesoquick on Highway 1 in Foghorn, just north of San Simeon. This is my first time visiting there, but I can tell you before I even take a bite that I know I'll be back! I mean, *look.*" I brought an oozy interior side of the sandwich up close to the camera. "See that? They use a waffle iron to make their grilled cheese, which also means they cook up fast! This thing is going to be crunchy and cheesy in all the best ways. Yum!" I paused a beat, and then used my clean pinky finger to stop recording.

I stuffed half of the sandwich back in the foil to stay warm, then started eating. I half-shut my eyes in bliss. The two cheeses were imbued with different kinds of tangy, lemony sharpness that were fantastic with the tart-sweet olallieberries. The crust still tasted like fresh bread, even as crunchy and toasted as it was, and I kept discovering extra puddles of butter in the divots left by the waffle iron. Pure bready, cheesy heaven.

I inhaled the rest of the sandwich. After wiping my hands with a napkin, I tucked my phone into my jacket pocket.

Once I was home, I'd upload the video across social media – after I dressed it up a little, of course. I could add a holy beam of light shining down from some cartoon clouds and a snippet of music – oh, I could integrate an acapella choir that sounded downright angelic! That would get the point across nicely. I'd be sure to tag Dale's business, too. I wanted people to know the exact source of such goodness.

That post plotted out, I grabbed my reusable bags and headed across the parking lot to my next destination.

An automated chime welcomed me into Foghorn Grocery store. The man at the register, who I guessed was Sikh by his beard and headcover, was helping another customer but gave me a wave and a broad smile. I smiled back and grabbed a handcart. I envisioned my list in my head as I wound through the store, grabbing items here and there.

The biggest downside to moving to the northern edge of the Central Coast's population center was that I'd burn through a lot of gasoline and this area tended to have the highest prices in the state. Grandma had left me a good chunk of money, but my goal was to sustain myself – and build a profit off my business within six months. That meant I needed to be frugal.

I paused to double-take at a cardboard display of spring-themed chocolate bunnies. It wasn't even Valentine's Day yet! A shrill cell phone rang from the next aisle over. I jumped. My basket struck the display. It tipped in horrible slow motion. As I lunged to grip it, a loud voice called out, "Hello! Hi! I was wondering when you'd call back. Yes, I'm Rita. How are you today?"

I was still hugging the candy display, like I intended to haul the whole thing to the cashier, as Rita rounded the corner. She was a short woman with mascara almost as thick as her eyebrows. Her trim, salmon-toned pantsuit complemented her deep brown skin. She looked me up and down, askance, then continued past me, a large, hands-free phone receiver hooked over the top of her ear. "Thanks for the confirmation. I can send you those forms as soon as I return to my office. I'll be back at Slocombe House in ten minutes."

Good grief, this had to be the all-powerful Rita that Dale told me about.

"Way to make an impression, Bird," I muttered beneath my breath as I lowered the display onto its cardboard feet again. A couple of candy bars plunked on the linoleum. The contents of my handcart – eggs included – rocked against each other. I took a tenuous step back and picked up the fallen candies.

As I came up behind Rita in line, she ended her call. To my surprise, she whirled to face me. "You're Lucille Franklin's granddaughter."

"I– well– yes?"

"I remember when you used to come around here as a little girl. Your name is Bird, right?"

I didn't remember meeting Rita when I was a kid, but back then I tended not to pay much attention to people unless their noise disturbed me. "Yes, Bird Nichols. And you're Rita, manager at Slocombe House. I was hoping to speak with you." Her arched eyebrow encouraged me to continue, so I pressed on. "I run a cheese board business. I've been based out of San Luis Obispo for a while now, but as of today, I'm moved into my grandma's house. I'd be delighted if we could follow each other on social media and if I could give you one of the fliers I have in my–"

"I don't think that will be necessary." Rita's smile was

decidedly constipated. Her gaze flicked to the bold purple streak at the front of my short blonde hair, then back to my face. A gallon of judgment was packed into that two-second glance.

"Oh." Was I reading her right? Was I getting rejected, even though we'd just met? First time meeting her that I remember, anyway. After a few seconds of mental flailing, I resolved to be blunt. "Why is that?"

Past her, I caught the gaze of the clerk as he helped two customers decide on lottery tickets. His gaze at me was sympathetic. I found that even more discomfiting – what had I done wrong?

"You're Lucille's granddaughter." Rita shrugged, then seemed to realize that sentence was an inadequate explanation for me. "I'm sorry that she drowned, as that's a terrible way to go, but quite frankly, she was a troublemaker around here for a lot of years."

"A troublemaker?" As surprising and insulting as that statement was, I'd heard Grandma described that way before. By my parents.

"Mom had Bird in the car during a high-speed chase in pursuit of one of her 'suspects'!" I remembered my mom hissing at Dad as they argued in the bedroom. I had my ear pressed to their door. "The police were chasing her before they realized who she was after! She's always had an unhealthy interest in local investigations, but she's gone too far now. I love her, but…" Mom hiccupped in a sob.

"You talked to your mom after she had Bird doing reconnaissance for her in the crowds at Pismo Beach," Dad said. "I don't think talking to her again will be enough. We need to protect Bird."

They did. I'd barely seen Grandma after that, not until

I started college. By then, Grandma's diabetes and heart had slowed her down, but Grandma was still Grandma. She insisted on teaching me how to pick locks and bust out of zip-tie handcuffs; it was amazing what a person could learn with some help from YouTube. She listened to the police scanner and took notes throughout the day, too, but everything she did was more passive in nature. Her drives to the supermarket stayed at the speed limit.

"A troublemaker," Rita repeated. "You must understand, I'm more than manager at the House. This entire village is my domain. It has been my love, my passion, for over thirty years." She spoke with tears in her eyes. "Your grandmother – I never understood her. I don't even know how she managed to gain ownership of her acreage from Mr Slocombe, but he was grateful to her for some reason." By her frown, this was not a good thing. "The fact is, Lucille meddled. She knew everything that was going on and had her nose in it. If there was a bad car accident or a near-drowning or a fire, she was there before the police. She acted *like* the police! She talked to the media! She had contacts there, everywhere. Reporters called her before they called me, and I'm the media rep for Foghorn!"

"You're saying," I said slowly, "that you believe that she made Foghorn look bad." The other customers at the head of the line exited. The clerk shuffled around large cigarette boxes, one ear tilted toward our conversation.

"That's exactly what I'm saying."

"But she didn't *cause* these bad things," I continued. "You have other genuine troublemakers around."

"No, I'm not blaming her for causing these incidents, but she exacerbated them. She made them too public. There are proper procedures that must be maintained. Rules of law."

"Has that helped to stop people like Chase Perkins?"

Her mood darkened – as did the expression of the clerk. "He's a pest and a constant grief to his mother. The sheriff's department has a file on him, I assure you. If anything is vandalized or stolen around here, we know who to look at first. It's only a matter of time until he's locked up for good, and I'll toast to that with a glass of wine!"

"Maybe he can be rehabilitated first, maybe–"

"Some people are bad. They can't be saved. They need to go away." She wasn't just referring to Chase, but to Grandma. I took a step back as if I'd been slapped. I couldn't believe she'd said something that awful right to my face. New customers entered, chattering. The clerk cleared his throat, drawing Rita's attention. She advanced to the counter. "I hope you prove to be more of an asset to the community," she said to me over her shoulder. A few seconds later, her purchases were tallied. She paid with a tap of her phone and left without looking at me again.

My brain boiled with a weird mix of emotions as I set my basket on the counter. I felt defensive about Grandma, but I knew that Rita's comments were justified. I also despaired, because I'd really, really wanted to sell cheese boards for events at Slocombe House. That was clearly never going to happen through Rita.

"Hey." The clerk had kind eyes as he handled my items and placed them in my bag. "Rita, she is abrupt like that. She means well, but..." He shrugged.

"Yeah."

"That Chase, he *is* trouble. When he was younger, he used to do graffiti around here, steal things. We added cameras around the shopping center because of him. But unlike Rita, I hope – I must hope – he can be a better person."

"Yeah," I repeated. My brain was too fried to manage more.

I buckled into my driver's seat and stared into space. Even though I had a million things to do, I felt so sapped I couldn't even drive. I sat there for thirty minutes. I went ahead and uploaded the video of my grilled cheese sandwich with the added frills. I checked my email, noting I had several potential clients I needed to respond to.

Finally, I remembered that I had items I probably needed to get in the fridge sooner than later. January was cold, after all, but not *that* cold.

I drove slowly on the winding road away from Highway 1. My progress was sluggish, as were my thoughts, so I continued right past the mangled guardrail for a short distance before my brain recognized what I'd seen. With a check behind me for cars, I reversed.

The guardrail along the curve was ripped wide open, leaving a car-shaped hole, the metal on either side frayed into a dozen sharp knives. It definitely had not been like that before.

I parked on the top of the embankment. My heart began to pound fast. Phone in hand, I followed tracks of flattened grass down the slope toward the brush-thick creek. As I entered the shade cast by tall, old trees, I had a new worry: "Do I even get reception down here?" I asked myself, then checked my phone. Sure enough, I had only one flickering bar. Not good.

My feet skidded a few inches as the incline steepened. Taillights stared from a thicket like dull, red monster eyes. The back wheels were a solid foot up in the air, unmoving. The car was off. Sucking in a sharp breath, I recognized the car's blue-grey color and older make.

This was Chase's car.

With a fleeting worry about poison oak, I pushed my way through the broken bushes to peer into the driver's side door. In the blackness, I could make out a slumped human form. "Hey!" I called, beating the glass with a fist. No movement within. I pulled on the door handle with all my weight. It didn't open. It was locked or stuck because of the impact.

I stumbled out of the brush to the back end of the car to dial 911. As the operator picked up, sound dropped out with little pulses of static. Unsure how long the connection would last, I quickly rattled off the location and what I'd found.

"There's definitely someone inside. I'm going to try to get to them through the passenger side now," I said, rushing there. "The door is ajar! I can get in!"

"Use extreme caution," said the soft-voiced operator. "Your weight could cause the car to shift deeper into the foliage or even into the creek. Units will be there within minutes."

I'd already leaned a knee on the seat. The car only wobbled. "The passenger side is empty. I don't see anyone in the back. And the driver... it's Chase Perkins." He was limp, head tilted forward. Shock and grief formed a thick lump in my throat. "His seatbelt is on. It doesn't look like his head hit the glass. No airbags deployed." The car was probably too old to have an automatic system.

The operator said something, but only nonsensical buzzing came through.

I touched his hand. His skin was barely warm. His jacket had tight cuffs. I couldn't check his pulse at his wrist. I reached for his neck, taking care not to move his head. I knew about the dangers of neck injuries thanks to a college health course and various factoids from Grandma.

My fingers slipped underneath his dipped chin and found more warmth – and wetness, lots of it. My fingers curled as I recoiled. Horror knocked a gasp from me.

"Ma'am? Ma'am – are you–" More static.

"His throat. It's been slit wide open." I almost fell on my backside as I staggered out of the car. A beam of sunlight highlighted the thick blood that coated my right hand. "He's dead. He's bled out, and I... I touched *inside his throat*." I didn't scream. Instead, my own throat was suddenly so tight that I could barely manage words at all.

The operator's voice sounded distant, not simply because of the poor signal, but because of the roar of my own panicked heart.

Chapter Three

I registered a few faint assurances from the 911 operator that help was on the way to me before the call dropped out completely. I was left holding my phone, staring at my other hand in utter revulsion.

I wasn't perturbed that I'd touched a dead man. No, it was the blood and the fact that I'd *touched inside his neck*, and he had felt like *meat*.

I didn't rely on a cheese-centric diet simply because it was delicious, offered endless varieties, and was generally awesome; cheese was also safe to touch. I couldn't tolerate the texture of raw meat. I tried to make a meatloaf one time to surprise my mom when I was younger, and the texture of the hamburger plus the runny egg made me physically ill. Eating meat was fine, though; I just needed someone else to do the cooking.

My bloodied hand extended far from my body, I worked my way up the slope again as I stared at my phone screen, willing reception bars to appear. Chase was dead – murdered. Had his throat been slit before the car came down the slope, or did someone do that after he survived the crash? There certainly was nothing in the impact that could've injured him like that.

I reached my car. My attempt to re-dial 911 failed. I didn't know how far away help was, but I couldn't wait. I needed that blood off my skin, now, or I was going to go into total sensory-overload/panic attack mode.

I dropped my phone on my car seat and proceeded to use moist towelettes to clean my hand with the thoroughness of a surgeon scrubbing down for surgery. I was practically scouring the webbing between my fingers when I heard the approach of sirens. A few seconds later, a sheriff's car rounded the turn. I waved, the stained wipe in my hand like a pink flag. The deputy pulled off behind my car, silencing the sirens.

I became a lot calmer once the majority of the blood was off my hands and the sirens from the police car had stopped wailing. Two deputies approached. They both stated their names, which I instantly forgot. I described what I'd found in a dry recitation. Only when I caught a look between them did I realize that my matter-of-fact intonation may have struck them as suspicious. That frustrated me – what, would I look more innocent if I was in hysterics? That would only feel dishonest to me, and probably to them as well.

"What should I do with the bloodied wipes?" I asked, motioning to the bothersome pile at my feet. I was told to leave them on the ground, which felt wrong, but I sure didn't want those stained things in my car.

The male deputy headed down to Chase's vehicle while the female deputy babysat me as I leaned against my front bumper. She asked questions and continued to take notes.

An ambulance arrived next, followed by two more patrol cars in rapid sequence. Lights and sirens stayed on. When I asked permission to grab my noise-canceling ear plugs from my car, I was relieved when she didn't ask why but gave a nod of assent.

The ear plugs weren't enough.

As dusk descended, the narrow roadway was a cacophony of noise and color. My heartbeat galloped. This was worse than the singular time I tried to go clubbing with friends back in college. There, at least, I only had to linger in a bar line for five minutes before I realized this was not my scene. A friend waited with me outside for a bit until a ride-share vehicle came to take me home, where I needed a solid hour for that horrible pulsing beat to fade from my consciousness. Here, I had to wait until the investigating detective was ready to talk to me, and not just because I found the body. Although I had a solid alibi, I knew that I had to be a suspect. I'd told the deputies why Chase had reason to travel this narrow road to nowhere and about my confrontation with him alongside Grizz. I had reason to be angry with Chase.

Grizz did too.

Grizz had likely heard the sirens from his house, but we were fairly close to Highway 1 along this portion of road. He probably assumed an accident had happened along the coastal thoroughfare. I wanted to call and check on him, but with the deputy watching, that seemed unwise. I didn't need to make either of us look more suspicious. I mean, Grizz wouldn't have done this to Chase. Right?

I'd known Grizz all my life. He'd always seemed like an old man to me, the cranky sort who got tired of yelling at kids to get off his lawn so he moved where he didn't have a lawn or kids to bother him. He'd doted on me, though. When I was younger, I knew I could always run over to his house to get a slice of Portuguese sweet bread. At that point in my life, it was the only bread that I tolerated without a need for cheese or butter on top – but those toppings made the slices even better, of course. A few years ago, Grandma had let slip that Grizz had only kept sweet bread around because I loved it so much. I knew now that it tended to be a lot more expensive than regular store bread. That indulgence for my sake must've been an awful strain on his tight budget back then.

"Miss Nichols?" A deep voice roused me from the fog of my overwrought senses. "I'm Detective Merrick, with the San Luis Obispo Sheriff's Office. May I speak with you for a few minutes?"

I made an effort to focus on the figure before me. He was a black man maybe forty years old, attired in a long black coat over a trim suit. "Yes, of course." Anything to get this done so I could go home.

He looked around. "It's noisy out here. Would it be acceptable if we spoke in the back of an ambulance?" I must not have done a good job of hiding my askance reaction of I'm-not-going-off-alone-with-any-unfamiliar-man because he continued, "Deputy Johnson will be with us."

The woman deputy nodded. I made a point of remembering her name this time around.

"Okay." I followed him to one of the two ambulances on site. I climbed into the back to sit on a bench while he took a seat across from me, no gurney between us. Deputy Johnson stayed just outside. The open doors faced the road. I released a deep, relieved breath and removed my ear plugs. I could still detect noise, but it was muted. Even more, the visual chaos was gone.

"Thanks," I told him.

"Johnson told me you needed ear plugs, and I did a quick check on you online. Autism, huh? I have a nephew who's autistic. He's ten."

I shouldn't have been surprised that he'd looked up my public profile – a good detective *should* detect. I had hashtag-autistic in my biography on every social media platform. It was easier to be 'out' as autistic online than it was in real life. A lot of people were supportive on the internet, and if they weren't, I could mute and block them. Face-to-face was a lot more complicated.

"That's good that he was diagnosed when he was young. Most women and nonbinary folks aren't diagnosed until sometime in adulthood. My assessment happened right after I graduated college." I stopped myself there. This was a subject I could ramble on about for an hour, and this was not the time and place. "What more do you need to know about what happened here? I already answered a lot of questions."

"You told Deputy Johnson that you and your neighbor Grizz Ferreira warned Chase that he needed to clean up the mess he'd made on your property. How did Chase react to that? Did you feel like you might be in danger when and if he returned?"

That sounded as if the detective wanted to establish that we might have a motive to preemptively attack Chase. I spoke with slow care. "As I told the deputy here, he threatened me by verifying where I lived. He wasn't specific about what he would do to me, but his voice and manners made it clear that he was angry. Grizz had witnessed Chase and his friends using guns out there, though. I saw evidence of that – casings on the ground. Chase never brandished a gun, and I didn't see any indication that he had one in his pocket or in a holster. Was Chase's gun – or guns – even legal?" I paused to give Detective Merrick time to say something, but when he only tilted his head, I figured he

BETH CATO

wasn't going to reply to me, even if he knew the answer. "I like to think that I made it clear that I was giving him a chance to undo the damage before I reported him to the sheriff's office." I paused again. "I haven't been home for a few hours now but some of your cars went that way a while ago. Does everything look okay at our houses?" They had to be interrogating Grizz right now.

"Your place looked fine from the outside. In the morning, can I get permission from you to search your property?"

I felt a spike of panic. I didn't need this drama in my life right now! I needed to unpack and prep my next cheese order! I couldn't have strangers making an even worse mess of everything! I took a deep breath to portray stoicism. "You can search the back forty, sure. Is it okay if I supervise?" I desperately wanted to oversee the search to see what they found, if anything, but even more, I needed to portray cooperation. I couldn't risk looking more suspicious.

"Of course. You mentioned that you had just finished bringing your belongings into the house today. You must have a lot of unpacking to do." I wished that I could believe his sympathy.

"I have *all* the unpacking to do."

"Well," Detective Merrick said, rising, "I'll leave you to it, then. Would you like Deputy Johnson to accompany you home, to make sure things there are undisturbed?"

I glanced at her. Her smile was courteous beneath her hat. "Sure. Thank you. Both of you."

"I'll likely have more questions for you tomorrow," he said, to which I nodded. "We'll be there at eight in the morning."

"Eight. Right. See you then." As if I didn't have enough on my plate. Or my carefully partitioned cheese board.

Chapter Four

I returned home with salad that'd gone too limp to eat. After I threw that bag in the trash and dumped out the warmed milk, I checked the egg carton. Four eggs had cracked, probably during my tussle with the candy display. *Four.* As my college sophomore suitemate from China would've been quick to point out, in her culture, that was a number associated with unluckiness and death. I didn't put stock in portents, but they could still be creepy.

The events of the day had sapped my energy, leaving me with shaky fingers and a pounding headache, but I still staggered around the kitchen and bedroom to do some basic unpacking. I'd cleared out much of Grandma's dishes and clothes; she might've had money to outfit the Kitchen, but she otherwise reused the same things she'd probably had for over fifty years. A lot of my things were thrift store finds, but at least they tended to originate in the current century.

I needed to work on my latest cheese order, but I couldn't. I was fried more thoroughly than bacon broiled for an hour. A hot shower assured me that I'd scrubbed away every last remnant of blood and death. I used my hair dryer – on low, as always, to keep its annoying roar to a minimum – then I set my phone alarm for six o'clock before I collapsed into bed, literally.

I'm neither a night owl nor a morning person, but when my alarm went off, I felt only vaguely human, and most decidedly not owl-like either. My stiff back and bruised shins reminded me of the hard physical labor I'd been engaged in this week, too. I brewed tea as I whipped up an omelet using two eggs and a lovely dill-freckled Havarti out of Wisconsin. That hot, eggy, gooey deliciousness roused me more than the caffeine. I dressed and made the ten-foot trek to the Kitchen outside of my lower-case kitchen.

I stared and blinked for a moment.

"I didn't do anything in here last night other than check for vandalism, did I?" I asked, moving around the large central island. Several large cardboard boxes had been unpacked and laid on the floor, flattened. The sealed packs of six-by-six-inch boxes and the rimmed muffin cups that I needed for this morning were stationed in stacks on the counter right beneath the schematic print-out I'd stuck on the magnet board above. Yes, cheese boards require schematics. Anyone can toss ingredients in a partitioned box, but a proper cheese board is *art*.

I glanced at the clock: half past six. I had to get things done before the deputies came at eight – and they'd better come on time. I hated tardiness about as much as I despised loud, sudden noises. I needed them to wrap things up in quick time, too. My cheese needed to be delivered in Morro Bay about noon so it could be enjoyed after a beach wedding this afternoon.

I let myself flutter in panic for a moment, and then I got to work.

First of all, I assembled boxes. Forty of them. That took up the majority of my counter space, and the room had a lot of that real estate. Next up came the cheese: Young

Manchego and Cabra al Vino. My client really liked sheep and goat cheese. I sliced the Manchego into triangles that showed a sliver of the lovely, brown, weave-impressed rind. I repeated the same cut on the goat cheese with wine – it had the loveliest rind with a violet hue. With my gloved hands, I arranged the two varieties to stand on their sides with rinds facing right and left in an alternating pattern. They went into the six-by-six boxes in an up-hand corner. The sturdy muffin cups went beside them. Fortunately, I'd already prepared little mesh baggies of Marcona almonds and sweet, paprika-dusted walnuts; I only had to drop them into the cups. Into another cup went four large, dried California figs. The wedding was between a Californian Latina bride and a Spanish groom, and they both wanted their origins represented. That meant the boxes also included traditional membrillo quince paste, another thing I'd already prepared. I wedged the lidded plastic cups into the arrangement and then distributed cute bamboo spreaders to go with them.

Thin, crisp, gluten-free crackers came out next. I arranged them in fanned-out crescents around the fig cups. I'd discovered early on in my business venture that with gluten-free foods both popular and necessary, it was safest to make all of my basic boxes that way – unless someone made a special order to include regular bread. The crackers I used were so tasty that people sometimes freaked out, certain the crisps *had* to contain gluten. Nope!

Another clock-check: ten till eight. Now I almost hoped that Detective Merrick was running late because the most unpleasant, fiddly task was next: the Serrano ham roses. I switched out my gloves, sanitized my workspace again, then laid out the paper-thin meat, rolling it up like layers of petals. If the slices were sticky, I dabbed my fingers in water to make them easier to peel apart. I then arranged the completed roses into the empty nooks between two of the little white cups, thankful that charcuterie didn't trigger my revulsion the way that raw meat did. Brains are weird.

I was about halfway through my rose-making when a buzzer on the wall went off. "Couldn't you have waited twenty more minutes?" I grumbled, taking off my gloves before I pushed a button below the buzzer.

"Hello, who's there?" I asked. I really needed to update the system to include cameras and voice activation.

"Miss Nichols? This is Detective Merrick. We're here to conduct our search." Voices burbled behind him.

"I'm in the Kitchen outbuilding. I need about five minutes to put away what I'm working on. How many of you are here?" If I had been in the house, I would have heard the cars on the gravel, but the Kitchen was back far enough that I would've only noticed if someone honked.

"A dozen. May I come around to the outbuilding to speak with you?"

I hesitated. Grandma had told me to never, ever let a cop inside a building because they could then decide to search, if they wanted. I didn't trust these people, but at the same time, I wanted to act the part of an innocent person. "Sure, but I don't want more than a couple people in here. I need this space to stay sanitary." I kept my tone friendly but firm. In my imagination, Grandma's scowl was incandescent.

A minute later, Merrick and two other deputies, including Johnson, joined me. I was in the process of securing and moving the completed boxes into the larger boxes I use for transport. Those went into the industrial-size fridge. I still didn't know how Grandma had afforded that unit or the entire Kitchen. The deluxe fridge alone had to be five grand.

"This is quite a setup," said Deputy Johnson. She waved at my special staging zone, which had yet to be fully arranged. "It almost looks like a TV show set. You even have those fancy circular lights!" She'd been all cool and professional last night, but now she sounded giddy.

"Social media is my major source of business. Therefore, good photography is everything. I want my food porn to go viral." I belatedly realized that maybe that wasn't the best online lingo to use in front of law enforcement, but Merrick only emitted a soft snort. "Can you give me an estimate on how long the search will take? I really want to supervise, but I also need to make more ham roses before I haul everything to Morro Bay this afternoon." I shuttled my almost-done boxes to the fridge five feet away, panting from my quick back-and-forth movement.

"We'll try not to take up too much of your time," said Merrick. He wore the exact same outfit as yesterday, all the way down to the blue-striped tie.

"That is a useless answer," I said bluntly.

He shrugged. "We haven't gotten to the area in question yet. I don't know the size of the search zone or what complications may arise. If I told you it'd be an hour, I'd be throwing a useless number at you."

I grunted, conceding that he was right. He couldn't give me a fair estimate. I glanced around to confirm that everything that needed to be cold was being chilled, then grabbed my phone. "Let's get this going, then."

I sat in Merrick's black sedan for the short drive into the back-forty. About half the tables and chairs were gone. I pointed this out to Merrick, but he wasn't surprised. Those items had already been accounted for, he said. The officers split into search parties. Once they were underway, Merrick came back over to me.

"Your property ends past the tree line, correct?" he asked, pointing.

"Somewhere around there, yeah." I shifted, self-conscious of my ignorance. "My grandma would have known. Grizz probably knows, too. He's lived here for thirty years and rents the land he's on from Grandma – from me."

Shrewdness entered Merrick's gaze. "How long have you known Mr Ferreira?"

"My whole life." I resolved to be straightforward. "I understand that you need to look at me and him as suspects, but seriously, Grizz didn't slit Chase's throat. I mean, look around. Chase was actually cleaning up out here!" I noticed a deputy bagging some trash from among the leaves. "He was doing what we asked of him. There was no reason for us to kill him."

"We need to engage in due diligence," Merrick said in a patient tone. "How much do you know about Mr Ferreira's past?"

I shrugged. I knew absolutely nothing about Grizz's life before I was born except that he'd had his nickname since he was a teenager because of his surly, growling ways. "We don't talk about it. He's more interested in knowing if I've seen tri-tip on sale in town."

"You described him as 'warning' Mr Perkins yesterday." So, Merrick picked up on my conscious effort to avoid the word 'threaten.' "This isn't the first time he's made remarks about Mr Perkins in front of others, including the man's own mother. Mr Ferreira and our murder victim have been clashing for a long time."

"If you've talked with anyone in Foghorn, you know that

Chase clashed with most everyone here," I retorted. "I've been told that he has a criminal record, too. Not that such a thing excuses his murderer, of course."

"Your 'Grizz' has a police record, too. Did you know that?"

I shrugged again. "Grandma wouldn't have been friends with someone who was dangerous. She wouldn't have allowed him to be around me when I was younger." I *was* curious about Grizz's record, though. It had to contain worse crimes than mere traffic violations for it to be of note to Merrick – or did it? The detective might be trying to manipulate me to either distrust Grizz or to compel me to spill useful details.

Deputies shuffled by me, following some invisible grid pattern in their slow walk. A few colorful flags were planted in the ground. Grandma would have known what those meant.

"I knew your grandmother," said Merrick. That jolted me to look at him again. "She was… a known factor to the entire department. I was told about her when I first came on as a deputy. Your grandmother tried to 'help.'" He used air quotes. "She often got herself into trouble."

I didn't doubt him, but I was still irked at yet more negative comments about Grandma. Merrick and Rita could probably exchange notes on Grandma's nuisance ways. "My understanding is that she succeeded in providing that help sometimes, too."

"Sometimes," he said grudgingly. "I asked her once why she didn't join law enforcement herself, and she said that the job would have been too limited in scope. I never asked her what she meant by that. I think I was almost afraid to know."

I tried to dismiss that comment. "She was smarter than everyone and not shy about that fact."

Detective Merrick scrutinized me. "On your first day in Foghorn, you find a man dead. Lucille Franklin had a similar knack. She ended up as a suspect more than once."

"But she wasn't guilty, and neither am I," I snapped. Merrick looked thoughtful.

"If anyone could've gotten away with murder, it would be her."

He was right. As much as I hated that my parents had kept me and Grandma apart for a decade, I understood why now that I was an adult. I had a hunch that they knew Grandma had been up to shenanigans worse than speeding with me in the car or making me an accomplice in her investigations. I had tried to ask Mom about it a few times in recent years, and she always waved me off. "Let's not ruin your visit home with that kind of talk," she'd say.

Visits weren't possible now. I couldn't get those answers – or could I?

I was due a chat with Grizz.

The search concluded after another hour and a half. As far as I could tell, the deputies hadn't discovered anything big, but Merrick kept me far back from the main action. I wondered if I had been positioned at a standard distance for these kinds of procedures, or if I was placed in some anti-meddling spot.

When Merrick returned me to the house, I dashed inside and then on to the Kitchen. In my mind, the clock loomed over me and threatened to crush me flat. I had yet to be late with an order. I wasn't about to start now.

I vented my anxiety into the ham roses as I rolled them up in a steady sequence. I gave all of the boxes a careful check against the order and my schematics, worried that I'd forgotten something amid the chaos of the day, but things looked good. Since it was January and somewhere in the fifty-degree range outside, I normally would have driven straight to my destination without worry about cold packs. My wilted salad bag the previous night, however, had taught me to take nothing for granted. I rolled a layer of thick bubble wrap over my enclosed boxes and then secured ice packs around them. Now they would stay cold for hours.

To my relief, I had a smidgen of extra time. With the house and Kitchen locked up and my cheese stash loaded in the back of my car, I set off for Grizz's house.

Grizz was of an age where he didn't keep his phone within arm's reach at all times. His device was capable of texting, but he wasn't; he found the process to be confusing and frustrating. He wasn't on social media, either. If we wanted to talk, it had to be face-to-face.

His house stood at the end of a short, upward-sloping dirt drive, the trailer angled so that the front windows overlooked the road like a guard post. The hill behind him had patches of thick growth. I remembered his comment about the fire danger and made a mental note to hire someone to clear a broad fire break in the next few months. California could have bad wildfires as early as April. A tall wire fence encased an edible garden lot that was bigger than his trailer and already showed verdant growth. I'd been promised all the fresh strawberries I could eat when harvest time came in two or three months. They would go beautifully with many of my favorite cheeses.

As I marched to his door, I could only think that he'd

better keep that promise to me. He couldn't maintain his garden plot from behind bars.

Grizz heard me coming. He kicked open the screen door to admit me. "Come on in," he grumbled, waving me inside.

"I can't stay long. I'm on the way to make a delivery but I needed to – geez, Grizz." I hadn't seen him look this haggard since Grandma had gone missing. His skin had a gray cast, bags heavy under his eyes. He wore the clothes from the previous day, his thin hair flared out over his ears rather than making its usual valiant effort to hide his bald pate.

"I didn't sleep much last night." His ancient recliner wheezed as he plopped down in the seat.

"They didn't take you in for questioning, did they?" No need to specify the 'they.'

"Nah. They talked to me here for a long while, wanted to know about my history with Chase – and you. They didn't make you go to the station, did they?" Worry clouded his eyes.

"No. I had to wait at the scene after I found him–"

"Dear God! You found him? I wish you hadn't had to see that! Oh, Bird." He wailed my name.

I continued, softer, "I wish I hadn't seen that either, but I'm fine." I was now, anyway. I touched my hands together, as if making certain they were still free of blood. "They searched his party zone on my property, too, and just finished up, but you probably know that already."

"Yeah. Seeing those cars go by... I almost went over to see how you were doing, but–"

"It was better that you didn't." I sat in the wooden rocker across from him and leaned forward. "Grizz, Detective Merrick is treating you like the prime suspect. He was toying with me, saying you had a record–"

Grizz groaned and covered his face with both hands. "Stupid, youthful stuff. Not unlike Chase in some ways, which is a big reason why he peeved me so much. I hated seeing someone being as idiotic as I'd been. Your grandma, she helped me a lot back then."

"I didn't realize you'd known each other that long. Well, I'm the one who can help you now. I've already gotten the impression that Chase didn't have a lot of friends in Foghorn, but who hated him enough to slit his throat after he wrecked his car?"

His eyes widened. "You mean he didn't die in the accident?"

I paused to think. "What did they tell you?"

"That Chase'd been found dead, crashed in his car, under suspicious circumstances."

"Well, that's not wrong. When the police talk to you about this again, please make sure to mention that I let that detail slip. I don't want them to find you more suspicious because you know something that only the murderer – and me – would know."

"Got it. As for who'd want Chase dead: plenty of people, I imagine. He stole from most everyone around. Vandalized. Did joy rides. Pulled off that swishing, uh, swatting thing." Grizz's flippant list made me cringe, especially when it came to the swatting. His tone didn't give proper gravity to the terror created by that kind of attack. "Ran with bad crowds here and there until they got sick of him, too, and he'd be solo for a bit before becoming a new tag-along. No one liked him."

"Did he have any friends here in the past?"

"Chase does – did – have one loyal friend around. That kid… I dunno. Short time that I talked to him, he struck me as vulnerable, you know? Like he looked up to Chase as a big brother and would do anything he said. Ray – that's his name. Unlike Chase, he keeps a regular job. Groundskeeper at a mobile home park down in Morro."

"How do you know that if you've barely talked with him?" I pulled out my phone to jot down details in a note-taking app. I lived by my schedules and lists. I knew better than to trust myself to retain tons of details at once.

"I didn't find that out by talking to him. Remember when I scared off those intruders with my airhorn? I found these on the ground near where their cars were parked." He twisted to rummage in an end table drawer. "Figured they were mine now. Served the kid right to suffer the loss for hanging with that crowd. Ah, here we go." He held up a laden key chain.

I snatched it from his hand. There were about seven keys attached to a plastic fob that had a generic palms-and-sun logo for Tall Palms Mobile Home Park. Black marker on the back stated they were property of Ray.

"You're sure these belong to that friend of his?"

"Pretty sure, yeah. I saw him wearing a t-shirt for that same trailer park once, and I know he's named Ray."

"Good." I pocketed the keys. "This gives me a perfect excuse to go talk to him."

Grizz's jaw dropped. "No, Bird, that– You shouldn't– You could be in–"

"Please stop sputtering. This is exactly what Grandma would have done, and you know it." I jostled the keys. It felt good to act like Grandma in this regard. We'd been opposites in many ways – she was such a confident extrovert, lacking my many sensitivities and anxieties – but I liked to think we were alike in intellect. "You really shouldn't possess evidence like this right now, anyway. They might search your trailer next."

"Sounds like they might want to search more've your property, too. You shouldn't have the keys, either."

"I won't have them on me for long. I'm going to Morro Bay right now. I can return the keys to their owner."

Grizz shook his head, his hair strands waving like a flag in surrender. "Sure, Lucille would've done something like this, but you don't need to. I mean, won't this kind of confrontation be hard on you? With your, uh, condition?"

I gave him a look. "Grizz, don't you dare try to coddle me. I'm perfectly capable of talking to this guy. Now, if I walk up and he's using a leaf blower, that will be sheer torture for me, sure, but I can still deal. I have to."

"I could go with you."

My glare intensified. He wilted. "No, you won't."

His haggard face looked even more hang-dog miserable. "Bird, a lot of murders are done by someone close to the victim. Ray was his friend, but that also makes him a suspect. *He* could be the murderer."

I moved toward the door. "Maybe. Maybe not. I'll give you a call later to check in. Please try to answer or at least call me back soon."

Chapter Five

Construction traffic on southbound Highway 1 gave me time to think. I didn't want Grizz to be the murderer, but logically, I understood he did have motive: to protect me and my property now that Grandma was gone. Why hadn't I asked him straight out about his alibi? Why was it easier to confront a stranger than to have a forthright talk with someone who'd been like a surrogate grandfather to me?

Because I didn't want to know the answer.

Next time I talked to Grizz, though, I resolved to be blunt. I had to know the truth one way or another, because if he had done it, I needed to make sure he lawyered up. If he hadn't done it, he also might need to lawyer up. I could help him with Grandma's money.

I drove over a slight rise in the highway and the bay came into view. The small town of Cayucos lay between me and the water, its many roofs forming tiers that led toward the beach. Farther south sprawled Morro Bay. Along its shore towered three massive smokestacks. Behind them, however, loomed the biggest, oldest landmark: the Rock.

People who haven't actually been to Morro Bay don't grasp how massive the Rock is. They hear, "Oh, there's a big rock in the bay right by the town," and they think it's large, as in thirty feet high. No, the Rock is genuinely enormous and awesome – an almost six-hundred-foot-high, broad volcanic plug, the boldest in a chain of similar plugs along the Central Coast.

Driving around in picturesque Morro Bay wasn't quite as awesome. Cramped, sloped streets featured squished stacks of motels, rentals, houses, and apartments. I was glad this was a Wednesday because that meant I didn't have many pedestrians volunteering to act as speed bumps. Weekends were something else.

I navigated my way to the strip mall that held my destination.

The fifty-year-old shopping plaza featured a flat, squat roof and about ten storefronts along a tiny parking lot. I grabbed a prime spot.

I entered the bakery and breathed in the sweet, yeasty air. I loved how different bakeries smelled unique.

"Hola!" called the woman at the counter, grinning at my blatant bliss. "Can I help you?"

"I'm here to make a delivery for the reception, but wow, I'm now distracted." I studied the glass-domed counter loaded with goodies.

She laughed. "You'll want to go to the door at the back. Knock if it's closed."

"Before I do that, I need to buy a pink concha." I pointed at the row of large pastries designed to look like crackled seashells.

I paid and tucked the wax-bagged concha in my purse. With a wave and a final "Gracias!", I went outside.

The back door of the shop gaped open thanks to a creative doorstop: a milk crate loaded with large, smooth rocks. Inside, reception preparations were well underway. Two women fluffed out a white vinyl tablecloth while several other people were unfolding chairs. I recognized the bride's mother bustling about with the air of a highly caffeinated army general right before combat. I was assigned two people to help me bring in the cheese boxes. Two minutes later, that task was done. I usually liked to linger for a few minutes to help set up, but the tension of their flurried preparations boosted my own anxiety. From what I overheard, the groom's car had died, someone's beloved dog was missing, and family drama had the bride in almost-constant tears – plus, five other people were no-shows to help with preparations. I needed to get out of their way.

I sat in my car to do a phone search for the location of Tall Palms Mobile Home Park. To my relief, it was only a half mile away. I didn't even need to cross the highway. My next destination set, I pulled out my concha along with something else I'd thrown in my purse as I headed out: a small baggie of sliced goat cheddar from nearby Central Coast Creamery. I could tell by its pliability that it had reached an optimal temperature.

A lot of people freaked out if cheese wasn't kept chilled at all times, but the truth was that cheese exuded its true flavors and textures after being at room temperature for at least thirty minutes, and most could safely stay out up to four hours.

I took a bite of cheese and then decided to try something. I layered a piece of cheese with my concha and bit through. My teeth sank through softened cheese and into the crunchy sugar cookie pastry-top to find the soft yeast roll beneath. The combination reminded me of a thick piece of brioche, with the sugary bits adding general sweetness not unlike honey. The combo didn't clash at all! People in the northeast liked cheddar cheese with apple pie, after all. This was like a Central Coast take.

With my makeshift lunch done, I drove on to the trailer park.

The place occupied less than a city block in the middle of town, the promised tall palms lining the sidewalk along the north side with more trees scattered within the neighborhood. Past the chain-link fence twined with cut-back vines, I could see the rooves of several rows of permanent trailers, plus another full line of RVs. That came as no surprise considering this was snowbird season, when older folks from colder climates came to California and other warm locales to enjoy the temperate climate. The presence of a tricycle and rubber balls in a driveway right near the entrance, though, told me this wasn't a seniors-only park as some were around here.

I intended to take a winding route through the whole place, but I hadn't gone twenty feet before I spotted a young man trimming bushes along the main avenue. He wore a light-blue polo shirt with jeans, a bucket of garden implements by his feet. Nearby, I noticed a terra cotta pot that looked like it'd been backed into by a car, the early season white-yellow daffodils inside half-crushed.

"Hi there!" I called from about ten feet away. I could imagine Grizz's conniption fit if he knew that I approached a maybe-murderer who was holding sharp clippers.

"Oh. Hey." His smile was pleasant but strained as he faced me, setting down the clippers. "Have we met?" Before I could reply, he continued, "If you want to rent a trailer or a spot, the manager's in the office right now. It's in the trailer right at the entrance behind you, with the palms all around."

"I'm looking for Ray. I'm assuming that's you?" I gestured, indicating his name embroidered on the pocket of his shirt. "Did you lose some work keys recently?"

His brow furrowed and then he gasped. "I did, but– Oh."

I held up the keys. "They were found on my property up in Foghorn. Can I talk to you for a few minutes?"

"You mean you own that land... where Chase, where he had been... Oh, Chase." With a wail, he pressed both hands to his face and started bawling.

Oh, boy. This was awkward. "Hey, Ray. I'm sorry to upset you, I really am. Here, do you want to sit? There's a nice rock over here."

"Yeah, yeah, I should probably sit," he said through heaves, almost tripping over his own feet on his way to the small boulder amid the landscaping. "I've been trying to hold myself together, y'know? I got the news in the middle of the night, and I couldn't sleep after. I can't believe he's really gone."

"Yeah, it's hard to lose someone." The words sounded so generic, but I didn't know what else to say.

"I thought things were looking up for Chase. I can't believe that George got him." Before I could ask who George was, Ray continued babbling. "Chase was supposed to come by my house last night. We were going to play video games. He left his stuff with me. His mom had threatened to hock his best games and junk. I kept texting him, asking where he was, and I never got an answer. I was so mad at him for keeping me waiting." Ray sniffled, rubbing his nose with a wrist.

I'd have to circle back around to find out who it was that Ray was blaming. Right now, it seemed he needed some gentleness as he coped with this loss. "You didn't hang out at all yesterday?"

"Nah. My coworker took a trip down to TJ. I worked all day yesterday. I haven't seen Chase since the weekend." He rubbed his bleary red eyes. "Thanks for bringing me my keys, but who are you again?"

Oops. I should've started with that, but this conversation hadn't followed any kind of normal script. "My name's Bird Nichols."

"And you own that property where Chase was partying? Seriously? I told him over and over not to hang out there, but he thought it was really pretty and peaceful, y'know?" Ray's smile was wistful at the memory. "He loved that spot."

I really didn't understand how someone could find a place pretty and peaceful and yet completely trash it.

"Ray!" A high-pitched voice creaked from a trailer window across the street. A pale, kerchief-adorned face stared down at us. "Why're you sitting on the job? You're paid to get work done! You can't do that while sitting on your keister."

Ray didn't need to be harangued right now. "Hello, ma'am!" I called, making an effort to hide my indignation. "Ray's having a hard time. A dear friend of his died yesterday. The shock has hit him hard. Could you possibly get a glass of water for him?"

Her shrewish sneer vanished in an instant. "Oh. A friend died? Of course I can get some water!" She retreated.

Ray gaped at me. "You got Violet to do something *nice*, that easy? I know you said who you are, but now I'm wondering *what* you are, because that's some magic, right there."

I shrugged. I liked to think that most people were nice; some folks just needed an extra chance to act that way. I'd approached Chase with that same philosophy in mind. At least things had worked out in a better way here.

Violet bustled across the street. She was a short stick of an old white woman in a voluminous purple muumuu. "Here." She extended a water bottle beaded with condensation. I passed it to Ray. "This friend of yours, he was a young kid, too?"

"Yes, ma'am." He popped the lid off and took a long drink.

"Damn shame. Never right, when youngsters go like that." Her face softened. "Well, don't stay sitting there too long, you hear? That sunlight glaring down on you won't help. Just addles a person more." She grumbled beneath her breath as she hustled back to her trailer.

"Ray," I said softly. I had no doubt that Violet would attempt to eavesdrop once she was back at her window. "Since you were close to Chase, Sheriff's deputies will probably be by to question you. I'm surprised they didn't find you already." Merrick was going to be less happy with me when he found out I'd been here first and hadn't given him the keys as evidence, but so be it. When it came down to it, the keys had been removed from the scene prior to the confrontation with Chase. They belonged with their owner.

With that thought in mind, I handed the keys over. Ray tucked them into a pocket with a feeble smile of gratitude.

"Yeah, I figure they'll get to me eventually, but I don't need them coming here. My boss will freak out, and my mom will freak out worse." He motioned to trailers up the street.

So, he lived here in the park with his mom. "I can give you Detective Merrick's number. Maybe if you reach out to him first, you can meet him at the station."

He perked up at that. He was so close to my age, but seemed like such a kid. "Really? That'd be great."

I'd added Merrick's number into my phone during my

property search. That way, if he called me, his name would show up on my screen and I'd know to answer instead of ignoring it as I did persistent automobile warranty spam calls. Ray input the number into his own phone, then kept staring at the screen with tear-filled eyes.

"People keep texting me about Chase. They expect me to know what happened, but I just dunno." He shut off his phone and put it away.

"What have you heard?" I asked gently.

"That he died in a weird car accident. Deputies have been talking with my aunt and grandma and cousins. That's how I know this wasn't some normal crash. My mom watches lots of cop shows, so I end up watching them, too. I can figure things out." He must have seen the question in my eyes, because he continued, "Me and Chase are distant cousins, you see. Born like a month apart. We grew up more like brothers." He blinked back tears. "I told him to be careful, I told him, but he never listened to me. He always knew best about everything, but I had a bad feeling when he started inviting George around, I really did."

"George?" There was that name again.

"He's a bad dude who knows a lot of other bad dudes. He's made money in drugs, smuggling, whatever. Chase started picking up jobs for him. I didn't like George, I didn't want him around, but I think Chase felt like he was moving up, y'know? Getting away from the kiddie table?"

I nodded. That made sense. Chase had been the bigtime punk in a very small place. "Why do you think George would kill him now?"

Grizz had mentioned that Ray had struck him as being vulnerable. Now I understood why. I was a total stranger, but Ray was willing to tell me everything. As grateful as

I was for the info, I was starting to feel like I was taking advantage of Ray. I didn't like that realization, not one bit. At the same time, I treasured his trust, and I wanted to do right by him.

"Chase's been telling me he needs money bad. Recently, he's placed a lot of big bets, all that. Well, George sent him on a job last Friday to pick up money in Oakland. Three hundred thousand dollars, cash." His voice hushed in awe.

"Wait. Cash? Seriously?" I pictured that amount in a suitcase, like I'd seen in TV shows.

"Seriously. But I didn't see it myself. Chase says he didn't either. He went to the drop and cops were swarming the place. I guess someone gave them a heads-up. The guy Chase was supposed to meet was arrested. Anyway, Chase left. He says he never got the money, but George has a lot of questions about the timing of everything, right? Chase said he really got the third degree from him."

I had a lot of questions spinning through my head, too. I couldn't help but think of Chase's rumored use of swatting to get revenge in Foghorn. Could he have swatted his compatriot in order to abscond with the money?

"The arrested guy should be able to testify about what really happened," I said.

"Yeah, you'd think, but it's not like George can just walk into jail and talk to him. Or maybe he can and hasn't yet. I don't know. In any case, George had a really good reason to come after Chase for his money and some revenge."

"How has Chase been acting the past few days?"

"You mean, did he act guilty?" Ray hummed as he considered the question. "Not guilty, no, but weird. Pleased. He kept saying that he was really lucky. I thought that he was feeling that way because he wasn't busted in Oakland, but when I asked if he wanted to go gambling a few days ago, he said he didn't need to right now. That he had the right amount of money. If he was feeling lucky, I mean, wouldn't he want to use that?"

I nodded. "The right amount for what, though?"

"No clue. I've been wondering about that, too. He's owed me money for ages, and I was hoping he might finally pay me back."

I was increasingly glad that Chase wouldn't be around Ray anymore. I could only imagine how he had manipulated his cousin over the years. "Three hundred thousand... If he wanted a house, that'd be a down payment." Coastal real estate prices had always been horrible, and had only gotten worse over the past few years.

"He doesn't – didn't – care about houses. Not cars, either, really." Ray stared at his empty water bottle. "I got to get back to work." He caught my look of concern and smiled. "I feel better now. I'll be okay. As okay as I can be."

"That's good." I stepped back, giving him space to return to his clippers. I mulled over what he told me. George had motive and probably some experience in violence – and he had likely been on my property to hang out with Chase. That disturbed me. I didn't want a guy like that coming back by my place. "Be sure to tell Detective Merrick about George," to which Ray nodded. "You take care of yourself. I better head back to Foghorn." I needed to talk with other people there who knew Chase as I formed a list of potential suspects. George topped the column for the time being.

My gaze went to the nearby broken pot with half-smashed daffodils. "Would it be okay if I took those remaining flowers?"

Ray blinked. "Um, I guess? I was just going to throw them out. I have an old plastic pot I could–"

"I just need the stems." He gazed at me, still puzzled, so I continued. "I want to take some flowers to Chase's mom. Could you tell me exactly where she lives?"

Chapter Six

I ended up with about ten pretty daffodils. Ray cut them for me, but when he fussed about tracking down a nice vase, I told him I'd take care of everything else. I couldn't continue to distract him from his work, not with Violet and likely others watching.

A few blocks away was a thrift store I'd visited a couple times before. There, I found a cut crystal vase so nice I was tempted to keep it for myself. It was sure better than anything I would have gotten in a formal order at a florist. I added water from a bottle in my car, stuck in the daffodils, and had a lovely vase in my center console cup holder for the drive north.

Ray had told me that most of the people who lived and worked in Foghorn resided in a row of older bungalows and trailers hidden behind the strip mall. Parking spots were few, he said, so most guests parked in the main lot, which had more security anyway. He didn't comment on the fact that the security measures had probably been instituted because of Chase.

I'd just parked and unfastened my seatbelt when my phone dinged. The message from my friend Mollie in San Luis Obispo popped up on my watch a few seconds later.

"hey, this is where you moved right? u ok?" The message

cut off there. I logged into my phone to confirm she'd sent me a link to a *Breaking News* story on a suspicious vehicular death in Foghorn. Chase Perkins was named as the victim; other details were scant.

My quick reply said yes, I was in Foghorn, and yes, I was fine. I made sure my phone was on silent before I pocketed it again. Mollie's check-in would likely be the first in a barrage of texts and direct messages I'd be getting from other friends, distant family, and followers.

I parked in the middle of the Foghorn parking lot, which gave me a good vantage point of Quesoquick as I got out of my car. About ten people stood in line, with the surrounding area full of people eating in or around their cars. My concha and cheese had been tasty, but not the most filling thing in the world. Maybe I could stop off for a bite before I returned to the house.

I turned around to encounter someone decidedly less nice: Rita, her high heels striking the pavement with a distinctive fast click-click-click as she hustled my way.

"Bird Nichols." She paused to sip from a paper coffee cup that wafted steam into the January air. "You're already up to Lucille's ways. Your first day as a resident, and you find a dead body." She released a dramatic huff.

Figured that Rita would know more than the media did about what happened. She was the head honcho in Foghorn, after all – and had very good reasons to see Chase's criminal ways come to an end. That made me regard her as a suspect, too.

"What did you expect me to do, see a broken guard rail and keep on driving? Or leave him to rot in his car?" She opened her mouth to retort, but my rant was just getting started. "Trust me, this isn't how I wanted my time here to start. My to-do list is a mile long, and it did not include 'finding murder victim' on it, or wasting a chunk of my morning supervising a search of my property. I have cheese boards to make!" With that, I remembered that I needed to prep another cheese delivery for tomorrow. Ugh.

"You don't get it. Suspicious deaths were a regular thing here twenty, thirty years ago when your grandmother meddled with business operations, police investigations, *everything*. Now here you are, day one, and things start happening again. I don't know what is wrong with your family. You people are weird. It's like you attract trouble." Her gaze went to my purple streak of hair again as she grimaced. Yeah, she *would* be the type who thought colorful hair meant I was some kind of psychopath. If she knew I loved video games, too, oh boy, she'd be even more convinced. Never mind that if those traits were real indicators of pathology, there would be a lot more proof of that in society. Sadly, some people automatically equated being different with being evil.

Grandma had been different, too. And not necessarily in positive ways. That didn't mean I was about to tolerate Rita blaming Grandma for everything that had gone wrong in Foghorn for decades. That accusation was just ludicrous.

"Rita, you're ignoring the other common factor in all of these crimes: *you*. Now, how many times have you complained to the sheriff about Chase Perkins? How much money have you spent cleaning up the messes he created? How did you feel after he likely swatted Slocombe House and created a legal quagmire?"

Rita's eyes widened in shock. I guess she hadn't expected me to go there. "Are you accusing me of killing him?" she asked, incredulous and shrill.

"No, but I *am* saying you had motive – but did you have opportunity?"

Her cheeks flushed. "I was at the House and here at the center all yesterday afternoon and evening. I told the police as much. I also told them I saw Chase driving away from here with someone in his car. I even gave the footage to the police! Not like that is your concern," she added, clearly annoyed that she'd spilled those details.

I considered her, head tilted. Her alibi would likely be easy to prove. "Could you identify who was in the car?"

"That's not your business." She took pleasure in shutting me down, as if she was attacking Grandma by proxy and relishing it.

Actually, if Grandma hadn't publicly vanished on an ocean swim, I'd consider Rita to be a top suspect in her disappearance and presumed death. She had clear motive for that as well.

I shrugged and walked past Rita, the daffodil-filled vase in my hands. "Grizz is being looked at as a suspect. You better believe this is my business."

Only when I was twenty feet away did I release a long, shaky breath. I hated arguments. I hated that I had to defend Grandma from Rita's ridiculous claims. I hated that Grandma was gone, period. She shouldn't be. I hated that my parents were dead. I really wished I could vent to my mom about now. She had a cool-headed, compassionate way of assessing situations that I could only hope to emulate.

I still felt trembly as I followed the sidewalk through a gap between the strip mall buildings and then took a right, as Ray had advised. There, I found a street with pothole-ridden asphalt and a line of aged homes. It was essentially an alley. Down at the far end was the access road that led up the hill to Slocombe House. Lots of tall trees loomed around that junction, hiding this shabby neighborhood from the hoity-toity sort who would want to spend money at the B&B.

"Mustn't expose the nobility to the sight of the dirty help," I quipped in a posh accent, continuing to a white house with peeling paint. 'PERKINS,' read a crooked wooden sign affixed to a short chain-link fence around a mostly dead front lawn. As I lifted up the latch, I jumped at the loud bang of a slammed front door. A woman exited the house, her back to me as she started to do the lock. A plastic pet carrier swung from her other hand.

"Um, excuse me. Belinda Perkins?" I called.

She whirled around. The carrier smacked into the door sill with a dense thud. I cringed. "Yes, who're you?" she barked at me, fierce as any dog.

I instantly regretted the whole idea of coming here. Her pale face was red, her eyes puffy with tears. "I'm sorry to bother you. I'm Bird Nichols. You might've known my grandma, Lucille? I brought you some flowers!" I brandished the vase.

At my grandma's name, Belinda's expression softened. "Of course! Lucille! I adored that woman. I can't believe she's dead. She was too tough to die, you know?" Her lip wobbled. "I'm sorry. I'm an emotional wreck right now."

"No need to apologize, I–" A fierce, agonized yowl cut me off.

"Shut up, you." Belinda gave the carrier a shake. "This is my son's cat. I can't... I can't deal with him right now." Her arm began to shake violently. I had the sudden awareness that she was going to drop the cat. Setting down the vase, I lunged forward to grip beneath the carrier right as she lost her hold. The cat's next yowl ended with a surprised question mark as the carrier lurched up and down. The whole thing weighed a lot more than I expected. I retreated a few steps to set the carrier down on the red-paver sidewalk next to the daffodil vase.

"I'm sorry," I said, not sure what else to say.

"For all of Chase's inadequacies, the one thing he could do was take care of this stupid cat. I can't cope with the litter box and all that thing's neediness. He has to go."

So the cat was male. "Go where?"

"I don't even care. Away." She gestured to the wild blue yonder.

Oh no, no, no. Was she actually going to dump this cat in the hills? With all the cars, coyotes, wild dogs, and owls around? "There are animal shelters–"

"I don't have time to call or drive around. I need to... I need to talk to the police again. I need to make funeral arrangements. I need to clear out his things, and I need to work soon, because I need the money more than ever. Even dead, he's bringing me deeper into debt." Belinda's bitter laugh made it clear how close she was to shattering completely.

"I'll take the cat." The words emerged, and only then did I realize what I'd said.

"Good." Tears started streaming down her cheeks. "Thank you. I... I think I need to sit down." She made a controlled collapse onto her concrete front stoop.

"Have you eaten anything today? When did you last have water?"

"Are you a mother?" Her laugh was weaker, less bitter.

I shrugged. "I'm serious. You need to take care of yourself, especially right now."

"You sound like Jessie. She's young, but she harps on me, too."

"Jessie who works at Quesoquick?" I asked. She nodded. "Everyone knows each other here."

"Small town. Very small. That's how it goes. Everyone sure knew Chase – knew him and hated him. Can't say I blame them, either. He practiced pissing off people like it was his job. The only things he took seriously were gambling, video games, and that cat. He couldn't hold a normal job anywhere."

I had struggled to hold normal jobs myself. I'd needed to get creative and find my own way to make money. Maybe Chase could've found legal employment that worked for him, under other circumstances.

"It sounds like this has been hard on you for a long time," I said.

Belinda had to be somewhere in her fifties, but she looked closer to Grizz's age and far more fragile. The squarish bones in her shoulders were visible through the weave of her thin sweater. "Chase almost killed me when he was born. He never stopped being a trial. Always the bully in school. Rebelling against anyone and everyone. And now he's dead. I'm sad, but I'm relieved, too. Does that make me a terrible person?" She cast her eyes upward. She wasn't asking me for absolution. "Jessie is going to set up an online fundraiser for his funeral, and in all honesty, I don't know if anyone will donate. If they do, it's because they feel sorry for me."

"No, it'll mean they care about you," I said. The assurance felt trite. On the verge of a lie.

"Chase was always going on and on about all the money he was going to make, and when he had a win and would lose it again, he'd say, 'I'll have better luck next time.' That was his mantra." She rubbed her face between her palms. "Guess he finally ran out of luck."

I didn't know what more to say. The cat at my feet emitted a querulous yowl. I welcomed the change in subject. "About this cat – what's his name?"

"Bowser."

I stooped to look through the metal hatch. "Good grief. He's like an orange bowling ball." Yellow eyes glared from the shadows.

That evoked a lighter laugh from Belinda. "An orange bowling ball. Yeah. That sounds about right." She teetered as she stood. "I'm going inside. I need to… do things. So many things." Her eyes half shut as she wavered for a second, but she regained her bearings before I could approach. She turned and fumbled with her keys to reopen the door.

"Hey, before you go, can I ask–"

The door closed. The vase of daffodils still sat on the walkway. My new cat yowled, a sound of blatant frustration. "Yeah, you said it," I told Bowser, sighing.

Chapter Seven

"Well," I said to Bowser as I hoisted him up. This cat had to be what the internet dubbed a mega-chonk. Twenty pounds, minimum. "Time to go shopping! I'll get you basics so I can make you cozy in the hall bathroom for at least tonight." Just what I needed, more items on my to-do list.

I walked away, continuing to worry about Belinda. Grief was a complicated thing, as I knew all too well, and she seemed deep in the anger stage of bereavement. No way could I include her in my list of suspects, though. For one, she was his mom. Two, she seemed physically incapable of the act. Actually, no; I shouldn't make that kind of snap judgment. Sorrow could debilitate a person. The only thing I could be certain of was that she *currently* struggled to complete tasks.

"I really feel for Belinda," I murmured to Bowser as we took the sidewalk between the wings of the strip mall. I carried the vase in my other hand. "She's dealing with a lot right now."

Bowser yowled agreement. And kept yowling at a decibel like a fire alarm. I cringed every single time.

I acted nonchalant as I went to my car, but I could sense the weird looks I was getting from all around. Yesterday the lot had been so empty, yet today it was bustling. A small child nearer to Quesoquick piped up, "Mom, what's that weird noise?"

"I hope this yowling isn't a regular thing for you," I told Bowser. I opened up the back passenger-side door to set him on the floor. "I'm going to pop over to the store to grab supplies really fast. Please don't pee in my car. Please?" I started the car long enough to partially roll down two windows. The day was quite cool, but I wasn't going to take any risks. I left the vase in the cupholder.

"I'll be right back," I told Bowser as I locked up.

As I approached the shops, I noted what looked to be a small shrine with flowers and candles beside the door of Salon & Nails. Oh, good, I had a place to set my own offering. As much as I liked the vase, I had a feeling that the combo of new cat and breakable vase would not end well for anyone.

New cat. What was I thinking? This had to be temporary. I'd get him to a shelter tomorrow. I mean, I did love cats. I'd grown up with three tabbies, and Grandma had a Siamese-mix cat until he died of kidney disease a few years ago. I really didn't need extra drama in my life right now, though. I had to finish moving in, handle my cheese orders, take care of Grizz by solving this murder.

I did a quick U-turn to grab the vase again. Bowser was still screaming. He kept it up as I walked across the lot.

The memorial consisted of two flower vases, a teddy bear, several unlit candles, and some flowers laying on the ground. Chase's name adorned one ribbon, but everything else addressed Belinda.

"Hi there! Oh, pretty daffodils. Early in the year to see those!" The voice at the open door jolted me. I glanced, then did a double take. The woman who smiled at me looked an awful lot like Belinda. Not so much in their faces – they wouldn't pass for sisters – but they wore the same business-casual floral shirts like I'd see at Target, same dyed blonde hair with dark roots showing, same fiftyish age range. This woman, though, was of a healthier, curvy build.

"Hi! I brought these for Belinda." I set my vase in the shrine.

"Thanks. I'm sure she'll be by to see them later. She's off the schedule for a few days, but she lives right nearby. Are you a client?"

"I actually just moved here, but I know Belinda and Chase."

"Oh! There are so few homes here, local newbies don't come in often. Tourists, though. We get so many tourists! You'd be amazed at how many women stop in on a coastal road trip because they had a nail break along the way." Her gesticulation drew my attention to her blue nails with little snowmen painted on each one.

"You're a nail technician here?"

"I'm *the* nail tech. Plus, I do hair." She corrected me with a friendly smile. "I'm Ella May. I've been here about as long as Belinda."

I hesitated a second and then resolved to be nosy. "I'm really worried about Belinda and how she's taking this. She seems so... fragile these days."

Ella May glanced inside. One woman sat under a hair dryer helmet, attention on the phone in her hands. Ella May let the door close so she could stand outside with me.

"Belinda is trying to act like everything's fine," Ella May said in a low voice. "But she's barely been eating the past six months. She is under a ton of stress, most of it caused by Chase. I mean, that's why she picked up the evening job at the warehouse down in Grover, right?" I nodded like I knew about that as I experienced a new surge of sadness for Belinda. Her physical struggles weren't something new and episodic after all. She had truly been overwhelmed by awful life stuff. "That was totally because of Chase's legal bills. I wonder if there's more going on, though."

"I hope she's still keeping up with doctor appointments even though she's working two jobs," I said.

"She has been doing that, yeah. She's taken off a few hours here and there. She normally tells me everything, but these days..." Worry clouded her eyes. Some measure of hurt, too. "Hey, if you need to get anything done today, it's a slow afternoon. I could work you in." Her gaze went to my blank, bland fingernails.

I posed a smile on my face. No way could I tell her that the one time I tried acrylic nails back in college, due to roomie peer pressure, I ended up ripping them off within a week. My natural nails had taken ages to heal. The feel of the fake nails, the way I couldn't feel *my* nails, had even made me awaken at night in a panic. "It's not a slow afternoon for me, sorry. I actually need to dash into the grocery store then rush home and do my own work."

"What do you do?" Ella May asked as I took a step away.

"Artisan cheese boards."

She gasped. "For real? I love cheese!"

"All the best people do," I quipped, pulling a business card out of my purse. "If you're on social media, look me up. I have loads of pictures."

"I'll do that! My sister in Pismo is getting married later this year. This might work for her. She's trying to avoid a cake because of the sugar. Can you believe that? A wedding without cake? Isn't that blasphemy or sacrilege or something?"

I grinned. "I've actually made cheese-cakes for two clients so far, and I don't mean the Philadelphia kind with cream cheese. I'm talking whole rounds of cheese, stacked in tiers, with accompaniments and crackers."

"Oh, God yes. Can I get another card? That might be an even better kind of cake. Maybe I won't disown her after all." I could hear the salivation in her words. I pressed another card into her hands. I could hardly believe my luck. Ella May wouldn't quite have the connection power of Rita at Slocombe House, but she'd know everyone and everything going on around here.

"Send me an email or text if you have any questions," I said. "Nice chatting with you!"

"Thanks, you too!" Ella May stared at my card as she went back inside.

Meanwhile, Bowser continued to yowl, his voice carrying like that of a yodeler on an alpine mountain. I hurried down the covered walkway to the grocer. To my relief, they had a small pet section – and to my dismay, it had few foods and only miniature bags of cat litter. No scoops, no litter boxes, no liners.

I purchased what I could. A young white guy with acne-freckled cheeks worked the counter today. He didn't offer any conversation, which was fine by me.

As I finished loading my purchases into my car, a young man jogged straight toward me, waving. He held a familiar aluminum pouch in his hand.

"Hey. Your name is Bird, right? Jessie sent this." He panted as he held the sandwich out to me. Now that he was close, I could see his polo shirt had an embroidered logo of a waffle-patterned, oozy grilled cheese sandwich with tiny wings and motion lines.

I shook my head. "I didn't order anything from Quesoquick."

"We're closing up for the day. We had some extra stuff we'd otherwise dump. She said you like cheese a lot."

Well, how could I argue with that? "I do. Thanks. What kind is it?" I asked, accepting the bag. It exuded heat.

"The GOAT." He said it with emphasis that informed me that this was the acronym for Greatest of All Time. "Smeared fresh goat cheese, shredded mozzarella, California-made date preserves, all on sourdough. We're out of white," he said, like he needed to apologize. His tan skin flushed.

"Wow. You have no idea how much I need this dose of cheesiness right now. Thank you."

His gaze went to the unseen noisemaker in my car. "That cat sounds mad."

"I guess so. I just met him. I haven't had a cat in years, but I couldn't let this little furry guy get dumped somewhere." Stressed as I was, once I started babbling, I couldn't stop. "I just went into the grocery store, but their cat care selection is sadly lacking – what are you doing?"

He'd pulled out his phone and started tapping, rapid fire. "Dale has cat stuff galore. He's fostering two batches of kittens."

I blinked, absorbing this news. "He does?" The man couldn't be more saintly if he wore a halo. "Could he take in Bowser?"

"Nah." The young guy didn't look up. He had to be barely out of high school; tall and skinny with close-cropped black hair. "No way does he have room. Okay, Dale replied. He can't leave his house right now. He's on hold with a supplier and has to stay at his computer. Can he go by your house in two or three hours?"

"Sure. Does he know where I live?"

He texted again then nodded. "He just said he does, yeah. Jessie told him. Not like there are loads of houses around here. So anyway, I need to start on tomorrow's dough." He pocketed his phone and set off without a goodbye.

"Hey!" I called, causing him to turn around. "What's your name?"

"Maurice."

"Thanks! For everything!" He gave me a wave as he jogged back to the restaurant.

I shook my head in awe as I settled into my seat. "A free sandwich, a free cat. Good things come in threes, right? What's next?" I asked Bowser, who continued to holler. How was his voice not sore by now?

I sanitized my hands then opened up my sandwich. I made no pause for a 'Gram-worthy video today. I was frazzled, hungry, and I took my comfort in queso bliss. The mozzarella had melted into gooey strands even as the goat cheese created soft cheesy puddles. Fig preserves went well with so many cheeses, and wow, was it good in this sandwich with its soft, crunchy, waffle-iron-blessed bread.

"I need to see if they have a tip jar on their counter or online. I owe them big," I told Bowser.

Another person crossed the lot toward my car: Jessie from Quesoquick. She had a notable limp. "Hey," she called out to me. "Just a quick chat. That cat that's screaming – is that Bowser?"

Bowser yowled the affirmative.

"Yes," I said, clarifying for his sake. At the question in her eyes, I continued, "I stopped by to talk to Belinda Perkins.

She was... about to dump him, I think. I couldn't let that happen. I said I'd take him."

"Oh, good God." She pressed her hand to her neck. She wore a thick red scarf above the collar of her uniform polo shirt. "I'll talk to her. That's not right. I mean, I know she never liked the cat, but she could've at least called up a shelter."

"Don't bother her about it. He can't go back to her. She's clearly not up to taking care of him. I'll make sure he's settled into a new home."

"Okay. Yeah. I'm glad you were able to grab him. I should have thought about Bowser as soon as I heard about Chase. Not like I can take in Bowser myself, though. Me and my roomies, we have a Chihuahua. Bowser would probably eat her." She tilted her neck, stretching and wincing.

"How are you feeling?" I asked.

Jessie's smile was faint. "Tired. I was up all night. New semester, y'know, getting schoolwork done after my shift here. And, ugh." She stretched again, wincing. "I tried doing gymnastics moves yesterday. Showing off, I guess. I hadn't tried those in five years, and man, I feel it today. If this is what getting old is like, it's going to suck."

"I hear that. I've been moving boxes all week and I have the bruises and aching muscles to prove it. Hey, how much do you know about Bowser? Does he have an established vet? How old is he?"

"Um." She tapped her fingernails on the open car door. "Chase got him as a kitten like three years ago. I think he had him fixed at a place in Cayucos. Kittens and Friends, or something like that." I nodded. I could look up that place. "I doubt he's kept up with stuff like shots, though Bowser was about the only thing he loved." She said that matter-of-factly.

"Sounds like you knew Chase well," I said.

"Sure. He was a grade ahead of me in school. We rode the bus together every day until we both got cars in high school. He was my first boyfriend. We were together for a year, and that was like three-hundred and sixty days too long. Maybe it was good that my first relationship was so awful. I learned a lot, the hard way." She reflexively touched her own neck and then recoiled, seeming to realize she'd revealed too much.

"What, did he—" I stopped myself. "Sorry, it's not my business."

"Nah, you're good. He was abusive. Manipulative. Stuff like that." Jessie said it dismissively, and what she didn't say said everything. "He'd steal cash, credit cards, whatever he could get. My dad banned him from the house after some family jewelry went missing. We ended up finding it in a pawn shop in S-L-O. He pawned away a lot of stuff from his own house, too. I kept telling Belinda that she needed to kick him out, let him go to jail or straight to hell, but she kept trying to save him." Jessie hiccupped as tears started. "She's worn herself down to nothing for him."

"Belinda said you were setting up an online fundraiser to help her with funeral expenses," I said as softly as I could while still trying to be heard over Bowser.

"Yeah. It's the least I could do, you know? She's been like a mom to me since I was a kid. I'm closer to her than I ever was to Chase." She sniffled. "She's been having a hard time lately. Someone swatted Slocombe House a while back. She's certain Chase did it out of spite."

"Grizz mentioned that to me. He said it ruined a wedding."

"It did more than that. One guy ended up with a concussion and a broken arm when an officer tried to restrain him. Several other people were hurt in a stampede when law enforcement flooded in with guns up. An old lady had a heart attack and had to go to the hospital, but I think she ended up okay. Swatting is so freaking scary." She shuddered.

"It really is. I've had to deal with trolls online, and one of my big fears is that I'll be swatted, too. Do you think Chase was behind this incident?"

Jessie looked subdued. "It seems like the cowardly way he'd attack someone. What scared me about the swatting is that it set a precedent, right? Chase liked to try out different stunts, like stealing different models of car or breaking into buildings. If he succeeded, he'd keep repeating the crime, trying to get better at it. He referred to it as leveling up, like in a video game. What drove me nuts was that he started posting videos online of the stupid crap he did, and he got an even bigger thrill out of all the likes and shares his posts got. I told him that advertising his crimes would make it even easier for him to get busted, and he laughed at me. Like he was invincible. He wasn't, though. He really wasn't." Tears streamed down her cheeks.

"I'm sorry. I didn't mean to make you upset. I do have tissues here, if you–"

"No, I need to get back to work, get the place set up for tomorrow. You're not waiting for Dale here, are you? I think he's stuck at home for a while."

"No, I need to–" My phone started to vibrate. I glanced at my watch to see who was calling. An all-caps name filled up the tiny screen: DETECTIVE MERRICK.

"Oh, no. What does he want?" Seeing Jessie's puzzled expression, I continued. "It's Detective Merrick. I need to answer this." She nodded in hearty agreement as I pulled out my phone and accepted the call. "Hello, detective?"

"Hello, Miss Nichols, how are you today?" His tone was crisply professional.

"Busy." Bowser screamed from his cage in the backseat.

"What on earth was that?"

"A cat," I said, matching his initial tone. I didn't want our conversation to go off on a tangent. "How can I help you today?"

"I need to speak with you. Can you please come down to the station in Los Osos?"

My breath caught. He was having me come in? "What's this about?"

"We have matters that we had best discuss in person as soon as possible."

"You mean you want me there right away."

"Yes, within the hour. Are you in Foghorn right now?"

"Yes." I pressed a fist against my chest, as if I could help keep my panicked heart inside my chest. Had he found something that somehow incriminated me? Was I going to get arrested? Or was this about Grizz? Did I need a lawyer right away? I didn't want one, I really didn't, even though I knew Grandma would say I should get one. I wanted to handle Merrick on my own. I needed to. But what if I couldn't? No, no, I could do this myself. I just needed to give myself time to think through my responses. I'd look less guilty to Merrick if I cooperated.

"Very well. I'll see you soon. Goodbye." And just like that, Detective Merrick hung up. I pulled my phone away from my ear to stare at the screen in disbelief.

"He's making me drive all the way to Los Osos," I said to Jessie, who looked on me with deep sympathy. "That's like... forty-five minutes away."

"That really sucks," Jessie said. Bowser yowled as if in agreement.

"What am I going to do with the cat? I can't take him with me! He'd probably pee in my car." Thoughts zoomed through my head like a spaceship going at lightspeed. "Okay. Okay. I need to get Bowser to my house first. I can dash to Los Osos from there."

"Good luck with everything. I had to speak with a deputy earlier, too, but we did that here. I think they talked to everyone who works in the area." Jessie stepped back from my car. "That detective needs to stop pestering people in Foghorn and go find the criminals that Chase was working with. Really, the biggest surprise is that it took Chase so long to end up dead."

Did Jessie know about George? There was no time to ask. She gave me a final wave as she limped back toward the restaurant.

I proceeded to break multiple traffic laws in my rush to get home.

Once there, I hauled Bowser into the hall bathroom. A beach theme decorated the white and blue room, a shadowbox of sand dollars from Morro Bay on the wall. I pulled down the starfish-covered plastic shower curtain and removed the half-full roll of toilet paper. A litter box! I still needed a litter box! In my bedroom, I dumped stationery from a plastic tote box with low sides. The small litter bag filled it about two-thirds high. Perfect. I'd kept a couple of Grandma's old melamine bowls in garish 1970s yellow and green. They'd do for Bowser's food and water.

I closed the bathroom door with us both inside, then sat on the closed toilet as I unlatched the carrier door.

"Come on, Bowser," I crooned. I needed to hurry to meet Merrick, but I had to make sure the cat was okay first.

Bowser crept onto the toilet rug, audibly sniffling. "Wow. You are a mega-chonk," I said in admiration. Bowser was big-boned, like a bulldog in feline form, with a bright orange tabby coat and a long tail with a major crook at the end. I would need to get that checked to make certain the injury had healed okay. Bowser glanced up at me as if he wanted to take my measure too. His face seemed to be made up of a sequence of chubby circles, like a cartoon cat, sea lion-like white whiskers drooping from each cheek. The white fur that framed his yellow eyes was long and tufted, resembling crazed old man eyebrows.

"You look healthy, as far as I can tell," I murmured. "I'm sorry you lost your person. And your home. I hope you can settle in here, at least for a bit. There's food over–"

To my shock, he leaped onto my lap. As I began to stroke his head, a motor-loud purr radiated from his body. He spun in circles. I angled my chin up to avoid taking a tail to the mouth.

"I wonder if Merrick would excuse me from our appointment if I told him that my new cat needed some therapeutic lap time?" I asked, laughing as Bowser continued his happy spins. Clouds of orange hair drifted around us. "Probably not, huh? Well, I'll go bananas if I don't know what Merrick wants to talk about. Come on. Hop down." I gave Bowser a nudge. He shot me a baleful look as he landed, then approached his food bowl, sniffing. I took that as my cue to leave. I closed the bathroom door behind me, took a deep breath, smoothed my fingers through my hair, and then ran through a mental checklist. I could get to his office on time, I could do this. And everything else I needed to do today.

As I headed to the front door, a querulous yowl boomed from the bathroom.

"I'll be back soon!" I called, my keys in hand. I then realized I had no idea what was about to happen. I couldn't trust Merrick or any other cop. I could be on the verge of being arrested for some inexplicable reason.

"I'll be back soon. I hope," I amended, then left.

Chapter Eight

The Coast Station for the Sheriff's Department consisted of a blocky gray building on a street corner. I drove by, searching for a public parking lot. Finding nothing, I looped back around to park on the curb across the street. My anxiety had decreased on the drive as the traffic had been mercifully light, even through the highway construction zone. Now, however, all of my worries doused me like a full water bucket.

As I crossed the street, I reminded myself to make a conscious effort to act like I was a composed neurotypical person. Stand up straight, even though I wanted to curl up in a fetal position. Keep my hands still, no fluttering. Don't do anything to attract special attention.

I hated that I had to mask my natural behaviors, but it was a survival technique for a hostile world. Merrick might have some experience with autism within his family, but that didn't mean he could appropriately assess my reactions.

I entered and approached the front desk, a practiced smile on my lips. "Hi, I'm Bird Nichols. I have an appointment with Detective Merrick?"

The uniformed woman scrutinized me with a glance. "Take a seat."

I claimed the only open chair. A man beside me sat with his knees spread wide, like he was braced to wrestle a polar bear. I wiggled to sit on the far edge of my chair, leaning over a side table with a scattering of wrinkled magazines. I checked my watch. Exactly an hour had passed since Merrick's call. He couldn't criticize me for being late. That made me feel a little better.

I felt decidedly less better as the next thirty-six minutes rolled by. The guy next to me left, to be replaced by a gray-haired woman who hummed to herself as she scrolled on her phone. I resisted the urge to put in my ear plugs, as I knew that'd make me look rude, instead sitting stiffly as I tried and failed to ignore her off-key undulations. People in other chairs came and went. A toddler was slamming a toy truck hood-first into the carpet about six inches ahead of my toes when I spied Merrick approaching through a canyon of low cubicle walls.

"Miss Nichols," he said with a tight smile, beckoning me. "I'm sorry to keep you waiting."

I schooled myself to walk with slow deliberation even though I felt like I was fleeing purgatory. "That's okay," I said, in immediate hindsight realizing that my shrill tone made my lie obvious. When he cast me a curious raised eyebrow, I continued. "I raced to get here. At the speed limit, of course." Another lie. "Then I had to wait."

"Again, I'm sorry. Active investigations tend not to obey tidy schedules. Can I get you a water bottle?"

I shook my head. I was thirsty, sure, but as rattled as I was, I'd either choke or end up wearing the water. As we both sat down on either side of a broad desk, Merrick's gaze lowered to my chest for a few seconds. Knowing he couldn't be ogling me – he just didn't seem that sort – I glanced down to find my navy-blue shirt was coated with long orange cat hair.

"Is that hair from the cat I heard in the background when I called?" he asked.

"Yes. I rescued him from being dumped in the wild." No way was I going to reveal who had previously owned the cat, not unless I absolutely had to.

"I'm glad you stepped up," Merrick said with surprising passion. "Coyotes and owls get a lot of outdoor cats around here. Years ago, my uncle had a stray he took care of. We couldn't catch the cat no matter how we tried – he was too smart for any traps – but he was the handsomest cat with black and white spots. I got to where I could sit twenty feet away and draw him, and he'd purr." Merrick shook his head. "It wrecked me when I found his mauled body."

"Oh." I was stunned at the personal revelation. "How old were you?"

"Ten. I tried to do a forensic analysis to determine what killed him. I think that's when my family knew my future career path."

"You grew up around here?"

"San Luis Obispo. My uncle lived over in Arroyo Grande." Merrick cleared his throat, resuming his stoicism. "You did the right thing for this cat."

"Thanks." Time for me to get down to business as well. "Where are you in your investigation of Grizz?"

He gazed at me levelly. "I cannot discuss that investigation."

"Meaning he's still considered a suspect."

"Everyone is being considered, including you. Which is why we needed to speak."

In that instant, all of my anxiety was validated. "But I have a solid alibi, and I found Chase dead! There have to be cameras around the shopping center in Foghorn. They'd prove where I was."

"Such evidence doesn't exclude you from involvement."

"True. I *could* be a co-conspirator or an accessory or something of that ilk." I paused. I was beginning to understand why people lawyered up first thing. Nervous rambling was not going to help my case. I suddenly remembered Grandma once mentioning she kept her attorneys' numbers in her cell phone. That phone was in a drawer back at the house. I'd need to charge it, but if it brought up the info of someone she used regularly – as I was beginning to suspect might be the case – it could be useful. As if I didn't have enough to do. "What do you need to know?"

"Foremost, I want to share what I've discovered. I did some research on you and found the news about your parents' deaths. I'm sorry for your loss. The past year must have been quite difficult, losing them and then your grandmother in quick succession."

I deeply inhaled, a hitch in my throat. "Yeah, you could say that."

"It must have compounded your grief to see charges dropped against Duvall Harmonson."

I stiffened, my temper rising along with my need to rant. "No. That had no effect on my grief. Did it *infuriate* me? Yes. Did it make me lose faith in the criminal justice system? Yes. The guy was seventeen when he drove drunk and plowed into their car dead-on. He lived and was barely dinged thanks to the brand-new massive truck that his daddy bought him. My parents were killed instantly in their smaller car. There was no question of Duvall Harmonson's guilt, but he got off with an 'oh, this poor rich boy made a bad decision one night, but he has his whole life ahead of him.' My parents weren't even fifty. They had lots of life left to live, too."

Detective Merrick held up both hands as if to placate me, which only made me angrier. He started this fire. He should've been prepared to get burned. "I'm not arguing with you there," he said. "The system doesn't always get it right. Trust me, I know." He gestured to himself with a grimace; yes, as a Black man in a profession with a proven pattern of discrimination, he would have experienced and witnessed the inadequacies of American law enforcement firsthand. I conceded his point with a nod, my rage cooling some. "Have you followed news about Mr Harmonson?"

I mulled how to reply for a moment, acutely aware of Merrick's focus and the many black-domed cameras throughout the station. I had no doubt that anything I said would be used against me in a court of law. "I actually followed Duvall Harmonson on social media for a while. When the case was being considered, he kept things private, but when he was freed, he switched to public. After a few weeks of seeing him post pictures of his new truck and snowboarding and selfies with pretty women, I decided that it was best for my mental health to keep my feeds focused on everything cheese-related."

"You haven't heard from the Fresno County officers involved in the case?"

Where was he going with this? What did this have to do with Chase? "No, not in months. I reached out to them after Grandma, you know, to let everyone know that I had to be the contact person from now on since she was missing."

"Then you don't know that Duvall Harmonson is dead."

I stared at him. "He's dead? Really? How? When? Why didn't anyone tell me?"

"I can't answer that last one. Someone should have contacted you. It would only have been right. As to the how and when, right before Christmas at his apartment in Clovis. An accidental drug overdose."

The world suddenly seemed very quiet even though I had faint awareness of other people jabbering in the room and the distinct, muffled beat of mariachi music playing outside. Duvall Harmonson was dead. My parents' murderer was dead. No more parties, women, and living the high life. His parents would be alive and suffering, too. They had proven themselves to be awful people like their progeny. They'd gone on the local news, trying to blame my parents because they'd been out on a date night. A toxicology report proved Mom and Dad both had a glass of wine hours before their deaths. Alcohol was detectable in only trace amounts. They were sober. Not at fault.

The Harmonsons had thought their baby could do no wrong. Now they'd had to endure their first holiday season without Duvall.

Good.

I didn't smile. I didn't whoop with joy. I couldn't even say I was happy. What I felt was… relief. Schadenfreude. A strange sense of satisfaction.

Merrick was clearly studying me for a reaction, and that irritated me all over again.

"What, are you going to try to blame me for Duvall's death, too? Or blame Grizz? Good luck with that. He hates the Central Valley. He couldn't even tolerate driving to Fresno for my parents' funeral."

"I'm not trying to place blame at all, but I do find it curious that Mr Harmonson is dead and now you find another body a month later."

"Give me the particulars on when Duvall Harmonson died and I can probably give you an alibi. Up through Christmas,

I was doing ten-hour night shifts every day stocking at a grocery store in S-L-O. My co-workers came down sick, too. Food poisoning. I picked up a lot of overtime. In what little free time I had, I threw my cheese orders together."

"You worked yourself hard. Not even a day off for Christmas."

"You already checked on my whereabouts. Of course you did."

"That's my job," Detective Merrick said.

"I admit, I had an excellent motive to want Duvall Harmonson dead; but Chase? I met the guy once."

"And if he'd continued to be a nuisance?"

"I would've contacted the sheriff's office and hoped they did something. Honestly, if I was going around killing people who annoyed me, I'd be a serial killer. And I'm not." I added for emphasis.

"Your grandmother once told me, quite calmly over coffee, that most people were the equivalent of mosquitoes."

"That sounds like something she'd say." I paused a beat. I was unsurprised he'd had coffee with Grandma. I wondered how long he'd been in the department before making detective. "Are you trying to say *she* was a serial killer?"

"I don't know what your grandmother was." Merrick's tone was a mix of awe and frustration. "Outwardly, she didn't have a job, nor had she inherited any wealth from her husband's death. I asked her once what she did for a living, and she said she did puzzles. She wouldn't elaborate, but I knew she didn't mean the jigsaw variety."

I felt like I should be indignant on Grandma's behalf again, but instead I shook my head and sighed. "I don't have answers for you." Inheriting her estate had made me wonder about her financials too. "There's a lot about Grandma I don't understand."

"Hmph." He considered me with pursed lips. "I recall that you were kept away from her for much of your childhood."

"What, is that in my file, too?" My words were sharp.

"Actually, no. Lucille mentioned it to me once a few years ago when I found her lurking around a terrible car crash scene in the middle of the night. I'll spare you the details, but it was suspicious for her to be there." He shook his head. I knew he had to be considering how she'd long plagued the department with her meddling ways. "I was exasperated and asked her what her family must think of her prowling about during the night, and I must've hit a nerve. She snapped that her family didn't understand, that she'd been kept away from her only grandchild and was only getting to see the girl now because she'd started college at Cal Poly. Lucille went on to say she was just starting to regularly speak with her daughter and son-in-law again, but that their conversations could never compensate for so much lost time."

Tears stung my eyes. "Yeah. Things stayed weird between them right up until they died. I think that made her grief even worse. She wanted to make up for those years of strained relations, and she couldn't."

"There's been a lot of death and grief in your family this past while."

"But here I am, still alive, right? Are you going to look at me as a suspect in Grandma's disappearance, too? You probably know that I was questioned months ago as a matter of procedure since I'd recently been named a co-owner of her estate. You should also know that her distress in the ocean was witnessed by dozens of people on the beach –

and I wasn't present. I was working." I shook my head in disgust. "That's old history. Chase's murder is the issue now. Why aren't you going after suspects with a much stronger motive to see him dead, like George?"

Oops. Definitely should not have mentioned him. "George?" Merrick's voice went sharp. "How do you know about George?"

I shrugged, abashed. "Everyone knows everything about everyone around Foghorn."

Merrick looked downright irate. "You *are* like your grandmother." In light of what he'd recently said about her, the comparison felt more disparaging than complimentary. "Who else have you spoken with today?"

That was my cue to finally act smart and keep my mouth shut. "Am I under arrest, Detective Merrick?"

He considered me over his twined hands as he leaned forward on his desk. "Not at this moment."

I stood, my hands clutching my purse. "Then I should get going. I need to go cut cheese." I paused, realizing I'd accidentally made a fart joke in a very serious moment, but at least the man didn't laugh and annoy me even more. "Goodbye, Detective Merrick."

"I'll see you later, Miss Nichols." His smile was forcefully pleasant, the threat of his words ominous.

Chapter Nine

I returned home to find the bathroom door cracked open. Bowser was gone.

"I know I closed it; I heard it click!" I whirled around, trying to catch sight of him, but he had a hundred places to hide with all the boxes and bags around. Well, Bowser would come out when he was ready. I totally understood if he needed to hide from the world for a while. I was feeling much the same.

I'd lost almost three hours of the day because of my trip to Los Osos. I had to start on my cheese order for tomorrow. Instead, I pulled out my laptop and looked up the news on Duvall Harmonson.

The local paper and two of the news stations in my hometown had mentioned his death in passing. An initial report on Duvall's death had actually labeled it a suspected suicide, which the family had publicly refuted ('our son had too much to live for'). His parents had the nerve to suggest donations in their son's name be sent to a local drug recovery agency. People needed to support that place, sure, but the Harmonsons didn't deserve any credit.

His name also brought up stories about my parents and the court case. I read those again by compulsion, the way I might pick at a fresh scab, then went back to my search results. I found his obituary. It, of course, sainted him. He'd been a fun-loving guy with a passion for football, barbecues, blah blah blah.

I closed all the tabs at once and shut my laptop. Breathing hard, I rubbed my palm against my forehead. I had to stop reading this garbage. I had to. Mom and Dad were dead, and Grandma was missing and likely dead, but Grizz was alive. He was the family that I had left.

I tried calling him. Despite my earlier pleas for him to keep his phone close and to actually answer it, the thing rang and rang and went to voice mail. I left a message, exasperated. "Grizz, this is Bird. I'm attempting to check on you. Pretty-pretty-please call me back today. Bye."

Now I had to hope he remembered to check his voicemail – and how to do it, because I'd already walked him through the procedure five times.

Locking up the house, I headed to the Kitchen. I shuffled through my printouts and replaced the schematics above my workstation. I stared at the plan, suddenly and profoundly exhausted. Of course, the next order couldn't be for some fancy date-night platter for two that would take under an hour. No, it was for my largest kind of cheese board, and a current major fad: the grazing table.

I assembled my wax-coated boxes. I used large boxes – think cafeteria-sized casserole dishes – to create my framework, then on the inside I arranged various small boxes to fit together like a successful game of Tetris. A traditional grazing table used the full span of a surface as a cheese and charcuterie board; I did the same but used my organized boxes. In this business, grazing tables were gold mines. Depending on the table, they could cost thousands of dollars. They were also tons of work. This order was for a woman's 50th birthday party and included four packed platters; it was my biggest order since New Year's Eve. The payment – deposited in full three weeks ago, so I could buy the cheese and accoutrements – was more than I would make in two weeks of full-time work at my old job as a stocker.

The centerpiece of each box was an eight-inch round of an American-made cheese in the style of French Brie. Each one had achieved perfect ripeness. Yes, soft rind cheeses have levels of ripeness. I could usually tell one was too far gone by a sharp ammonia funk, not unlike cat urine.

These cheeses, however, were perfect. They had a clean smell and felt like ripe peaches beneath my fingertips, softly fuzzy with the slightest bit of give. When they got to room temperature for serving at the party, they'd be thick and ooey-gooey, perfect for smearing onto the accompanying crackers.

Today, I was incredibly thankful that these centerpieces could travel intact to the event. No need to slice them or make them into some elaborate arrangement. However, I still had additional cheeses to prepare. I grabbed the twelve-month Irish cheddar first, the blocks pure white thanks to the fine milk of cows that grazed on the verdant countryside. The dusting of powdery white on the outside was often mistaken for mold, but was really an ideal development called calcium lactate that could also speckle crystallization throughout the interior of aged cheddars. These blocks definitely had some luscious crystal action going on. The knife crunched through the paste as if I were cutting through large-grained salt. I made the pieces into long triangles, filling a tray to tuck back into the fridge.

Next up was a pretty cheese from Rogue Creamery,

Oregon Blue. The white-blue veining reminded me of a beautiful sky. It was made in the style of French Roquefort, but I found it more approachable and milder than its inspiration, making it a good entry-level cheese for people wary of blues. I chunked it and placed it back in the fridge. Big logs of creamy Northern California goat cheese from Laura Chenel were likewise fast to prep; I sliced them into disks. I'd arrange them in a snaking domino pattern within their smaller boxes when I finalized everything tomorrow.

The last cheese was a special favorite of mine: a California original from Vella Cheese – a dry jack with an especially hard rind that had been rubbed with oil, cocoa, and black pepper. I used my short-bladed Parmesan knife to carefully break it into slivers and chunks. The deep succulent nuttiness was great with fruit and meats, but I found it to be outright divine on salads. Whenever I served it at an event, I always had tons of feedback as people discovered it for the first time.

I glanced at the clock and yelped. I stripped off my gloves long enough to plug in my phone and place it in a cradle over my station. "Sorry that I'm late to tune in, Mollie," I said to my friend even though she couldn't hear me. I opened the Twitch app to start her twice-weekly livestream as she played through classic role-playing video games. Her show, Your Friendly Neighborhood Cleric, had racked up thousands of paid subscribers. Just as my online cheese business was starting to make me a living, Mollie was paying off her nursing school debt by playing games with an engaged audience.

"Ugh, my health bar is nearly empty!" The tiny screen of my phone showed a view of her headphone-framed face as she played through the game. I set my phone on its side, hiding the text-based chat window. There were seventy people logged in right now, many of them typing at once, and I would struggle to track that level of inundation even if I was using my bigger-screen laptop. On my phone, it was impossible. Besides, I was there to enjoy the background noise of my friend's voice and show her my support. She'd see that I was in attendance. My username was CheeseBird, complete with a commissioned avatar of a sparrow-like bird made of stereotypical holey orange cheese.

As I listened to Mollie and the game's battle music, I pulled out my boxes of accompaniments. This order included two kinds of crackers and one mini toast. Those, I could go ahead and arrange in the large boxes, as I could close the lids and keep them fresh for tomorrow. As I lined up the mini toasts on end, Mollie chatted with her audience. She had a personable, easy manner that I'd envied for years. We met in a classic video gaming club at Cal Poly. My parents had also loved old games – it was how they met – so I grew up watching them and then joining in to play Nintendo, Super Nintendo, and Sega Genesis games. Seeing Mollie play through some of those same games made me feel nostalgic and cozy, like I was, by extension, playing with Mom and Dad again.

"I see what you said there, Seth of Death 94," Mollie said, addressing some remark from the text chat. "Yeah, vintage game cartridge prices have gone ca-ray-zee these past few years. I'm not buying as much right now for that reason. Sure, I'd love a particular game with a mint condition box, instruction manual, and cartridge, but pay five hundred bucks? For real? And the battery likely wouldn't even work, so I'd have to replace that if I wanted to play the cart. All that fuss for a game that I already own in like five different digital versions since they keep remaking it. No thanks!"

I guffawed in agreement. As Mollie talked about another high-priced video game online auction, my hands slowed down as I became lost in thought. Chase Perkins had been a big video game fan, too. His mom said that his games and cat were the only things he cared about. Ray had mentioned that he was holding onto Chase's game collection because Belinda had threatened to pawn it. What had Chase specialized in, I wonder? Had he owned high-priced vintage games or more recent physical copies?

I pulled out hand-sized plastic cups and two slotted serving spoons. I was filling a third cup with whole Castelvetrano olives when I heard the ding-dong of the house's front doorbell. I stripped off my wet gloves so I could hit the button to initiate the speaker on my end, then spun around to mute Mollie on my phone.

"Hey, Bird! This is Dale!" His voice sounded breathy, like he had leaned close to the unit at the door.

"Oh, gosh, hi!" Good grief! Amid the intense stress of the afternoon, I'd totally forgotten that he was coming by. "I'm in the Kitchen out back. I have Bowser stuck in the bathroom in the house – well, I did, but then I discovered he can open doors. He might be part velociraptor." Dale got my reference to the first Jurassic Park movie, as he laughed. "I'll be there in just a sec!" I shut off the speaker, then cleaned my hands to put away the olives.

I grabbed my phone to send a direct text to Mollie. "GIHA." That was the code we used with each other: Guy In House Alert. Mollie would be live streaming for at least thirty more minutes, but when she was done, she'd follow up to make sure I was okay. I'd done the same for her more than once. As dating was a low priority in both of our busy lives, we used the code more often because of repair or delivery guys rather than for romantic outings.

I'd need to clarify with her later that Dale was just a new friend who happened to be cute and love cheese and cats. Which, I had to admit, wouldn't present a very convincing "we're just friends" argument for the long term. Mollie would probably cackle and ask where I could set up a wedding registry that included artisan cheese.

I rounded the outside of the house to meet Dale on the porch. A loaded cardboard box sat at his feet. I recognized the jutting plastic edge of a litter box plus the colorful tops of two bags of dry food. He sidestepped to give me space to unlock the door.

"I'm being vigilant about locking up. Murderer on the loose and all," I said. And here I was, letting a new acquaintance into the house with me alone. Like most Foghorn residents, he probably had good motives to hate Chase. Maybe I needed to create an extra code to use with Mollie: PMIH. Possible Murderer in House. "My place is a mess, by the way. Sorry."

"No need to apologize for that! You only moved yesterday, and you've been kept rather busy."

"That's the truth. Let's dash inside. I have no idea where Bowser is or if he'll make an effort to get out."

Dale took this in stride, cat-fostering pro that he was. We slipped inside. I almost slammed the door behind us. No orange cat was in sight.

Dale set the box down as he gazed around the cramped living room. "How are you, by the way? I heard you were the one who found Chase."

"Yeah. Here I thought that yesterday was going well, too.

Your sandwich was totally the highlight. I guess things could only go downhill from there."

"Thanks for sharing the video of your grilled cheese, by the way. Quesoquick added some three hundred new followers since you posted that, which is incredible. You're quite the cheese influencer."

His blatant admiration made me blush. "I just share what I love."

"I'm with you there. My social media feeds consist of cats and grilled cheese sandwiches. Oh, I have a big bag of litter in the car. Make sure I don't forget to bring that in."

"You're a lifesaver." I realized, to my chagrin, that I could've stocked up on supplies when I was driving back from Los Osos, but I was such a stressed-out mess that it hadn't even come to mind. "I don't suppose you brought a litter scoop, did you?"

"I did! Right in here." He nudged the box with his foot.

"Oh, thank you a million times over. I was afraid I'd need to don a pair of disposable gloves and sift by hand." My shudder of horror was not exaggerated. "I should go see if Bowser found the temporary litter box I put out."

"Maurice and Jessie's texts said that Belinda was going to dump this cat?" His brows drew together in a fierce scowl as I nodded. I motioned him to follow me. "She's a regular at Quesoquick. I know she's going through a lot, but I hate to think of her doing such a thing to a creature."

"She acted like she was on the verge of a nervous breakdown. Maybe a sequence of breakdowns."

"I can only imagine. Jessie's been very worried about her. When I first met Belinda, I actually thought she *was* Jessie's mom. I referred to her as such, and she surprised me by laughing with delight. She said she could only hope for such a daughter."

I paused. "Did Chase come around Quesoquick, too? Like, as a customer?"

"Only occasionally for food. More often than not, he lurked around to hassle Jessie. He'd call her 'girlfriend.' I could tell by his tone that he was doing it to irritate her, and it worked. He wanted to tell her everything that was going on in his life. He thought it was bragging, I suppose, but his accomplishments were petty. Every so often, he wheedled her for money or favors. I think she often gave in, just to spare Belinda from suffering his attentions." Dale sighed. "I told Jessie more than once that she should get a restraining order, but she refused. That paperwork would've made it difficult for her to help Belinda."

"It's a wonder Belinda didn't kick her son to the curb," I said.

"She did a few times, I think, but she tried to be a good mother. She couldn't let him be homeless."

"What an awful situation all around." I motioned to the open door in the hallway. "Here's the bathroom I tried to lock Bowser inside. Oh, good, he actually did use the box! Hmm. I don't need everything crammed in here anymore. Maybe I should move the litter box and bowls to the laundry room since he's roaming the house."

"I need to ask, is his stay going to be a permanent arrangement? No judgment if it's not. You're already doing right by him even if this is temporary."

"I *thought* it was just for tonight. I've only gotten to pet him once, and yet…"

Dale laughed, a sparkling, joyous sound. "Cats can infiltrate your heart quickly. Is it okay if I offer some advice?"

I nodded for him to continue. "Keep this current litter box in the bathtub. Set up the one I brought in the laundry room." He motioned at the doorway across the hall. "Once he starts using that as well, then you can cease keeping the small one in here."

"I wouldn't have thought of that. Thanks! This will be my first cat as an adult."

"Welcome to the club. That's how it starts. I now have two permanent overlords and I'm fostering two passels of kittens, with one batch on the wee side. I'm up every two hours to feed them. I'm afraid to know what the next few months will be like as kitten season truly gets going."

I shook my head. I didn't know how he could handle that kind of responsibility on top of his business. I'd be a nervous wreck under such a load. "Let's bring in that cat litter before we forget."

We went outside. I held the front door open – keeping an eye out for Bowser – as he hauled in the bulk-store-sized litter. The bag had to be forty pounds.

"How did you know that I was going to be tempted to keep Bowser for more than one night?" I asked. "Do I have a vibe that says 'Future Cat Lady'?"

Dale hesitated. "Yes...? But please understand that from me, that's a high compliment."

I laughed. "I do, I totally do. I find it hilarious. I've already been so stressed with the move on top of my work, and now this murder, plus a cat. But who am I to complain? You're running a larger small business and have a coordinated feline incursion in your house right now, yet you made time to come here. I don't know how you're managing it all."

"I prioritize what matters," Dale said. I wondered how to interpret that as he smiled at me. "I've also learned to delegate. When I first started out, I tried to do everything myself. I soon reached a burn-out point and accepted that I'd been daft. I'm lucky I have good employees to share the burden at this point. Even as we speak, Maurice is at 'Quick, shaping loaves to slow-rise in the walk-in until I come in at four. I will admit, though, today has been... a lot. A deputy spoke with me for a solid thirty minutes early this morning, which threw things off from the start."

"How early did that happen?"

"Six. Right as we opened. At least they bought bread puddings and coffee while they were at it. I told them about my experiences with Chase and some vandalisms. My alibi is solid, thank goodness. Jessie needed to leave early, so I had to close shop. We have a camera at our window."

I didn't want to tell Dale about how Detective Merrick had questioned me at the station earlier. Not because I was embarrassed, no, but because I didn't want to confess my sad family backstory and delve through those deep emotions yet again. "I'm worried that the sheriff's department is fixating on Grizz for the murder. The problem is, he does have a good motive: protecting me."

"Grizz wouldn't kill someone." Dale's face darkened in a scowl. "The deputy brought up Grizz this morning, too. She wanted to know if I'd witnessed altercations between Grizz and Chase, which I hadn't. Jessie mentioned being questioned about the same thing. Everyone in the village might've been asked."

"You live right in Foghorn?" I asked.

"Yes, within sight of the House."

I had the sudden sense that I was being watched. I glanced up. Behind Dale, atop a high stack of boxes, Bowser stared at me. He was cozy as could be, his paws tucked under his body and almost invisible. I gestured with a nod. Dale turned and laughed.

"What a fine specimen of moggy you are! The very shape and color of an orange! Glad to meet you, my ginger cousin." He outstretched a hand. Bowser sniffed at his fingers.

"I think he likes you," I said as Dale began to rub Bowser's fuzzy white chin.

"Cats know their people. Are you in need of a referral to a vet? I can text you some places – and some warnings."

"I can use both, thanks. Jessie gave me a lead on the place that might've neutered Bowser, but from the sound of things, he's likely overdue for shots and check-ups. Hey, if you're up for chatting more, do you want to come to the Kitchen? I need to finish prep on a big order for tomorrow."

"Sure!" Dale said with one of his easy smiles.

"At least the Kitchen is neater than the house right now. Bowser, you guard the place, okay?" I said to the tiger on the tower. He yawned, flashing some impressive fangs. Thank goodness that stack of cardboard could hold his considerable bulk.

I walked Dale through the house and along the covered path to the Kitchen. Once inside, Dale released a low whistle of admiration as he spun in place, taking everything in. "I'm gobsmacked. This place is professional. That oven...! The storage! Can I open the cabinets?" He clasped his hands at his chest, his blue eyes wide and pleading.

I laughed. "Sure, but know that things do need to be reorganized. All Grandma's items are still in there, crammed with my stuff. Do you mind if I get started again?" I sidestepped to the island sink.

"No, please don't let me distract you. I'll continue to gawp." He parted the double doors of the fridge to stare inside. "Ah, the cheese hoard. Wonderful space for whole wheels. An industrial-sized unit like this is truly essential in your line of work."

"That's why I've been renting a space in a commercial kitchen in San Luis Obispo. I just downgraded my rental agreement there – they'll still accept cold deliveries for me. I know from Grandma that Foghorn is the last drop-off on delivery drivers' routes, and that means an overnight delivery might take two days instead. No way do I want my cheese spoiled." I resumed arranging my crackers.

"That's the sad truth of deliveries here. I can get packages as late as eight o'clock near the holidays." He closed the wing-like fridge doors. "Have you worked as a cheesemonger? Are you certified?"

I loved that he knew about the high echelons of cheese. "Becoming a certified cheesemonger was something of a childhood dream. But, reality." I shrugged.

"I'm sorry. I didn't mean to pry," Dale said, abashed.

"No, no. It's fine. I've gotten past the disappointment. You looked me up online. Did you notice the hashtag that states that I'm autistic?" I said this casually, but as ever, it felt weird to speak about it.

"I did." His tone was frank, which I appreciated.

"Well, being autistic has definite perks, right? My fixation on cheese is part of that. Cheese was one of the few foods I could tolerate as a kid. I had – still have – major sensitivities to things I touch or put in my mouth. I also have a hard time getting work done if I'm surrounded by people. School was a nightmare for me until a teacher in high school suggested I use noise-canceling earplugs. However, that accommodation only does so much on an actual job site, because there's more going on than noise. People are bustling around, and I feel that energy. There is random clatter. Constant interruptions. My nervous system reacts like I'm under constant attack.

"If I moved to a big city, I could probably work nights at a cheese shop, and that might be okay for me. But in S-L-O, there are only a few artisanal cheese vendors even though we have awesome local cheese makers. My friends believed I'd get a cheese-related job with no problem. I believed I would, too. But then I completely bombed two interviews because I nervously babbled the whole time. I was finally hired to work day shift at a grocery cheese counter. I lasted one day."

"Oh, Bird. That must have been hard on you."

"It devastated me." I said that in a chipper tone as I pulled out jars of pear mostarda and fig-walnut preserves. "I was in full deer-in-the-headlights mode during my shift. My smart watch monitored my heart rate and documented that it stayed steady at over one hundred beats a minute for a full eight-hour shift. I made it back to my apartment and physically and mentally crashed. I slept fifteen hours straight. To my relief, my bosses were supportive. I switched to night stocking in the general grocery department. That, I could do. No customers, just monotonous labor and clear expectations." Not much pay, though, especially as my college loan payments kicked in.

"That's what you did up until recently?" he asked.

"Until last week! Three years there, since I graduated college."

Dale leaned to examine a fig-walnut preserve jar and nodded approval. "I should stop gawking and lend a hand. You're flitting all over the place while I'm being a lazy bum." He started washing his hands.

"You've been up since four. This has to be your wind-down time. That said, there is one way you could be a major help."

"Anything," he said fervently.

"Way up high, I have bags of honey-roasted cashews and cocoa-candied pecans. If you could grab them, that'd be awesome. They're in cupboards to your right, top shelf. I'd need my stepladder to reach."

"I'm happy to put my freakish height to use on your behalf." He reached into the cabinet, which was just about his head level. "Huh. That was odd."

"What?" I kept my focus on my crackers.

"I overreached the bags and tapped the back wall. It moved."

"Wait, what?" I had to stop to see what he was talking about. "Is it broken? The Kitchen is pretty new. I didn't think I damaged anything when I was putting away supplies." I frowned in thought. "I didn't use the little stepladder when I put the nuts up there. I just stood on tiptoe. Can you take a closer look for me?"

"Certainly." He set the two large bags on the nearby counter then reached up into the cabinet again. "This is... How peculiar. There's a sliding door built into the back. It was slightly off track, which is why it moved when I brushed it." I heard a small pop that could only be the door being shifted back into place.

"Is there anything back there?" I thought of Grandma's suspicious antics with a spike of concern. Why would she have had a hidden nook built into the high cabinet – and were there other such spaces in the Kitchen? In the house? If so, what had she used them for?

And did I really want to know?

Dale turned on the flashlight mode on his phone. "I don't see anything." He leaned forward to probe with his free hand. "No. It's empty." He glanced at his fingers. "Another odd bit: there's no dust."

"No dust?" I echoed. "I cleaned the normal cabinets in here about a month ago. They had dust." I was pretty sure I'd blindly dusted the upper cabinet using a duster wand. Even if I'd knocked the door askew when I did that, some filth should've accumulated inside. The ceiling vent was feet away.

"I don't know what to say, but it's clean as if someone just dusted it. This would be a good hiding spot for Christmas presents. Do you think there are other hiding spots around?" He sounded delighted by the mystery.

Presents, as if it would be something so innocent. Grandma had been all about organization. Things in the kitchen – or the Kitchen – were to be used for cooking. What kind of cooking-related items would need to be hidden up there?

Something illegal. Something toxic. Maybe something that was a bit of both.

My shaky fingers resumed work on the crackers. "Maybe we can search the other cabinets later. That'll need to be an all-day effort. The lower levels have a lot more food inside that'll need to be moved elsewhere. Here, I'm just about done. The nuts are next."

"I'd be happy to help with a cabinet search. Just let me know when you have the time."

"Another thing for the to-do list." I already intended to procrastinate. I was afraid to know what we might find, creepy dust-free spaces included. I ripped open one of the bags. "Here, do a quality check for me." I tossed a couple of cashews his way. He obliged me, thoughtfully closing his eyes as he chewed.

"Those are downright scrummy, as the culinary high priestess Mary Berry would say. Where do you get them?"

I was glad he was easily distracted from further ruminations about Grandma's cabinets. "From a retired kindergarten teacher in Grover Beach. She sells small batch seasoned nuts at farmer's markets around. Nicest lady you'd ever meet. I get a special deal on bulk bags."

"I'd like to find a way to use these." By the gleam in his eyes, he contemplated new recipes.

"Her sticker's on the bag."

As he took a picture of the information, his phone buzzed in his grip. Dale's brow scrunched as he looked at the screen. "I'm sorry, this is Maurice, I can't think why he's calling. He never calls."

Deep in my gut, I suddenly knew that something awful must have happened. Our generation – and those younger than us – didn't call people except in an emergency. We lived by text.

Dale accepted the call. "Hello, Maurice– Wait, slow down." Even from a few feet away, I could hear the high panicked voice blaring from his phone. Dale hit the speaker mode. "Start again, Maurice, slower. I'm here with Bird. What happened?"

"Dale, Dale, it's Ella May. I just found her beaten up behind the dumpster. I think someone tried to kill her!" Maurice burst out in hysterical sobs. Mine and Dale's eyes met, our expressions grim.

Chapter Ten

"Maurice, listen to me." Dale's voice was crisp and patient. "Did you ring the police?"

"A customer did! I started screaming and I couldn't, I just couldn't." Maurice hiccupped between his words.

I closed the rest of my large boxes. The remainder of the nuts could wait. They would have to wait. It'd only take me twenty, maybe thirty minutes to finalize the assembly tomorrow prior to delivery. The past hour had been like the eye of the storm, and now a new disaster had struck Foghorn.

"Are emergency personnel there?" Dale's free hand tufted through his wild red hair, making it even wilder.

"No, but they're on the way!"

"Maurice," I called out. "How badly is Ella May hurt?" I could hardly believe it. I had just met Ella May earlier in the day. She'd been so nice!

"She's unconscious. She... There's so much blood..."

"We'll be there in just a few minutes," I said, projecting my voice to be heard over Maurice's renewed sobs. Then, at a lower decibel, I added, "I need my purse from the house. I'll drive, you talk Maurice through his panic attack."

"Thank you," Dale murmured, tears in his eyes.

I dashed into the house. Bowser remained on his tower,

now stretched out on his side, his head cocked in curiosity as I hurried to my bedroom and back. I shook my pointer finger at him. "I meant what I said before. Guard this house." With that, I rushed out.

Dale paced back and forth beside my car. I remote-unlocked the doors as I approached, and we threw ourselves inside. Gravel squealed under the tires as I backed up, the rear camera giving me a screech of warning as I came close to Dale's car. Oops. I was not used to another vehicle being there.

"Deep breaths. In through the nose, out through the mouth," Dale was saying, good advice for both me and Maurice. I cast him a sidelong glance as I paused at the end of the long driveway. This man knew how to work through panic attacks. The sound of sirens filtered over the phone – and wailed from Highway 1 up ahead. We were going to be right on the bumpers of the first responders.

"But, but, my nose was already stopped up because of allergies," Maurice choked out, "and now that I'm crying, it's all–"

"Then deep, long breaths in and out through the mouth," Dale amended his advice. "Is Jessie still there? Oh– No, she asked to leave early again. She needed to help Belinda."

"Yeah, yeah, she's gone but I have people here with me. Oh! Dale, there's a cop car pulling up, I, I, I should–"

"Hang up and talk to them. I'll be there in five minutes. You'll be okay." The call ended but Dale continued to stare at his screen. "You'll be okay," he murmured.

"Dale, the dumpster he mentioned. Where is it? I need to know where to park so I don't get blocked in." A second incident in little Foghorn in as many days would draw even more emergency and media attention.

"It's at the far end of the strip mall behind the grocer, not visible from most of the lot."

"Are there cameras there?"

His mouth opened and closed as he considered his answer. "There used to be. I mean, there still is, but I don't know if it's functional. After those storms last month, Rita put out a bulletin saying some cameras had died and they were currently on backorder. I don't recall an update."

Just dandy. I stopped at the junction with Highway 1. "Okay, so, where should I park?" Once I made the turn, I only had a quarter mile until Foghorn. I couldn't move until I knew where I was going.

"Take the road toward the House and do a U-turn to park on the street. I doubt they'll close off that unless they have a very good reason." By the grim line of his mouth, we were both thinking the same thing: with the way things had been going, anything was possible.

The sun tilted toward the horizon, the sky over the Pacific cast orange and pink. The time of day meant thicker traffic. I waited a minute to make my right turn. Flashing lights shone in the distance behind me. More responders. Merrick must surely be on the way if he wasn't here already. This might connect to his existing investigation, after all, but how? Why Ella May?

"Does Foghorn usually have much crime beyond mischief and car accidents?" I took the next right.

"No, not in the couple years I've been here. That's the nice thing about Foghorn. It's quiet. Usually. Most of the recent problems were caused by Chase or his associates." Dale paused, thinking. "I've heard old timers say things used to be worse a few decades ago – some legit serial killers, poisonings, spy rings, all sorts of shenanigans. I'd dismiss it as one person's fish stories, but I've heard the same things repeated time and again."

I snorted, remembering how Rita had tried to blame Grandma for that past drama – and would blame me for these new developments. I did the U-turn Dale advised. "Let's assume this attack on Ella May is connected to Chase's murder due to the locale and time frame. *But how?* Chase is dead. His throat was slit before or after a car crash. Ella May has now been assaulted. Belinda is a direct tie between the two. Oh. *Belinda.* She's the key." I faced Dale as I shut off my Kia.

"What about Belinda?"

"She and Ella May look a lot alike. Same hair, age, fashion style." We speedwalked into the main parking lot.

"You think someone may have tried to attack Belinda and got the wrong woman?" He still had his phone out, which reminded me of something else.

"I need to give you my cell number before we separate. You'll need a ride back to your car."

"Good idea." He tapped his screen, sparing me a look of admiration. "You think ahead."

"Sometimes too much," I said with a tight smile. I rattled off my number and he input it. His test text popped up on my watch a second later.

Two police cars, lights flashing and sirens wailing, had parked at the far end by the grocery store. Good thing I still had my ear plugs in my purse.

"There's Maurice!" Dale sprinted forward, waving. Maurice sat on a curb, deputies hovering over him. When he saw Dale, he held out his arms like a young child to his father. Dale embraced him, no hesitation. I hung back, not as eager to come under the scrutiny of deputies again.

The turban-adorned grocery clerk stood outside the open business door, his arms crossed. I gave him a nod as I walked by. His expression was inscrutable. I peered around the corner of the building. Past the shiny black hood of a sheriff's car, I could see a battered, rusty dumpster surrounded by bags and debris.

Among that mess lay Ella May. Her mottled floral shirt almost blended in with the rainbow array of trash. A deputy stood guard while another crouched and checked her vitals. I edged out a little further for a better view and sucked in a sharp breath. Ella May's face was covered in blood. One of Grandma's factoids rang in my memory: scalp wounds bled terribly, whether or not they were serious injuries. This seemed on the serious side, though – Ella May looked utterly limp and unconscious. No one had made an effort to move her. That likely meant they were wary of head and spinal trauma.

Sirens increased in volume behind me. As awful as the noise was, I was relieved that more help had arrived. I backtracked toward the grocery store.

"This. Terrible, so terrible." The clerk spoke loudly to be heard.

"Did you see who might have done it?" I asked him. He stood about as tall as me. I guessed him to be in his fifties, his skin a warm brown with plentiful laugh creases at his eyes.

He shook his head. "Ella May, she must have come here right before it happened. Bought her smokes, as she often does after work. She's parked right there." He waved at an older white SUV about twenty feet away.

"Do you have a security camera?"

"Miss Rita monitors most of the cameras around Foghorn."

Most, not all. Curious. "Dale was telling me that some cameras were nonfunctional after the storms last month. Do you know if they were fixed yet?"

"I do not, no." A slight smile curved his lips beneath his curly white mustache. "You remind me of your grandmother. Always asking questions."

I flinched as more sirens drew close. I popped in my ear plugs. "I keep getting told that, but not everyone considers the resemblance to be a good thing."

"To me, it is. Lucille was a friend. I am Mr Singh." His words were muffled but I could make them out with focus.

"I'm glad to know you, Mr Singh. I'm Bird."

"I know. I remember when you were this high." He held a broad hand to about his hip level. "Back then, we had a counter where we scooped ice cream. You would always get two scoops of vanilla in a cup with strawberry sauce on top. Nothing else."

"Huh. I'm amazed that you remember that." I had only the vaguest memory of coming here for ice cream with Grandma. I still loved eating that simple ice cream pairing, and it was reminiscent of my all-time favorite way to eat triple creme cheese, adorning gooey slices with dollops of strawberry preserves.

His bright smile faded as he glanced toward the scene of the attack. "The good things on this planet must be appreciated and remembered, because there will often be tragedies. That spot has experienced such drama before."

"Oh?" He had me intrigued.

"Your grandmother. She saved Mr Slocombe there." He paused as if waiting to see if I caught the reference. When I only cocked my head, perplexed, he continued, "This was before you were born, but I thought she may have spoken with you about such things. Late one evening, there was a car chase from the highway and through the parking lot. Lucille, she drove for Mr Slocombe quite often those days. She took his car behind the main building here, but the men in their car, they chased her." Mr Singh shook his head. Questions danced through my mind. I knew Grandma had been close to the eccentric Mr Slocombe – she'd somehow acquired her property from him – but she'd been his *chauffeur?* "I heard the squealing tires, and I came out in time to see what happened. Both cars had stopped right near the bins. The men who'd chased her had guns and were demanding she relinquish Mr Slocombe, but they never even had a chance to fire. Lucille, she was like... like Bruce Lee. She didn't use a gun, though she'd told me before that she carried one. No, no, instead, she flew at those men. Slap, slap, thud." He waved his hands around. "Both ended up on the ground. She saw me staring and told me, in a chipper voice, to go back inside and to not ask any questions. I did as she bid, then, but later when I asked her in private about what had occurred, she said it wasn't safe for me to know the answers."

I couldn't help but think of the childhood incident I'd witnessed in Morro Bay, how she took down the abusive man in public. Grandma might've been a chauffeur for Mr Slocombe, but with her skills, she'd definitely been more than that. "And... that was it? You never found out more?"

"Some people, you can press with questions and they'll eventually cave. Not Lucille." His lips were compressed in a thin smile.

He was right about that. "What was Mr Slocombe doing during all of this?"

"Sitting in the back seat of his car. He was frail in his later years. Nothing like he'd been in his youth, but that can be said of many of us."

"So you don't know what happened to the other men or their car?"

He shook his head, his frizzled beard illuminated by headlights. "I only know that fifteen, twenty minutes later when I poked my head out, everyone was gone. I don't know how she accomplished that. Cell phones were around at that time, but were barely functional, especially out here. My store, it had the only payphone in Foghorn. My father had it installed soon after he began to lease the property." He motioned to the nearby wall where the obsolete technology had once stood. "It's now been gone almost ten years."

"Security cameras wouldn't have shown much then, either, even if they'd been installed," I muttered. "Quality was pretty bad back in the 1990s."

"As if your grandmother wouldn't have known how to eliminate such footage." He clicked his tongue.

Huh, Mr Singh definitely viewed Grandma as a woman of many talents. I opened my mouth, ready to ask more about the weird connection she had with Mr Slocombe, when a voice boomed out behind us. "Bird Nichols!" Detective Merrick had arrived.

Mr Singh gave me a look of sympathy and retreated inside his store. I released a huffy sigh. I'd need to talk to him more later.

"Why am I not surprised to find you here?" Merrick said, glowering at me.

"Is that because I'm like my grandma?" I asked. "That seems to be a theme in my conversations over the past day."

His expression was droll, his fast stride whipping his coat tails around his knees. "How long have you been here?"

"Five minutes, maybe. Right after the first two responders. Should I take it as a positive sign that I'm not being promptly accused of assaulting Ella May?"

"I would like to know about your whereabouts over the past hour."

Of course he would. I heavily sighed. "If you must know, I've been working my cheese" – I paused, realizing how weird that sounded out of context – "as I have a large order due for delivery tomorrow. Dale Keswick from Quesoquick came by with more cat supplies for me, which I greatly appreciate."

"You two were discussing cheese, I assume."

"You can always make *that* safe assumption of me, Detective Merrick. Yes, we talked about cheese, and the events in Foghorn over the past day, of course. Then Dale got a panicked call from Maurice, his employee. He'd found Ella May and was freaked out. I drove Dale here so he could focus on calming Maurice over the phone. You can see them over there." I waved that way.

"How long would you say Mr Keswick was with you?" Several more patrol cars entered the lot along with an ambulance.

"I think… thirty minutes, at most? I was home alone before that, unless we count Bow– my new cat, and we probably should since he's the size of a small child." I barely remembered to omit Bowser's name.

"I don't think the cat can provide you with an alibi." Behind him, traffic seemed to be slowing on nearby Highway 1. The flashing lights and sirens at the shopping center would probably cause rubberneckers to crash, causing even more drama.

"Don't underestimate the power of a cat, especially on social media."

Merrick shook his head. The man didn't appreciate my tangents. "You speak of the victim as if you know her."

"I do. We met earlier today. I left flowers in front of the salon." I gestured far past him. Overhead lights showed that the memorial had grown in the past few hours. "Ella May came out. We had a nice talk. She's really worried about Belinda." I debated mentioning my theory about Belinda being the intended target of this attack on Ella May, but I held off. I needed more evidence.

"That's the only time you've spoken?" he asked.

"Yes. Before yesterday, I hadn't been in this shopping center since I was about ten or so." At his furrowed brow, I continued, "I never had cause to visit Foghorn. I always drove north on the highway and took the exit to Grandma's place. If she needed anything, I brought it, or we did a big outing and went to Morro Bay or elsewhere."

Merrick frowned. "Had she really become that feeble in recent years?"

"Feeble? I wouldn't use that word. She had slowed down, sure, but she could still drive without a problem. My parents' deaths hit her hard, though. After she vanished, investigators asked me if she had been depressed or made mention of suicide. But you probably know that since you were looking at my file."

"Such reviews are important." What a useless answer. The guy could be in politics.

Meanwhile, I was endeavoring to provide real answers, but with extreme care. I might not have called a lawyer yet, but I hoped I'd learned something from my visit to the station earlier. "Not denying she was depressed and grieving, of course. I mean, I've fought through those feelings, too," I said, matter-of-factly. If he dug deep on my Instagram, he'd find that last year I'd done a Thursday Cheese Therapy video series for about six months. The short clips gave me a chance to chat about a favorite cheese and how it personally gave me joy as I mourned.

"Detective Merrick!" Rita stalked toward us.

"Hello, Mrs Ramos," Merrick said in a level voice. "What can I do for you this evening?"

"Turn off all these lights and sirens. They make Foghorn look terrible!"

I blinked. Was she really expecting the emergency response to go stealth mode at her whim?

Merrick showed no surprise, but then, they'd probably known each other for years. He must have expected something like this. "You know we can't do that."

"You can." Rita stopped about five feet away, fists balled at her narrow hips. "Your people can keep working, but without this obvious fuss! Everyone driving by will think this is a disaster zone!" She glared at me, the newly arrived harbinger of woe for Foghorn.

"Mrs Ramos. The emergency response is not the problem. A crime was committed here. Someone who lives and works here was attacked."

"How long until the media is here then, huh? Are they going to come and broadcast from our parking lot to get video for their programs tonight?" She sounded angry, on the brink of tears.

"We will place barricades to keep them farther away from the crime scene, but the television stations do as they will." He didn't sound enthused by the prospect either.

Rita moaned. "The PR, it's on me. I don't need this."

I couldn't hold back anymore. "Rita, are all of the security cameras around the center functional?"

She looked at me as if I'd sprouted three extra heads. "What?"

"The cameras. Are they all online again after the winter storm disabled some?"

"How do you know about that?" Merrick asked quietly, then shook his head, as if accepting that *of course* I had to know. Genetic legacy and all.

Rita's expression of disgust told me she'd reached the same conclusion. "That is none of your business."

"Actually, it is, as I live here and frequent many of the businesses." Or had for the past day. "I won't be the only one asking you this question. Dale and Mr Singh are also wondering."

Rita sighed in resignation. "Then you can tell them, as you are nosily talking to everyone, that three of the cameras are still offline, and that–" Her phone rang, the same high-pitched tone that made me jump into the candy stand the previous day. The pitch even stood out against the sirens. I stepped back, my hands at my ears.

Rita glanced at her screen as her cell rang again. "Detective, can I answer this? It's the corporate team."

"You may, but please stay within the parking lot. I need to speak with you shortly."

Rita nodded, her mouth a grim line. "I won't be going anywhere while this is happening." She hurried away as she raised the phone to her ear.

Several deputies approached. Merrick turned to me. "I need to confer with others."

"Am I confined to the parking lot too?" I asked.

"No. I see no reason for that, but try not to get into trouble."

I gave him my most indignant expression as he walked

toward the crime scene with his fellow deputies. I hesitated for about twenty seconds before following him.

Peering around the corner again, I found the area had become congested with officers and EMTs. Ella May now lay strapped onto a gurney, a neck brace on. Her head moved – her eyes were open! I released a long, relieved exhalation. Consciousness was a good sign. Hopefully she'd be okay, and maybe she'd also be able to identify her attacker.

Merrick glanced back. I ducked behind the corner. He hadn't forced me to stay, but he certainly had the power to get me kicked out.

The sky had gone a deep purple, night almost fallen. I could no longer find Dale and Maurice in the crowd, but I had trouble discerning anything in the mix of darkness and bright lights. I blinked fast as if that would help my brain process the world better. It didn't.

I retreated down the strip mall past Salon & Nails. Getting forty feet from the chaos made a huge difference. My thoughts became clearer, my vision sharper. My damp clothes told me I'd been sweating heavily despite the coolness of the evening.

My watch pulsed with a text notification. Was it from Dale? Was he ready to go? I could only hope.

I glanced down. No, it was Mollie: "streaming done. u OK?"

I'd forgotten to follow up on the GIMH text I'd sent her. I pulled out my phone to reply: "OK. Not home now. Person I know was attacked in Foghorn, went to check on them. Lots of police."

Mollie sent an emoji of a head with a brain exploding. "what is going on there?!"

That was a very good question.

While I had her available, I typed back, "I need to take cheese to S-L-O tomorrow midday. Will you be around?"

"yessss. til 3. cya then. don't get killed."

Good advice about now.

A slow driving vehicle caught my eye. The driver's side window was down, the familiar face of the driver pale and wide-eyed. Belinda.

"Belinda! Hi!" I called, waving as I jogged her way.

Chapter Eleven

I moved around the backside of a parked sheriff's car to approach Belinda's white SUV. I suddenly wondered what Ella May's car looked like. A glance across the dark lot confirmed that deputies were investigating another white SUV parked closer to the grocery store; that had to be Ella May's vehicle. The cars looked almost identical. Wow. There were plentiful reasons for this attack to have happened due to confused identities – but I still needed an answer to the big question: 'Why assault Belinda OR Ella May?'

Belinda squinted as she focused on me. "Oh, hi! Your name was– Crow, was it?"

"Close! My name is Bird." Under other circumstances, I might have laughed. I'd been called Swan and Sparrow before, in all seriousness. Brains do funny things with word associations. "Did you hear about what happened here?"

"No. I just woke up from a nap." She sounded like she was still half-asleep. Had she taken a sleep aid? In any case, she was in no condition to drive.

"Can you stop and talk with me?" I asked. After a moment of groggy hesitation, she nodded. "Park over here. Hopefully you won't get blocked in." But if she did, that might be for the best. I'd be able to get a better idea of her cognitive abilities after a chat – and I wasn't afraid to ask Merrick for help in ensuring she stayed put for her own safety.

Belinda parked in front of a vacant store. As she climbed down from her high SUV, she started to slip. I lunged forward to offer a hand. "Thanks," she said ruefully. "I'm not at my best today."

"Of course you're not." I kept a hand on her shoulder as we walked together toward the covered walkway.

"Jessie helped me with funeral paperwork this afternoon. Before that, I went through Chase's things. The cops had already done that, too, and made a mess of everything. In a way, that made it easier to bag up the lot. I'm going to take everything to one of those thrift stores with a night drop box on my way to work."

"Work? Tonight? You didn't even do the salon today." This other job had to be the warehouse one that Ella May mentioned. No way was Belinda up to that.

"I had to do phone calls and forms during daylight hours. But now… I realized, I *need* to go in tonight. I need to make money." There was a desperate edge to her voice.

If George had killed Chase over the missing money and hadn't found it yet, he could still be on the prowl. Maybe George had mistaken Ella May for Belinda; could explain why she was assaulted. I had the horrible realization that if George tried to beat the truth out of Belinda, he'd probably kill her even if he wasn't trying to. Frail as she was, a stiff breeze could cause her to tumble and shatter on the pavement.

"Does Jessie know you're going to work?" I asked.

Belinda's smile glowed with love. "Yes. She tried to talk me out of it, but she understands. She's been helping out every way she can, but she can't keep pushing herself so hard for my sake. She has her own life to live." Her lip quivered. "I'm so proud she pulled A's and B's in her classes last semester. I don't want her GPA to fall because of me."

Ugh, how was I supposed to break the news about Ella May to her? "Maybe we should sit down somewhere."

"Was there a fire?" She gazed around, more muddled by the chaos than I was.

"No fire. Someone was hurt."

"Not Jessie!" Belinda cried. "She shouldn't be here; she had schoolwork to do tonight–"

There was no delaying the truth now. "Not Jessie. Ella May was attacked."

I gripped Belinda as she began to dip. Her legs had gone as soft and rubbery as Taleggio. "I've got you. Mostly." Belinda was skinnier than me by a lot, but we were the same height. My muscle strength came from toting cheese wheels, not human bodies.

"We can go in the salon. I have my key," she said faintly. We staggered the remaining ten feet to the front door. Hand over hand, we turned the key. Once inside, she pivoted against the wall and tapped in a code at a security system panel. The system hadn't so much as beeped as we entered. Her body largely blocked my view of the keypad.

"Can you help me to a seat?" she rasped.

"Sure." I guided her a few more feet to one of the hairdressing chairs.

"Where's the light switch?" I asked. The room was somewhat illuminated by outside lights, but it was still spookily dark, emergency red and blue pulsing within the broad mirror.

"The switch is behind you, above the door stop – that's

it." Light bloomed overhead as I mashed the switches. A ceiling fan began spinning.

"Can I get you anything?" I asked.

Belinda shook her head. "I think sitting is what I need right now. I'm not normally shaky like this. I was cutting hair just fine yesterday." She stared at her trembling hands.

"Shock can do that," I said, but figured this was something more.

We both jerked up at the sound of a heavy knock on the glass. Detective Merrick was on the other side, Deputy Johnson with him. Belinda beckoned them in.

"Mrs Perkins," Merrick said. "Miss Nichols." He didn't sound as pleasant when he said my name. "We saw the lights come on. Are you all right?"

"I think so. Bird here told me what happened to Ella May and it was like my feet were knocked out from under me. How is Els? Can you tell me?"

"She's conscious," he said in a gentle tone. "She wasn't, at first. She's been beaten."

"Beaten!" Belinda's hand fluttered as she brought it to her mouth. "Who could have done this? Do you think– Could this– Chase–"

"We're investigating as if the two incidents are connected due to related factors. Mrs Perkins, can we speak with you for a few minutes?"

I got the hint. "Should I go?" I asked Belinda directly. I sure didn't want to. I wasn't a lawyer or close to her like Jessie was, but I felt like I needed to protect her.

"No. I want a friend with me. I can't be a suspect in this attack. Can I?"

"I'm only gathering facts right now," Merrick said, grimacing. He didn't seem happy that I had permission to stay. Behind him, Deputy Johnson had a pen poised in her hand, ready to take notes. "What have you done over the past six hours?"

Belinda furrowed her brow. "Threw Chase's things in bags. Made twenty calls. Set up the funeral. Napped. I've heard sirens over the past while, but I assumed an accident occurred on the highway. Only as I drove by did I see something had happened right here in Foghorn."

"No one had contacted you about what happened?" Merrick asked.

"You know, that sur–" Belinda patted her hip. "Oh, my god. My purse. I don't have my driver's license or wallet or anything." She became impossibly paler as she realized she'd said this in front of deputies.

"Mrs Perkins, please, don't worry about that. You're a minute's drive from your house. You sometimes even park here in the lot overnight, right?" His tone was especially gentle. She nodded.

I resolved to be less subtle. "Belinda, you should not be driving tonight. At all. You're a danger to yourself and others. Don't be a reason there are sirens on the highway."

"Yeah. I get it. I can't believe I left my phone, of all things. It's usually glued to my hand." Belinda shook her head in awe.

I studied the room we were in. The place looked like a stereotypical salon with walls painted green-grey, a framed poster of the Eiffel Tower on one wall, a canvas print with the word "coffee" in different languages crookedly affixed over a coffee maker. In the corner high above the entrance, the small black ball of a security camera stared down at us.

"You have security cameras inside the salon?" I asked. Merrick and Johnson turned to follow my pointing finger.

"Are they on a separate system than the exterior ones that are in Rita's domain?"

Belinda blinked and looked up, too. "Yes, we have three inside, and they belong to us. Me, really, since I'm the manager."

"Mrs Perkins, can you please send that footage to us as soon as possible?" Merrick asked.

"No," Belinda said as she slowly pushed herself from the chair. She paused, seeming to realize what she had said. "I mean, I can send it all to you, yes, but I want to see it for myself right now."

"I don't want to pressure you."

"Ella May is my friend. I need to know what happened to her. I can't bear to wait."

I caught the sidelong look that Merrick gave me. I managed a pleasant smile in return. He was trying to keep me out of the investigation. That wasn't going well for him at the moment.

"Give me a minute. The tablet will be locked up in the back. I'll get it." Belinda was oblivious to the drama between me and Merrick. Her feet scuffed and dragged on the linoleum as she made her way to the back room.

I waited in awkward silence along with Detective Merrick and Deputy Johnson. "I don't suppose you'll tell me if Ella May said anything about her attacker?" I asked softly.

"Have you met with Grizz Ferreira this evening?" Merrick asked.

Was he implying that Grizz had assaulted Ella May? I knew for a fact that Grizz would do no such thing. "How was your drive up? I'm guessing you weren't too far away, as you made good time?"

His brow furrowed. He didn't seem to like that I'd played

his game by answering a question with a question. Merrick opened his lips, but they closed again as Belinda returned.

"Here we are." Belinda shuffled back into the room, her focus on a tablet in her arms. It had a credit card reader fastened to the top edge. "Let me open up the app." She sat down and waved us over.

We clustered behind her to gaze over her shoulders. The screen showed three live windows for each of the cameras. One was at the far end of the room, showing us in the distance with a fish-eye distortion. Another was of an almost-black room. The third featured a great view of us, with Belinda most prominently shown.

"I'll bring up the history for the day. Did the attack happen when Ella May usually leaves?" She looked to Merrick for confirmation.

"To the best of my knowledge, her daily pattern remained the same up until her assault."

"But was she leaving, or was she taking out the trash? She was found by the dumpster shortly after leaving the grocery store," I said.

"The dumpster!" Belinda quivered. "She was laying there, with the trash?" Merrick scowled at me. I guess he'd wanted to hold back that detail.

I leaned to one side to check the trash can on the other side of the sink. "This has been emptied."

"Did she have her purse?" Belinda asked.

"No," said Merrick.

"Where would it be kept here, ma'am?" Deputy Johnson asked. "You can stay put. I'll go look."

"The cabinet that's straight ahead of you," Belinda called as Johnson walked that way. "We keep our purses in the woven bin on the bottom shelf."

"So did she go to the store, then come back here? She wouldn't have taken trash with her when she bought her cigarettes," I said.

"She usually has a smoke and a snack before she drives home to Cayucos. She doesn't like any trash left in the shop overnight," Belinda said. I nodded. The order of events made more sense, then. Shopping trip, break at the salon, then take out all of the trash, including her own fresh refuse.

A soft thump and some rustling could be heard from the next room. "Her purse is still here!" Johnson called.

"That helps me figure out how far back to go in the recordings." Belinda's finger was shaky as she dragged it across the red bar on the screen, rolling back the digital footage for the camera that loomed over us. The screen depicted a dark room with overhead fixtures shut off but plentiful light from outside. Curtains flanked the window but hadn't been drawn shut.

"If someone watched her from outside, they'd see her emptying the bins, and they'd have time to hurry down the corridor to intercept her," I murmured, "if they weren't already lurking in anticipation behind the building."

"There's a camera on the dumpster, but I think it's broken," Belinda said.

"We're aware of that issue, Mrs Perkins," said Merrick. Johnson rejoined us to gaze at the screen.

In the footage, Ella May moved into the frame. The timestamp read an hour and a half ago. She bent to dump the contents of the bin into a larger black trash bag and then continued to the back of the room.

"Now that we know the time…" Belinda murmured. She tapped out of that tablet window and switched to the feed from the black room. That space was windowless and gray as Ella May passed through. She pulled the door open, admitting a brief bright flash, then out she went.

"Can you scan the footage forward, slowly, to see if anyone entered through the unlocked back door after that?" Merrick asked.

Belinda obliged with a steadier hand. Her forward scroll showed no one in view up until she had fetched the tablet. Merrick made a thoughtful hum.

"So the back door was left unlocked. Was the front door already locked when she was gathering trash?" I asked.

"Yes," said Belinda. "We do that right after the last customer leaves. The back door is always locked – until we take out the trash at the end of the day. I guess we need to be more careful about that in the future. If this place has a future."

I wasn't sure how to answer that note of despair. Merrick and Johnson remained quiet too. "Belinda, when I came into the salon with you, you immediately turned off the alarm system, but I didn't hear any beeps. Is it a silent alarm?"

"Huh." Belinda craned her head around to look at me. "You're right. It should've started beeping right away when we entered, but it didn't. I hit the buttons out of habit. Setting the alarm would've been the last thing Ella May did before leaving for the night."

I kept my thoughts to myself to avoid more scowls from Merrick. Whoever attacked Ella May definitely hadn't done so to rob the place; and if their intention had been to mug her, they would've been disappointed as well, as she hadn't been carrying her purse.

Maybe there had been no robbery because this was about Chase and George's missing money. The sums at the salon would be paltry in comparison.

"How much footage should I send you?" Belinda asked, looking between Merrick and Johnson.

"The whole day, please," Merrick said. That made sense; a suspect might have lurked in the area for a while. "Deputy Johnson can help you send that along. Miss Nichols, if I might have a word?" He gestured outside. I glanced at Belinda with the hope that she might ask me to stay longer, but she was immersed in a conversation with the deputy.

The flashing lights were all the more aggravating in the black of night, and though no sirens wailed now, the sheer number of gathered people created a terrible cacophony. I put my back to the chaos, facing the front window of the salon. Merrick grasped what I was doing and sidestepped to enter my gaze.

I spoke up first. "I'm worried about Belinda's wellbeing, detective. She and Ella May look alike. I'm afraid that someone might have attacked Ella May mistaking her for Belinda."

"That's possible." I must have not done an adequate job of hiding how that non-answer frustrated me, as he continued, "Miss Nichols, I wanted to privately remind you that we're looking out for Mrs Perkins. We know how to do our jobs."

"Of course. My apologies." My apology was sincere, even though I lacked faith in their diligence. I didn't want to irritate Detective Merrick too much.

Johnson knocked on the glass. We went back inside the salon.

"We have all three files, sir," Johnson said.

"Thanks for your help, deputy, Mrs Perkins," said Merrick.

"Just please, find whoever who did this." Tears filled Belinda's eyes. "I can't cope with someone else getting hurt, I can't. If Ella May dies…"

"She's getting excellent care," Merrick said.

Belinda gazed around the salon, her focus lingering on the nail station with its wall racks of polish bottles. "She decorated this place, you know? Her presence is everywhere here. My son's presence is everywhere in my house, too. Or was. I can't deal with his smell there, as if I'll turn a corner and see him." Her fists opened and closed. "That's why I cleared out his room today. I had to get his things out of there, I had to. I don't want to do the same thing here in the salon. This place wouldn't be right without Ella May's touch."

Detective Merrick made a small sound of sympathy. "Don't assume the worst of her condition, Mrs Perkins. I still advise you to hold off on disposing of your son's belongings as well. Grief can make us act in haste. You may realize you want to keep more items because of emotional or monetary value, and it'll be too late." This sounded like an argument they had started earlier today.

"He had nothing of value," she said with a sigh.

I thought of Chase's video game collection, currently in Ray's possession. If his items were vintage, they could be worth a ton, but I couldn't bring that up. It meant admitting I had tracked down Ray first.

"It's almost all clothes," Belinda continued. "He got rid of everything else he had of worth – and my things, too. You people already searched his room. If you want to take the bags over in my car and search them again, fine. Keep them. I don't, I won't, want to see them again."

"We don't need his clothes, Mrs Perkins," said Merrick. "But you might, later."

"I can take the clothes for you," I blurted out. Maybe the deputies missed something. "I'm driving to S-L-O tomorrow. There are lots of thrift shops I can go by."

"Can you?" Belinda perked up.

Merrick shifted his feet. "Mrs Perkins, you really should–"

"Oh, you're such a sweetheart." Tears glimmered in Belinda's eyes. "Thank you. Let's go move those bags."

Merrick and Johnson shared a look. "Ma'am," Deputy Johnson said to Belinda, "if you trust me with your keys, I can carry them for you."

"You already looked in my car. I don't care if you nose around again," Belinda said, holding out the key ring. It was the same one that had opened the salon. "There are three trash bags in the back. Please leave my emergency kit and my reusable bags."

"We will, ma'am."

"Good." Belinda remained planted in her chair. "Thank you again, Bird. I appreciate it." Gratitude quivered in her words.

"I'm glad to help, Belinda." I gave her a light pat on the shoulder.

Johnson walked out with me. "You're pushing Detective Merrick's patience, ma'am," she said in a low voice. A blonde strand had fallen free from her ponytail to drape by her ear.

I looked at her, surprised by the advice. "I'm not trying to irritate him, but I really want to find out who's behind all this."

"That's not your place, ma'am," she said with blunt patience.

I opened my mouth and then thought better of speaking. Nothing that I said would justify my investigation to these people in the sheriff's department. They would continue to be affronted and annoyed because I couldn't trust them, and ignore the fact that I had very valid reasons not to.

The deputy and I worked in companionable silence to

transfer the bags. As I shoved the final one into the back of my car, I heard approaching footsteps. Deputy Johnson shifted a hand near to her belt. There were few lights along the grass-lined street, so it took me a second to recognize Dale about twenty feet away.

"It's Dale," I said in a low voice. I had to make sure he wasn't about to get shot. Only when Johnson relaxed did I call out, "Hey, Dale! How's Maurice?"

"Oh, good, there you are, Bird! Maurice is better. Ella May woke up right before she was loaded onto the ambulance. That was a huge comfort to him, to both of us. I just walked him home."

"I know you're close enough that you could walk home, too, but you probably want your car. Can I go?" I asked Deputy Johnson.

The judgmental look she gave me had clearly been learned from Merrick. "You didn't need to be here at all, ma'am. Good night." She left, Belinda's keys jingling in her grip.

Dale looked between me and Johnson. "Ouch. Isn't that sort of brutal retort what youngsters these days refer to as 'a sick burn?'"

"Yes, but it's not like you're *that* old. Are you?" I motioned him to get in my Kia.

"I'm twenty-nine. Truly." We both buckled up.

"We're not that far apart in age. I'm twenty-five," I said.

"That is quite a minor age gap." I heard the smile in his voice, though I didn't dare try to see it for myself. I had to look both ways to make the left turn onto the highway. "What are you up to tomorrow, besides irritating the sheriff's department? Which, as far as hobbies go, is probably not the most prudent."

"You're right. I'd be better off creating a scale model reproduction of Foghorn using cheese." I turned, putting on the gas. My faithful car's engine roared as we outraced the oncoming traffic. It was probably in my favor that the north and southbound lanes were sluggish due to the major emergency response visible in Foghorn.

"Hmm. Have you made many medieval-inspired villages out of cheese?"

"Not medieval by a long shot, but I once made a very temporary reproduction of Stonehenge. I ate it."

"A worthy effort all the same! That site is in Somerset, too, not far from the origins of cheddar cheese in Cheddar."

This man had a way of making me grin. "Back to your original question about my to-do list for tomorrow: I need to deliver that cheese order before lunchtime. Then I'll do as many errands as possible while I'm in San Luis Obispo because I may not be back for a week or so."

"Ah." The single syllable radiated disappointment. "I was hoping I might deliver you a sandwich lunch and see how that beast of yours is settling in."

I regretted all of my plans for tomorrow as I made the turn onto my access road. "I'm available the next day. Friday. That's my designated stay-home-and-do-all-the-things time. I don't have another order due until Monday." We passed Grizz's place. I could see his truck parked beneath the car port. I still needed to talk with him. "You know what, as much as I love your sandwiches, I've now had two freebies from your restaurant. Jessie was nice enough to give me another one earlier," I added in response to his questioning eyebrow. "I need to reciprocate with a meal. What if I make us a mini cheese board to share at my house? We can chat, admire Bowser, talk about the latest hoopla in Foghorn, etcetera. Do you have any allergies or preferences?"

"A cheese board by you? I'd be honored to partake! I fear I have your average Englishman's intolerance for intense spice. I touched a piece of Hatch chile once and my finger felt like it was on fire for the next six hours. My tongue is even more sensitive."

"I don't favor spicy cheese myself. I'll make our food from my personal cheese stash, anyway. The spiciest I eat is cheddar with peppercorns, and I don't have that currently."

"Ah, cheeses from your 'personal stash'!" The bumpy gravel of my driveway made his laugh waver. "I have a feeling you're more adventuresome than I am. I've stayed quite traditional with good melters for my sandwiches. Please, enlighten me in the greater ways of cheese. Be my cheese Jedi. I will be your Padawan."

Oh, more confirmation that he was a fellow geek. I was so glad we were becoming friends. "The Force will be with us," I intoned. I parked beside his car.

"Now, do be careful this next while," Dale said. "If you see something suspicious and don't want to bother the police, please, bother me. I'm not far away."

"I'll keep that in mind. Thank you. On that note, after what happened to Ella May, should Jessie be working alone? Or Maurice? Or you?"

"Jessie is tough. She's done wilderness survival training and martial arts. If we were getting robbed, I'd stand back and let her pummel the villains. Maurice... I worry about him. I told him he can take as much time off as he needs. Now, I had best get on. A mob of kittens and cats require their wet food."

Sudden movement on my front porch made me jolt. I

leaned over the steering wheel. "Is someone in my front window? The curtains are moving." I pointed. Dale leaned forward as well. The curtain's sway became more dramatic, the cloth rotating around to reveal the massive bulk of cat that hovered in space. Bowser was a solid four feet off the ground, and creeping up the fabric.

"Oh no!" I cried. We both bounded from the car.

"Do you need any help?" Dale asked.

"Maybe to shop for new curtains. I've got this."

He grinned, his face pale and bright in the porch light. "I believe you do. Good night, Bird."

"Good night, Dale."

I waved to him, his headlights arcing over me as he turned around. I hefted the first garbage bag of Chase's belongings on my back, as if I was Santa Claus delivering gifts. In a way, maybe I was. Bowser might be ecstatic to nose around in clothes that still smelled like his former caretaker. Hopefully they'd distract him from continuing to use Grandma's old lilac curtains for his parkour practice.

Chapter Twelve

I considered prying Bowser from the curtains right away, but I also remembered one of my childhood cats used to pull such antics, and attention had only reinforced their behavior. Therefore, I did my best to ignore him as I shoved boxes closer to the walls to clear space on the old wooden floor. I dumped out one of the bags. The clothes reeked. Chase had used one of those nasty spray-on deodorants with a scent that could only be described as a combination of hot asphalt and concentrated pine-themed floor cleaner. I generally wasn't sensitive to smell, but ugh, I did not like this name-brand funk.

After a quick side quest to acquire neoprene gloves, I sat on the edge of a rug and began to sort through Chase's castaways. I picked up a worn gray sweatshirt bearing the Cal Poly insignia, the kangaroo-style pocket empty. That shirt started my discard pile. Next were some jeans, then elastic-band shorts, then some white T-shirts with yellowed armpits.

Bowser trotted over, a bounce in his step. His approach shuddered through the floor. "Hey, Bowser," I called. "How's this smell to you?" I offered him one of Chase's shirts only for him to headbutt it aside so my hand could rub his ears instead. I obliged.

His deep, throaty purr revved up as he paced in front of me, getting pets on every pass. He had no imprint of a collar in his fur – maybe he had never worn one. Had he had any flea and tick treatments? I definitely needed to buy some drops for him. I never intended for him to go outside, but he still might sneak out or I might track in bugs myself.

Bowser found the sleeve of the old Cal Poly sweatshirt, kneading it with mitt-like paws, sharp claws extended. I dug through more pants pockets. I found a ripped ticket stub, no info on it. A scratched-up penny. Some string. Those were my big finds. With a huff of frustration, I bagged up the clothes – except for Bowser's choice bed – and started on the second bag. There I found a few random personal items thrown in with clothes and bedding. There was a small wooden wall shelf, a participation trophy for a 5th grade run-a-thon, a thin floor rug. A fitted sheet had holes worn through it. A pillowcase featured Chase's name in marker in a young child's handwriting, the S backward.

I sat back as a wave of sadness hit me. Chase hadn't been a pleasant person, but he'd been a person. He'd been loved. He loved his cat. He was still someone to mourn; he still deserved justice.

I packed up that stuff and moved on to the third bag. "I wish the deputies had been a little more incompetent with Chase's things, just for my sake," I told Bowser. "They could've been nice and left me some clues."

Instead, I had underwear. Some dirty, some clean. Even though I wore gloves, I still plucked up each article by the waistband and transferred it at arm's length into a brand-new trash pile. The thrift store didn't need these things. Some pants pockets held bits of paper, and I doubted Chase was using invisible ink to jot notes.

Bowser continued to make biscuits in the sweatshirt, his yellow gaze steady on me.

I finished up the bag with a groan. For my efforts, I had seven cents, paper shreds, three half-ticket stubs, pocket lint, a paper clip, and some old-fashioned tokens for a video game arcade in San Luis Obispo that I knew had been closed since 2020. I had a hunch that some of these clothes had been stuffed into a drawer and hadn't been worn since high school.

"I guess it was too much to hope for a paper with George's full name on it or maybe a bank deposit slip," I said to Bowser. "Not that Chase seems like the type to put his stolen lucre in a bank, not when he intended to use the money for something. But what? And where is the money now? When my freshman roommate's boyfriend was busted for stealing, his take was found hidden in a desk at his work. Chase didn't have a standard job, though."

But he had been spending an awful lot of time on my property. Frowning, I faced east as if I could see through the walls. Could he have hidden the money out there, burying it in an old metal coffee can or something? I tried that with my allowance once when I was eight because I'd read about it in some book. I'd done a lousy job of sealing the can. Six months later, I unearthed a moldy twenty-dollar bill.

Shedding the gloves, I scrubbed my hands clean and rubbed in moisturizer. Normally after a day with lots of errands and conversation, I was exhausted. Instead, I felt just as energetic as I did after a big cup of tea, and I intended to take advantage of that energy while it lasted.

"I need my supper foremost," I told Bowser, who had followed me into the kitchen to stare at me with solemn expectancy. "I'm feeling inspired after talking to Mr Singh earlier." I didn't have ice cream around – I'd almost emptied my freezer prior to moving – but I could make a cheesy take on my childhood favorite frozen treat. I pulled out a chunk of Face Rock Creamery's Aged Cheddar from Oregon, its paste a deep ivory. I cut it into thick slices that crumbled somewhat, which didn't bother me one bit. Not a single morsel would go to waste. On one side of the plate, I dished out a heaped spoonful of Grandma's strawberry preserves. According to her neat penmanship on the label, it was made two years ago. Likely from Grizz's harvest.

I paused. I could try calling Grizz again – but no, I'd go talk to him in person. He would be home at this time of night.

I didn't need crackers with my cheese. I kept things simple and delicious. I sat at Grandma's round oak dining table and used my fork to add dabs of fruit to my cheese before I brought it to my mouth. The flavors and textures were complex yet harmonious, a welcome dose of nostalgia. The purring cat perched between my feet was pretty nice, too.

Grizz was home. He had to be. His truck was parked under the carport, same as when I drove by an hour before. But I rang the doorbell and knocked and hollered to no avail.

Was he sick? Had he fallen and hit his head? He was of sound physical health, but a body could fail suddenly at his age. After all, Grandma had been a strong ocean swimmer throughout her life, then one time she went under and didn't come up again. Or so people said; part of me found it more believable that she'd gone to live with merfolk.

"Come on, Grizz!" I yelled, frustration raising my voice to

a shrill pitch. I didn't want to call up the sheriff's department for a wellness check. As far as I knew, he was having issues in the bathroom and simply couldn't get to the door. The last thing he needed was for law enforcement to bust in while he was on the toilet.

I leaned my forehead on the door and took in deep breaths to calm myself. I'd find Grizz, somehow, somewhere.

I considered the lock. Grandma taught me how to pick them – that was one skill she drilled into me in my younger years that I'd somehow retained. I remembered sitting on her living room rug, where I'd just sorted Chase's things, as she handed me various doorknobs and padlocks, challenging me to use the correct pick and technique. I didn't know where my set was at the moment amid my boxes, but I had seen Grandma's personal kit a few days before as I shifted things around in a closet. I'd give Grizz ten more minutes before I returned to the house to get it.

I walked around the back of the trailer. A motion-sensitive security light blinked on, blinding me for a few seconds. I continued, taking a circuitous route around the caged garden beds. Far beyond the reach of the trailer's lights, trees formed a crowning silhouette along the rounded ridge. Out in the distant meadow, a dot of light moved. Someone was out there. Should I grab a stout stick in case I needed to whop a trespasser? I stared a moment more then realized there were really two lights. One was a flashlight, bobbing and jostling with strides. The other moved in parallel, but higher and more stable in its movement.

I pulled out my phone, ready to call 9-1-1 if trouble was incoming. "Who goes there?" I shouted.

The lights froze. "Bird?" came the questioning reply.

"Grizz! Thank goodness! What're you doing out in the

dark?" The lights began to move again, faster now. As he drew closer, I could discern that he wore a headlamp and also carried a long flashlight. I walked to intercept him. "What are you doing out here?" I repeated. "Are you trying to break a leg?"

"I went for a walk and time got away from me." Sweat beaded his face despite the night's chill. "Good thing I always bring some supplies with me, in case." He had on a saggy backpack.

"You went for a walk?" I echoed.

"Yeah. It's January, you know? Resolutions? I needed to get my steps in."

I gawked at him in disbelief. Maybe it was a generational thing, a stubborn remnant of old-fashioned machismo, but Grizz had told me more than once that he only exercised through useful labor like digging in his garden and chopping wood.

"How long were you gone?" I asked. "I left you a message this morning."

"Sorry. I forgot to reply to that. I think I left like… three o'clock?" We began to walk together back toward the trailer, his breaths huffing.

I groaned. "And of course, you were by yourself. No alibi."

He stopped cold. "What? Why would I need an alibi *today?*"

"There was another incident in Foghorn. Ella May from the salon was beaten unconscious."

"Dear God." Grizz motioned the cross, a rare show of his childhood Catholicism. "Is she– Could she die?"

"She was awake by the time the paramedics loaded her up, which was a few hours ago now. Do you have your phone on you? Come on, pull it out. How far did you walk?" I considered the nearby ridge as he pulled out his cell. "You probably lost your signal pretty quickly. Now look at your calls and messages. How many times did Merrick try to reach you?" We stopped beneath his back door light.

He pried off the headlamp, the unit and the straps leaving a sweaty, red imprint on his balding head. His phone cast ethereal light onto his face. "Huh. Six missed calls."

"How does that look, Grizz? This is the second time you don't have an alibi for an attack! I bet deputies came by here, too, and no one answered the door."

His whiskery jaw had a stubborn set. "I'm not under arrest. I can go where I want to go. That detective said so just this morning."

"Wait. You talked to Merrick this morning after I visited?"

"He had me go down to Los Osos, sure."

"What did you discuss?" Worry sent a vicious chill through me. I'd foolishly thought I could handle a station chat with Merrick. I hated to think of what Grizz may have let slip.

"Chase. How long he's been trouble. About my own past. You, some. Your grandma." His voice broke. "I told him I couldn't keep talking about her, though. It hurt too much."

"How long were you there?"

"Oh, we chatted for an hour and a half or so."

He was there a lot longer than I was. That scared me. I wasn't going to tell Grizz that I'd been officially questioned too. He would freak out. "Sure, Merrick can't restrict your movements – yet – but he'll expect you to account for where you've been and why. Can you answer that for them?" And softer, "For me?"

"Bird, I was out for a walk. I needed to clear my head. That... That's all." Grizz was a rotten liar. Now he wasn't even pretending to count his steps for some nebulous exercise goal.

I'd gone from frustrated about his whereabouts to even *more* frustrated about his whereabouts. He didn't need to look guiltier for Merrick. Fighting tears, I said, "At least answer this much for me: You don't have a still out there, do you?" Grandma had mentioned once that Grizz was an alcoholic, but to my knowledge he'd been sober over my lifetime. Grandma's death had hit him hard, though. If anything could've driven him to drink, it would have been that.

Grizz's gaze jerked up, shock in his expression. "Oh, Bird. No. I'm not drinking, and I'm not distilling anything, either. I can promise you that."

His words carried a ring of authenticity, and yet – I took a deep breath, not to calm myself, but to assess his breath. I didn't even detect a whiff of mint being used to mask other smells. "Okay. Good. If you do feel like you need help with that – please let me know, okay? Don't be embarrassed. I helped a friend in college who struggled, too. I know of local resources."

"If I need your help, I'll tell you. Your Grandma made me promise that I'd go to you if I needed that kind of support." It struck me as poignant and sad that he didn't even use the word "alcohol" in any form, as if it was Voldemort.

"Really?" I wiped away a tear. "I wish you could tell me what else is going on, though. You need to listen to whatever messages the sheriff's office left you and respond right away, got it? And if… No, I won't say 'if.' You need a lawyer, first thing tomorrow. Absolutely don't go to the station again without one."

"Fine, fine. I'm sorry, Bird. I guess… I guess my walks have had bad timing."

Walks, plural? Was he walking in the dark when Chase was killed, too? I didn't even want to get into that again. Whatever second wind of energy I'd gotten this evening was fading, fast. "Promise me you won't do any other walks into the middle of nowhere while you're under investigation. And that you'll pay attention to your phone."

To my surprise, he readily nodded. "I don't have an immediate need to do another walk. I'll stay around here. If I need to go to town, I'll leave a note on the door."

"You can also do this thing called 'texting' and let me know what you're up to. It's pretty handy."

His smile was small. "I don't know. I still think I'm too old and these fingers are too big and clumsy to do that kind of thing, but we can talk about that more soon."

If we had that option. If he remained a free man.

I hugged him with both arms. He froze in surprise – we probably hadn't hugged since Grandma vanished – and then he relaxed, his hands resting on my shoulders.

I stepped back. "I'm going back to the house now. Please take care of yourself, Grizz. You're the only family I have left." With that, I walked away as I fought off more tears.

Chapter Thirteen

Morning dawned gray and damp, though no rain had fallen. It was the kind of winter morning that made the doors stick in their sills and reasserted that a warm bed and blankets were about the coziest place in the world. My bed was extra cozy thanks to the new ginger snuggled close to me. Not Dale, of course – I didn't move that fast in human relationships – but Bowser.

When I'd gone to bed the night before, I had shut him out of my bedroom. That lasted two minutes. His repeated yowls cranked up for the first time since he'd come home with me. I tried my noise-canceling ear plugs. They muffled his cries, but his agony still cut through to my ears, to my heart.

"Come on, you big orange thing," I had muttered, letting him in. He made a quick circuit of the room to sniff and rub against some boxes, then joined me in bed. He curled up at my side, purring. His massive, white-socked paws flexed, but the claws remained retracted, much to the gratitude of both me and the quilt that Grandma had owned for some forty years.

I slept well through the first half of the night, but after about two o'clock, my brain became restless. I kept thinking about Chase, Belinda, Ella May, Grizz, and the mysterious "bad dude," George. How did all of these pieces fit together? How could I help Grizz, whether he was innocent or guilty?

First order of business had to be finding out which one he was.

I gave up on sleep at dawn when the birds outside became enthusiastic. That prodded Bowser to awaken too. I came out of the bathroom to find his thick neck wedged between the wooden blinds, his stout caterpillar-like tail lashing against the surface of the nightstand at a steady beat. A tissue box had been knocked to the carpet.

"Come on, you. Oof." I grunted as I hauled him from the room. "I have half-unpacked boxes that you shouldn't get into. At least for now, you're only allowed inside the bedroom if I'm present to supervise." When had I even started on those particular boxes? The past few days had been so weird, things had blurred.

I comforted Bowser with dry food and fresh water, and prepared myself some comfort by brewing tea. I poured that into a travel thermos, threw on a fleece hat and gloves, and set off on a brisk walk.

I went down my driveway, crossed the street, then took a shortcut across the calf-high green grass. There, right past a cluster of oaks, I found the narrow dirt trail that Grizz had used the previous night.

"Well, Grizz, you *have* been walking this route often, for one reason or another," I muttered, following the route deeper into the Santa Lucias. The path cut beneath oaks, then up a slope, then down again. I paused on occasion to sip my tea, keeping an eye on my watch. I'd started a hiking exercise mode as soon as I left my house. Therefore, my exact route was being tracked via my phone, complete with elevation changes and my personal exertion.

After about a mile on the trail, only wilderness lay ahead, and my watch informed me of something more important than my heartrate and my calorie burn: the time.

I had to turn around.

Frustrated, I hurried back to the house. The hike hadn't been completely useless, though. I'd confirmed that Grizz had indeed traveled a good distance, well beyond my property line.

I arrived at the house again, sweaty and cold together, and somewhat frantic.

I needed to finish assembling my cheese boxes.

After a quick shower, I was clothed, determined, and caffeinated enough to parse the schematics tacked on my board in the Kitchen. I mumbled gratitude to the me-of-yesterday who had cut, chopped, and portioned everything already. Now all I had to do was fill in the blanks. I did so, treating my counter like an assembly line, arranging cheese and accoutrements with sidesteps back and forth.

I finished right before nine o'clock. Perfect.

Time to load up. Cheese boxes in the trunk with some extra cold packs despite the chilly morning, thrift store donations on the back seat. I steeped more tea as I made sure Bowser had adequate food for the day. He'd reclaimed his tiger-perch on the same box tower in the living room, paws and tail draped over a long side.

My stomach growled, reminding me that I needed food for myself, too. I didn't have a lot of time to spare. Good thing I knew about a quick breakfast stop close by.

Foghorn Plaza was eerily empty after the hubbub of the previous evening. Quesoquick contained the sole sign of life. Four cars were parked there. I joined a fast-moving line of people that also included a guy in a suit who was mesmerized by his phone, three guys wearing neon vests, and a frayed mother trying to contain an energetic toddler who bounced around shouting, "Puddin'! Puddin'!"

As I shuffled closer to Quesoquick, I had a better angle of the end of the strip mall where Ella May had been attacked. A few yellow police ribbons whipped in the breeze. There had been two attacks in two days. Was a third one imminent?

I had apparently come at the end of the breakfast rush. When I reached the window, no one waited behind me.

Jessie brightened as I stepped up to the window. She wore a blue scarf adorned with snowmen above the thick collar of a red turtleneck sweater. The open window would be chilly at this time of year. "Oh, hey there, Bird! Trying out breakfast, huh?"

"That's right. I need something fast and tasty. Can you give me the nitty-gritty details on the breakfast bread pudding? And I love that scarf!"

"Thanks! We never get snow here, so we have to channel the season however we can, right?" Jessie rocked back on her heels, grinning. "As you can see on the sign here," she motioned to the menu board beside the window, "we reuse yesterday's bread for the morning's pudding. Today, that means it's all sourdough, since we sold out of white yesterday. We soak that overnight in beaten eggs and cream, then toss in a mix of shredded cheese. Not a lot. It's there as a binder and to add some different texture. People sometimes freak out at the idea of sweet toppings mixed with cheese, then they freak out when they discover it works so well."

I shook my head. "I've encountered those same reactions when people realize how well pairings work. Honey and fruit are chronicled as being perfect accompaniments for cheese even in the Roman era, but I swear every week the people I feed discover the delicious awesomeness all over again."

"Does that mean you've already tried maple syrup with cheese?" Jessie asked, then laughed at herself. "Wait, of course you have. How silly of me. Now, do you want just one block of pudding?"

"Yes, please." I studied the menu board. Topping options included butter, maple syrup, honey, and olallieberry honey. "I'm surprised you don't carry maple butter, but that is more of a Vermont and Canadian thing."

"Maple... butter?" I could barely see her moving around farther back in the kitchen.

"Yes, and it includes no actual butter. It's pure maple syrup that's heated and then beaten. It ends up with a thick consistency closer to creamed honey. You can spread it. But looking at the menu, I need to try this olallieberry honey. I've had olallieberries fresh, and as preserves, pie, and crumb bars, but never mixed with honey!"

"Oh! Here, let me get you a sample spoon of that. Olallieberry honey's texture is similar to creamed honey, too. You let it sit on the hot pudding for a minute to soften, then spread it around with your fork. That tangy berry flavor and the thick honey soak into all the nooks and crannies. It's so good! Dale gets it from a lady down near Cambria."

Cambria, small as it was, was essentially the olallieberry capital of the Central Coast. I accepted the tiny bamboo spoon she passed to me, the flattened bowl smeared with a thick, granular, and strangely violet-colored honey. I smelled it first, taking in the fruitiness, then used my teeth and tongue to scrape the spoon clean in a single pass. I closed my eyes for a moment to let the honey marinate my body and soul.

"Yeah, I need that on my bread pudding. Along with a touch of butter, if that's okay."

"Absolutely. Do you want a coffee, too? Our stuff is better than what they offer." She motioned toward the coffee place in the strip mall, which was weirdly dead for a purveyor of caffeine at this early hour.

"I'm not a coffee drinker, sorry. I have a hot tea in the car." I hesitated a beat. "Have you talked to Belinda today? How's she doing?"

"Yeah, I chatted with her late last night. She was badly shaken by what happened to Ella May."

"I hope Ella May is able to talk to police about who attacked her."

"So do I," Jessie said, voice quivering with emotion. "Maybe that'll lead them to whoever killed Chase, too. Oh, hey, the total's on the screen in front of you."

I paid, with a generous tip. "On that note, did Chase ever mention a guy named George to you?"

Jessie came into view again, a deep frown on her face. "How did you hear about George? Who've you been talking to?"

The somber shift startled me. "I've been asking around. Detective Merrick suspects that Grizz killed Chase."

"What? Why?" She looked astonished.

"Chase was camping on my property and trashing the place. Grizz came with me when I confronted Chase. Things didn't go so well. Threats were made," I said, to which Jessie grimaced and nodded. "I can't twiddle my thumbs and trust the police to do the right thing."

"I don't know. Maybe in this case, you should." Jessie

sounded genuinely worried. "There's a murderer on the loose, you know. They killed Chase. They attacked Ella May. They can strike again."

"Indeed they can. That's the problem. By your reaction, you *do* recognize the name George. Did you meet him?"

Jessie looked blatantly annoyed now. "Bird, seriously. You need to know when to leave things alone. No, I never met him, but Chase always blabbed when he *thought* he'd scored big. He bragged that he was smarter than George. Well, we know how that turned out." She shrugged. A timer behind her dinged, and she turned around.

"Do you know George's last name? Or where I might find him?"

She glanced over her shoulder. "Why are you looking for trouble? This George guy smuggles goods along the Central Coast. Drugs, contraband, whatever. He's not going to be nice."

"I don't expect to chat with the guy about cheese, but if he's up for that, hey, I'm game. Do you know *anything* that might help?"

Jessie's motions were slow, thoughtful, as she dabbed butter atop my bread pudding. A generous dollop of the olallieberry honey followed, landing in the center of the craggy bread square. "Chase mentioned that George came around here because he had a drop point in the area–"

"Not on my property, right?" I cut in.

"No, not there, but up behind the House. There's a gate past the B&B with a No Trespassing sign on it. Climb over that, and there's a trail going into the mountains. It gets steep fast. The drop zone is hidden near some boulders up high on the peak."

I furrowed my brow. "Why did Chase talk about things like that?"

Jessie snorted. "Chase was the only person in the world who thought he was smart."

"Does George… keep guards around there?"

"I don't know. It's Slocombe House property. Maybe some groundskeepers are in on the scheme. All I know is, Chase ferried goods for him, and that's where he went."

"Interesting." I drummed my fingers on the cool metal ledge. I wondered if this drop point was where Chase should've delivered the money he was supposed to fetch from Oakland.

"Do you think you'll take a look?" Jessie sounded worried. She approached the window carrying an enclosed cardboard box, the kind takeout hamburgers came in at some restaurants.

"I need to hit San Luis Obispo right now." I tilted my head, pondering. No way could I provide this lead to Merrick. I needed something more substantial. "You know, I think I will explore behind the House, but I can't do so until mid-afternoon. Maybe I can find something useful to direct Detective Merrick toward George."

"Be careful. You're messing with dangerous people," Jessie said softly. She slid the box to me, a plastic fork wrapped in a napkin on top.

"Trust me, I know."

I sat in my car to eat, engine on so I could run the heater as I dug into my bread pudding. The block was about four inches by four inches, the loaf chunks dense yet melt-in-the-mouth tender. Everything came together, sublime, sweet, and perfect. Jessie was right: that fruity honey melted into the nooks and crannies in a luscious way.

I sipped tea between bites, mulling my plan of action. I could only hope my second hike of the day would prove more productive than the first. Could George have traps around his drop zone? I didn't like the idea that House groundskeepers might be in on his operation, either.

But I still wanted to go. I needed to know what was up there. I was... excited by the possibility of danger. Intrigued. I remembered feeling this way as a kid when I helped Grandma in ways I didn't understand, then or now. One time, she had me spill ice cream on the clothes of a stranger along the Embarcadero in Morro Bay. I then waited by the car when she went to confront them in the bathroom as they cleaned up. Another time, I was told to act casual and sit on a bench at Moonstone Beach, and if I saw three men come along the path, I was supposed to turn on a battery-powered radio at a loud volume. I lurked there for an hour or so, then turned on the music when I saw the guys. They walked past me, deep in conversation. I don't know what happened to them, but I do know that Grandma was hiding nearby, doing something.

I loved being part of her mysterious operations – being helpful. These days, though, I was no longer content with being ignorant. I needed answers, no matter the risk.

Chapter Fourteen

San Luis Obispo was the county seat of the same-named county, a college town that still retained a small-town feel. It may have been founded around a mission in the 1700s like a lot of other vital coastal California cities, but it was never going to become a bustling metropolis. That vibe was a big reason why I wanted to go to school there and stayed around afterward. It was the kind of place where I felt comfortable cruising around by car, taking in the hilliness and abundant trees. Not like I could dawdle today, though. Between the construction traffic and the extra Friday fuss, I rolled up at my destination exactly on time. Fluttering, neon-bright streamers braided the chain-link fence at the front of the yard. The vines twining the white arbor over the front walkway had died back for the winter, and instead had grown gobs of balloons adorned with the number fifty. That number was repeated in three-foot-high painted cardboard placards tacked over the front porch.

"Gosh, I hope I'm in the right place," I said with a laugh as my client opened the door.

"I know, there are just soooo many fiftieth birthday parties going on." Estelle's black skin glowed with happiness, her laugh lines deep and proud. From the first time I met her, she had struck me as the kind of lady who laughed a lot and helped others laugh too. She turned around and hollered. "Hey! Gather around, people. We got to help carry in the *cheese!*"

Only a couple cars had been parked parallel along the street, but about a dozen people of all ages emerged to help. My platter boxes were so big, we had to turn sideways to carry them through the arbor and doorway. I was directed to a formal dining room that had been, well, generic, with white walls and modular furniture, when I'd come by for my in-person consultation.

"Wow, I love the decorations! It's like a unicorn vomited in here," I said, gazing in awe at the array of balloon bouquets and streamers. The ladies busted out giggling.

"We're celebrating color today. And me." Estelle held out her arms in a modeling pose. Her flowery, fluttery blouse featured bell sleeves and mottled splotches of yellow, blue, and red.

"As well you should." I helped arrange the boxes on one of the fold-out tables that now encircled the room. "Do you want lids on or off?"

"Off!" screeched an older woman. The others howled with laughter.

Estelle waggled a finger at me. "Now, cheese temptress, how long was it again that the cheese should sit out before we dig in?"

She'd started calling me "cheese temptress" at our consult. Next time I had business cards printed, I was going to include that term. "Thirty minutes is good to bring them up to temperature so the best flavors and textures emerge, but don't leave them out more than four hours."

"Girl, none of this will be left in two," said another woman, to a chorus of agreement. I opened one of my boxes. I noted that many of the platters on the other tables already had their lids off or their plastic wrap peeled back, too. Some were well picked over.

The group gathered around, chattering. Fingers eagerly reached forward to start sampling. Their ecstatic reactions brought a big grin to my face. I took in their cheese-joy like a sponge.

"Okay, I gotta take some pictures of the arrangement before it's full of gaps. Gorgeous, just gorgeous!" Estelle stood back to take some shots.

I joined her to do the same. "Great lighting in here. Oh, yes, that's a great pic!" I said, looking over her arm at her phone. By my boilerplate contract, I had to approve the social media pictures shared by my client – or I'd straight out supply them myself to ensure good quality. It sounded like excessive control, but the rule existed for a reason. There's no horror like being tagged on a picture of a box full of ugly crumbs and seeing the outreach extended to thousands of people. Drool-worthy cheese photography meant everything in my biz.

"Your presentations make it easy to get good pics. Speaking of good presentations, see what my meat guy brought me." She motioned to the next table.

"Meat guy!" chortled an older woman nearby.

I side-stepped to investigate. I'd already known she wasn't getting meat from me because she was going all-in with platters from a local charcuterie business. The two circular arrangements were extraordinary, like wheel-sized spirals of sliced and thin-cut meats. As much as I admired the artistry, I felt no desire to try anything. The various carnivorous delights touched each other and had been mingling flavors for hours.

"Isn't it amazing?" Estelle said. "This is my 'screw you, diets!' party. We got cheese. Meat. Cupcakes. Wine."

"Margaritas!" someone shouted from another room.

"Margaritas." Estelle grinned. "Sweet tea. Plus stuff to make that sweet tea harder than my abs have ever been." Laughter rang out. "Most of all, there is no ring on this finger anymore!" She brandished her bare hand, to whoops of support. "We are living life as God intended today and enjoying every last morsel. I've got twenty-five girlfriends coming over. This party's going until midnight, and all the neighbors are invited so they don't complain, either." This elicited an 'amen!' from an older white woman nearby, presumably a neighbor. "You are welcome to join us, too."

I wasn't often invited to join in on festivities I'd catered, and I'd never accepted the offers I'd had. I could imagine the decibel of the music and chatter here would soon be heard from a block away. "I'm honored, but unfortunately, I have other commitments today."

"Well, here. If you can't stay, then at least take some cupcakes. I ordered a hundred fifty. I mighta gotten carried away." She tugged me by the sleeve to the far table where frosting-swirled cupcakes were lined in perfect rows. Well, almost perfect. Each row already had a few holes.

"Wow. I like how you go overkill. These things look amazing. Who's the– Oh, there we go." I spied a small placard set off to one side that listed the baker's name and a QR code with their info. I snapped a picture. "Is that... candied bacon atop these? Oh, and is that maple flavor for the brown frosting?" I could detect a whiff of maple scent.

"You know about more than cheese!" Estelle laughed. "Yes, these are maple cupcakes with candied bacon on top. How many do you want?"

The big platters of mixed meat had grossed me out, but I was okay with bacon on maple frosting. I'd never understand how my brain processed things as delicious or repulsive.

I thought of my friend Mollie. "Two would be great, thank you. I can go to my car and get–"

"Nope. Maria, remember where that big ol' stack of take-out boxes are in the kitchen? Can you grab one? Thanks!"

A few minutes later, I left with my cupcakes. As I started up the car, I could still hear the laughter and jabber from inside the house. I felt a wistful twinge. Sometimes I wished I could enjoy gatherings like that. At least today I had a valid excuse to leave. In the past, saying "no" to that kind of event had left me in a funk, even though I knew if I'd tried to linger, I'd be miserable and ready to go within an hour.

Ah well. I had a happy customer and maybe I'd have more contacts from people who discovered my cheese today – plus, I had cupcakes. And now I was going to visit Mollie for the first time in a few weeks, after a brief stop at a thrift store. Chase's clothes were making my Kia smell funky in a way that I only tolerated from cheese. I needed those bags out of here.

A drizzle began to fall as I parked in the guest lot behind Mollie's apartment complex. I pulled up my hood and was glad that the cupcake box had a lid as I hurried through the center court and up the metal steps to the second floor. I did my signature knock on her door – the first few notes of the fanfare for one of our mutually favorite video game series – and she opened it about twenty seconds later.

"What's that?" she said, eyes on the box. She knew I

hadn't brought cheese – Mollie only liked cheese when it was melted. Not that this was a total tragedy. I could make a mean from-scratch pizza for our girls' gaming nights.

"Maple cupcakes with candied bacon bits on top, courtesy of my client."

"A quality lunch. Let me get water heated for our tea."

Her microwave started with a purr. I wondered how Dale would react if he knew I drank microwaved tea water on occasion. A few years ago, I'd seen a viral video that depicted British people reacting with horror to such American practices. Probably best if I kept Mollie's water-heating method a deep, dark secret. At least I had an electric kettle at home.

"So, tell me about this new guy of yours," Mollie called. I laughed. It was like she knew I'd been thinking of Dale at that very moment. "Don't you dare say 'what guy?' either. I want to know who was at your place. Did he go to that crime scene with you, too?" At my nod, she rolled her eyes. "Gurrrrl, you have issues."

"Catalogs of issues," I readily agreed. I stacked vintage video game strategy guides to one side so there was room for our steaming mugs on the table. By the thud of the cabinet, she was starting the tea steeping process. "Dale's not really my guy, though. We've hit it off as friends. We have a common bond of cheese."

"Listen to yourself. Anyone involved with you, as a friend or something more, would need to like cheese in some way. Okay, so he's not 'yours,' I won't push you on that." She knew me well enough to understand that she'd get nowhere with that angle. "But you like him? He's cute?"

I had to answer positively to both. I told her all about Dale. British-born. Bread baker. Cheese-lover who needed guidance to more deeply cultivate his passion. A total gentleman. She squealed at every new detail as we enjoyed the tea along with our cupcakes, which were as delicious as they looked. Estelle had exquisite taste in her party purveyors.

"Okay, yeah. We need to visit this Quesoquick place to get lunch sometime so I can vet him for you," Mollie said. "It can't be this week. Maybe next? Depends on if I get more overtime shifts. But I dunno. The way people keep dying in your neighborhood, there might not be anyone left by the time I get there."

"Only one person has died," I chided. "I wanted to talk to you about that, too."

Mollie leaned back on the couch. "I don't have a shovel you can borrow, but if you need my strength, I'm there for you." She made a bicep muscle, the bulge clear through her blue sweater. She was tall with thick curves, a total bruiser during her brief stint in roller derby in college. She hadn't had time to keep that up these days between nursing and video game streams.

"So, the murder in Foghorn," I said. "The victim was in a bad offroad car accident, but that didn't kill him. Someone cut his throat. How strong do you need to be to do that? How much… stuff do you need to cut through in the neck to kill them? I want details. Make me understand on a visceral level." I knew this would make me squeamish, but I wanted to grasp the science of Chase's murder.

She arched a heavily penciled eyebrow. "So in terms of strength, you know how when you punch somebody you kinda have to pretend they are not there, that your fist is just going to run through them and come out the other side?" I nodded. We'd done self-defense lessons together after there were a couple of rapes on campus. "It's the same with cutting a neck. It's not like sawing at a dense steak; you bring your knife hand across and the tissue resistance should come as a surprise but you keep going anyway. A moment later there isn't any resistance anymore."

"Spoken like someone who has done their share of cutting," I said.

Her smile was grim. "You better believe it."

I took a sip of Earl Gray, brow furrowed. "One of the saddest aspects about all of this is that Chase really isn't being mourned much by the people who knew him. He was a major troublemaker. A lot of people are relieved that he's gone. His mom definitely has conflicted emotions."

Mollie's laugh was brittle. "That's not odd, considering what I've seen of families. We see the worst kind of drama in a hospital."

I acknowledged that with a rueful nod. "The other thing about his mom: her health is pretty poor, and has gotten dramatically worse in the past couple days. She works in a salon. She was able to cut hair the day he was killed, but now she can barely turn a key in a lock."

"Shock messes with bodies like that. Don't underestimate what even a small, weak-looking person can do if they are mad, though. Adrenaline can help a petite gal lift a car off a crushed person. It can give them extra oomph with a knife, too. How was this Chase guy positioned? Where would the murderer have been?"

I explained how the driver's side door had been stuck and the passenger side was ajar. She took that in with a brisk nod, then motioned me to switch spots with her on the couch. "Okay, since that Rita gal said she saw someone in Chase's car with him, we assume that was the killer, right?"

"Until we know better, yes. I still don't know if his throat was cut before or after the car accident, but I'm guessing after. Maybe the killer hoped the accident would kill him, and when it didn't, they needed to finish him off. Of course, the murderer would have also risked hurting themself when the car went off the road, but maybe they jumped out first. Which is also dangerous." I realized I was rambling and gave Mollie a little nod to indicate I was done.

"Right. So, I'm the killer." Mollie shaped her right hand like a blade. "I have my knife, and I'm ready to cut his whole head off." She leaned over me, blade hand on the left side of my neck. "I'm assuming the killer is a righty, since most people are, and from what you said about when you touched his neck, the cut was shallower on the right side." I nodded, cringing at the memory of what I felt. "The knife is going to cut the left vessels first," the pinkie side of her hand scraped my neck, "then get deflected by the spine as it tracks around it. The trachea and esophagus will get sliced next, right below the larynx so that air escaping from the lungs does not make noise over the vocal cords. The knife comes back toward me, the killer, and takes out the vessels on the right as it lifts away. Ta-da! Done." Her hand drew back.

"It sounds like it would be fast."

"Necks are soft, vulnerable spots. If the guy was knocked out by the crash, it'd be especially easy. A choice-cut steak would be tougher to slice."

I considered Grizz and everyone else around Foghorn while staring into my empty cup as if I could scry the truth. "Sounds like I could do it, too, even if it squicked me the whole time."

"You've spatchcocked a chicken, girl. Slitting a throat is easier than that."

"Spatchcock" was one of our favorite words. We made an effort to work it into every conversation we could. At least the process of removing the spine of a whole chicken for speedier cooking time made sense within the context of *this* chat. We'd gotten some odd looks in public before.

"I'll need to keep you away from Detective Merrick or you'll give him even more reasons to consider me a suspect." I glanced at my watch. I'd wanted to get her perspective on Ella May's attack and recovery, but I hadn't the time. Winter days were short, and I had a literal mountain to climb.

I stood. Mollie stood as well, plucking the cup from my hand. "I'm sorry, but I need to go," I said. "You go to work in like an hour, right?"

"Don't remind me." Mollie made a face of revulsion. "See, I need to get another hundred thou' subscribers on my channel and then I can stream video games all the time, get some promo deals, live the good life."

"I need to finalize the new camera setup in the Kitchen and then we can do that cross-promo we've been discussing for years. That'll bring in followers for both of us."

Mollie's eyes glimmered like the starry-eyed anime maid on the wall poster behind her. "Yes! You do cheesy things, we talk games, our audiences mingle." She tried to intertwine her fingers, but the mug made that impossible. "Good things are about to happen for both of us, so you make an effort to not die next or anything, right? Text me every so often so I know you're okay! Don't wear a red shirt!"

I laughed at the classic Star Trek reference; the away-team member in the red shirt so often succumbed to a dire fate. "No need to worry there. I don't own a single red shirt."

I didn't tell her the other thought that came to mind: that blood could make any shirt into a red shirt.

Chapter Fifteen

By the time I made it back to Foghorn, the skies were blue, the air crisp and comfortably cool. I'd gone through a drive-through for a salad before I left S-L-O and ate it in my car. My attempts to bring salad fixings to the house had been jinxed thus far, so I figured a restaurant version would be a safe way to get greens inside me.

I passed my exit and took the next one into Foghorn proper, following the road straight past the strip mall to the grand estate of Slocombe House.

As I'd eaten my salad, I'd studied a satellite overview of Foghorn on my phone. The estate had two parking lots: a paved upper one immediately adjacent to the House that had a wheelchair-accessible sidewalk for guests, and a lower gravel lot located down-slope, tucked behind trees. My wheels growled as my car crossed the gravel to park among late-model sedans and rust-freckled trucks. This had to be the parking area for employees. My stalwart-yet-aged Kia Soul fit right in.

I took one of several walking paths toward the House. The tall, peaked roofs jutted over the high trees. The greenery up close to the buildings was beautiful, but I also found it nerve-wracking. If a fire started in the mountains nearby, a blaze had fuel to take it straight to the main House. At least the parking lots and a lower meadow acted as a buffer to protect Foghorn Village.

I skirted around the House, leery of confrontations with employees, especially Rita, though I barely saw anyone about. I didn't spy cameras, either. A dirt road took me up a steeper slope to a metal gate with a NO TRESPASSING sign that looked like it'd been shot multiple times with a pellet gun. I climbed over the metal bars, grateful for the flexibility of my yoga trousers, and kept on walking, plagued by a deepening sense of ill-ease. That wasn't just because I was trespassing – though I wasn't one to usually flout such rules – but because I felt like I was being watched. I kept looking over my shoulder, but I didn't see anyone following me.

Despite my misgivings, I had to keep going. I needed to make some kind of breakthrough on the case today. Maybe George had tagged the area in some way – or I'd score something like a packing slip. If I could uncover a last name for George, I'd have an easier time tracking him down... unless his name turned out to be something like Smith or Garcia. In that case, I'd need to try a totally different avenue of investigation.

Trees surrounded me as I slogged upward. The dirt road narrowed to a rugged trail. The earlier rain had softened the ground enough to make it extra slippery, which was only exacerbated by plentiful pebbles and shards. Birds screeched and sang. Such a beautiful afternoon for trespassing.

Through the trees, I saw something move in the narrow valley below. I froze. Was it a deer? The object moved again – it was a person in blue. Were they a House employee? Another trespasser? Someone connected to George, or the man himself? The person stopped moving.

They saw me.

I dropped to a crouch, my heart pounding like a 1980s drum machine. I stayed down for a long minute, then eased up to peek. I didn't see the other person. Should I try to follow them – would they try to follow me? A second later, I knew my initial question was stupid. No way was I leaving the trail. Cell phone reception would be horrible out here. I needed to stay where I could be found if I twisted an ankle or fell.

I emerged from the tree cover onto a broad ledge. I knew I'd been climbing upward, but I was astonished to see I was almost to the mountain top. If I'd been on the other side, I'd have a gorgeous ocean view, but this vista was amazing, too. The north-south aligned ridges of the Santa Lucias seemed to stretch on forever. Somewhere due east lay the southern portion of Lake Nacimiento and the city of Paso Robles, not that I could make them out from this far away.

I turned to take in the slope behind me. Boulders formed an impressive jagged wall, hardy shrubs growing from numerous cracks. The flat faces of the boulder had been painted in taupe that didn't quite match the natural rock. Had gang tags been left here – maybe in connection to George? Or had it hosted more tame graffiti, like so-and-so loves so-and-so? It felt weird to see evidence of other encroachers. I was maybe a twenty-five-minute walk from the House, and I felt like I was in the absolute middle of nowhere.

I approached the rocks, peering between them to look for parcels or papers, only to be confounded by the deep shadows. The sun faced the opposite side of the mountain. I pulled out my phone and turned on the flashlight mode. I revealed more rocks and plants. In warmer weather, snakes – rattlers, in particular – would lurk in a place like this. Brisk as the day was, I still wasn't going to poke my hand into those gaps unless I had thick gloves and a good reason.

The ledge narrowed as the path continued, boulders on one side, a steep cliff on the other. I put my phone away – not in my pocket, but in my purse, which I firmly clasped shut. No way did I want to risk dropping it.

A shadow crossed over me. I glanced up to find a large bird swooping overhead. A vulture, maybe, or even a California condor. I thought I recalled that condors had been reintroduced into the area after a close scrape with extinction.

Rapid footsteps pounded on the trail behind me. I turned, but before I could face the person, I was struck. Hard. A screech escaped me as I went airborne. I had a view of blue sky and the black blob of the bird, and then gravity gripped me. I hit the slope of the cliff. Breath was knocked from my lungs. I tucked in my knees and arms to protect my head and my purse, my face pressed to my forearms as I began to roll downward, downward, downward, bouncing against rocks and brush, my panic a roar in my ears.

Someone had shoved me. Someone was trying to kill me.

And as I continued to spin and painfully bounce my way downhill, I wondered if they were about to succeed.

Chapter Sixteen

A bush snagged me for a moment, stabbing through my jacket and sweater, but didn't arrest my movement. Rocks collided with my head, my shoulders, my hips. Something scraped the length of my calf, causing me to scream again. Oh, that hurt, that hurt, that hurt. Pressure jerked against my neck, briefly strangling me, and only after the sensation ended did I realize that the pressure had been my purse strap. I no longer had that little bundle tucked against my torso.

My roll ended as abruptly as it began. A broad bush caught me, the winter-bare branches snapping at the impact before dropping me to the dirt. I muffled a moan and sob against my arm, then made a conscious effort to be quiet. I didn't need my attacker to know I was conscious or alive, or they might try to finish me off – just as someone had finished off Chase after his car crash.

Huh. We'd both gone down slopes to land in the bushes. This attack on me fit the MO of Chase's death more so than the assault on Ella May.

I slowly stretched out my legs, hissing at the sharp pain in my right calf. I reached to examine it with my fingertips and I found shredded cloth and hot blood. No bones felt broken, but wow was I cut up and bruised. I sat with a look upward.

From here, the slope looked like it led up to the heavens. I had no sense of where the trail was, nor did I see anyone craning their heads to see where I landed. I returned my attention to my body. My pants had ripped around my calf, exposing a nasty cut that extended at a diagonal angle from my ankle to below my knee. An infection waiting to happen.

My right boot was gone, the sock almost pulled off. My arms and fingers seemed intact. My scalp felt hot in spots, but the bleeding was minimal. It'd hurt something awful when I took a shower later.

"Okay, Bird," I muttered, trying to find comfort in my own voice. "Focus. Someone just tried to kill you. Be smart so they don't figure out a way to still succeed."

I crawled up the slope on my hands and feet. The route I'd taken was easy to find. I'd broken branches and disturbed dirt along the way.

After a few minutes, I found my purse. I sat to investigate it with trembling fingers. The clasp had stayed shut. My phone screen looked fine, and it promptly turned on. No reception, though. I growled in frustration. The big cut down my calf was sending a spike of pain up my body with every step. A walk out of here was not going to be fun.

I tied a knot in my broken leather strap and again draped it across my body. My knees struck my purse and made it bounce around as I continued crawling upward.

Whoever shoved me might be waiting at the ledge. I couldn't climb up to the same spot where I fell. But I also needed to find my other ankle boot before I walked back to Foghorn. I scanned the slope around me, and after several minutes I finally spied it – some thirty feet from my downward path, sitting atop a shrub like a funky crown. It had sailed off on its own fun trajectory after being pried from my foot. I scooted back down to retrieve it. I secured the laces tightly, trying to ignore how much the pressure hurt my cuts and bruises. That done, I didn't climb much higher, instead working my way around the mountain toward Foghorn.

I reached the western-facing slope at a low elevation that didn't offer a view of the ocean, but did show the spires of Slocombe House beyond another ridge and trees. I also spotted a trail farther down that winded between the knolls. I let gravity help me hobble that way, every step radiating pain.

This new path felt more impacted, more used. Footprints and bike tracks were visible on the thin mud. This had to be one of the hiking trails advertised by the bed and breakfast – the House even rented bikes to guests. As I neared the more populated grounds, though, I realized I had a problem.

From this side, I'd need to go right by the House and along the full length of the guest parking lot before I could reach my car. I did not want to stop off for first aid at the House. No way would that escape Rita's notice. No way could I casually get to my car, either. I *looked* like I'd been shoved off a cliff. People would want to help me – and I wouldn't know if my attacker was among them.

I did want someone's help, though. That's why I kept going straight, taking a split in the trail that guided me toward the small residential area tucked behind the strip mall, where Dale said he lived with a view of Slocombe House.

I pulled out my phone. The sight of reception bars almost made me weep with relief. Dale answered after a single ring.

"Bird?" Urgency rang in the single static-filled word. "You're calling me. What's wrong?"

He knew it had to be serious because I dialed him directly. "Hey, Dale. I hate to impose, but I'm near your house and I'm rather banged up. Would it be okay if–"

"Banged up?" he snapped. I heard the harsh squeal of a rolling chair. "There's a black cat on my *pfftt zzzzz–*" static interrupted him, "–chain-link fence, green house. I'll head to the yard right *zzzz–*"

My path met the dead end of the narrow street. There were no sidewalks. I knew Dale had to be on the eastern side of the street based on his view. A few houses down, a wooden black cat affixed to a metal mailbox stood out above crabgrass. Dale bounded into view.

"Good grief!" he cried out, the words ringing through my phone and directly from him. I took that as a cue to hang up. Since my purse no longer dangled in the right spot, I fumbled my phone and almost dropped it in my effort to put it away.

"Good to see you, too." I lifted the U-shaped latch on the gate.

"What happened? What do you need?" His gaze raked me up and down.

"No ambulance, please. I don't want to explain what happened. If I can wash off the worst of my injuries so I don't bleed all over my car on the drive home, that'd be great. My upholstery is light gray. I didn't get black because it gets so hot in the summer, but today I regret that choice." Why was I babbling about upholstery? Did post-attempted-murder-shock cause that kind of thing?

"I have a full medical kit and some experience using it. I played rugby ages ago and did time in a roller hockey league in San Francisco."

"'Did time in a roller hockey league.' You must be a

particular kind of criminal to get that sentence." We entered the house through a tiny and tidy kitchen.

"Indeed. The team was started by an English literature teacher. We had to choose jersey names based on classic books. As a bread baker in training, I was Yeast of Eden. Oh, wait. The hall bathroom will need to function as our nursing station since it has a tub, but I need to get the kittens out first."

The small bungalow had to be from the 1920s, but based on the country goose wallpaper and striped-wood cabinets, the kitchen had last been remodeled sometime in the 1980s. A stand mixer sat on the counter, a clear bin of shelled walnuts beside it. An old-fashioned nutcracker jutted half-submerged among the knobby brown shells.

"I'll stay on the linoleum for now," I called as he jogged down a wood-paneled hallway. "I'd rather not bleed on your carpet." Though it was a nice dark blue; it'd mostly mask the blood, unlike my car upholstery.

I heard a rattle of metal. "Don't worry about that. I've cleaned up every possible stain courtesy of these beasties."

I tried standing on one leg like a flamingo, but my good foot hurt too much under my full weight. I gently lowered myself to sit on the floor. The cut in my calf still oozed blood. My sock had sopped up most of it. "You seriously played under the name Yeast of Eden? I can't decide if that's brilliant or horrible. It must be both."

His laugh sounded tinny. "We all had fun names. Another bloke was The Sound and the Furry. He was a pet groomer by day."

"Roller derby names are awesome like that, too. My friend Mollie used to play in college. Sometimes when I went to games, I had to cheer for rival teams because I loved their names so much."

A distant door opened, followed by mews and thumps. A moment later, Dale waddled into the hallway, a dog-sized cage partly resting against his legs. Inside were three meowing kittens – wee babes, as he might say, still small enough to cup in a hand.

"Oh gosh, they look too young to be from their mother. What are they, four weeks?" I asked, sliding over so he could set down the cage, blocking access to the fridge.

"That's about what I guess. They were found five days ago abandoned behind a motel in San Simeon." Two of the kittens were spotted gray and white, with the third all gray. Their mews were fierce but puny compared to the operatic roar of Bowser. "Follow me, Bird. You can sit on the toilet and start cleaning up while I get the tub disinfected." His brows scrunched with worry. "You've lost a lot of blood. Your whole leg needs to be washed down."

"Agreed. I can feel the bacteria crawling through my bloodstream." He offered me a hand to stand, his fingers soft and callused. The contact was brief yet welcome. I limped after him down the hall. The bathroom was surprisingly spacious, about as big as the kitchen. I sat on a fuzzy toilet cover, extra-fuzzy with cat hair while Dale dashed away. He returned with a laptop-sized white case with a red cross on the side. He set it on the counter to my left and lifted the latch. I let out a low whistle. He was serious when he said he had a full medical kit. The contents were organized much like my cheese boards, but with separated areas for different-sized bandages, sanitizers, and tools galore.

I pulled off my boots and socks. Wincing, I rolled up both pants legs to assess the full damage. In addition to the huge cut, there were a dozen minor ones, plus yellowed splotches of developing bruises. Both knees had scraped-pink splotches, the kind of injuries my mom used to call strawberries. I blinked back tears, surprised by a sudden yearning for her presence.

Dale returned with a spray surface cleaner. "While I clean, please, can you tell me what befell you?"

"Befell. Ha!" I scrubbed my hands clean in the sink, the sting of soap revealing more cuts. "Someone pushed me off a cliff, on purpose."

He paused to gape. *"What?* You're sure?*"

"If it had been an accident, I would have expected someone to yell that they were going for help. I'm certain I wasn't followed – the path was too exposed for much of the hike. They must have been hiding among the rocks." The harsh scent of the cleaning solvent made my nose prickle as he gave the tub a quick scrub-down.

"You need to call the police!"

Well, this was awkward. "Um, no. I'd rather not. You see, I was kind of trespassing behind Slocombe House."

"How does one 'kind of' trespass?"

"That's a very technical question that I'd rather not get into right now. Ow." I sat on the toilet lid and dabbed at my scalp with a cleansing wipe. "My assailant and I aren't the only ones to go up there, either. Heavy paint covered up graffiti."

"Ah, does that place have numerous boulders and a nice view?" Dale asked. I nodded. "I've heard my young employees talk about that as quite the snogging spot. That means kissing."

"I know what snogging means. I've probably watched enough British comedies and detective dramas to qualify for some lower tier of citizenship. Have you ever taken in that view yourself?" I belatedly realized what that implied and blushed. "I mean, hiking. Not actually using it. For snogging purposes."

"I'm an old man of almost thirty. I don't need a 'make-out spot.' I have a rental home of my own for the utmost in privacy, thank you very much."

My guffaw was soft, as I was distracted by new thoughts. Something here didn't make sense. Jessie had said that place was George's drop zone – but why would he use a place that was frequented by mischievous teenagers? Maybe George was using them as mules to deliver and fetch his goods, knowing that Slocombe House employees would assume they were trespassing for other reasons.

I considered the person I'd seen in the woods. They couldn't have attacked me. No way could they have outraced me up that steep, slippery path. Their fresh footprints would have stood out in the mud, too. Whoever shoved me must have climbed up along a different path, then had seen me coming and hid.

I glanced around me. "Sorry for the subject change, but where do you want me to put the trash?"

"Sorry. I had to remove the can because of the kittens. Pile any garbage on the linoleum floor. Here, I have the tub done. Bring your bum over here, Bird." Dale patted the rim of the tub, which was a more modern inset version. "Be careful. The ledge is narrow and sloped." He turned on the faucet and spoke louder to be heard. "Here are some washcloths–"

"They're white, I'm going to – "

"Stain them with blood, yes, and that's why God invented bleach, as my mum used to say in regards to my siblings' nappies. Do you want me to stay and help, or would you prefer to do this yourself?" His blue gaze was level and compassionate. Did the guy have any idea how sexy it was that he respected me enough to provide me with a choice? Ugh, Mollie was right to tease me. I wasn't sure how long I'd be content with being "just friends" with Dale.

I wiggled to keep myself seated on the edge with my feet in the tub. "My pride wants me to do it on my own so you don't have to see me cry from the pain, but my pride can also tell that if I try to stay seated here *and* wash up, I'm going to fall in the tub."

Dale laughed. "Shall we work together, then?"

"Together."

It was a teamwork unlike any I had known before. I kept myself propped upright with an arm against the wall. The water kept running as he poured cups of the liquid over my injured leg. With care, I dabbed at the cut with a washcloth, wiping away debris. My calf radiated agony. Dale kept his focus on my leg, carefully ignoring my sobby, snotty face. He didn't remark on my hairy legs, either – I wore my stretchy pants all year long in part because I hated shaving. I only scraped the hair off if it was absolutely necessary for me to wear a skirt for something like a job interview, a funeral, or a wedding.

"That's a pretty deep cut, especially in the middle," he said. "It could use stitches." My horror must have been apparent in my rigid posture. "But it could also do without. I have some large bandages we can use. It'll probably scar, though."

"A cut this big will probably scar even with stitches."

"True enough. I have a few dings that are proof of that, stitched and unstitched."

"I wear pants ninety-nine percent of the time, anyway.

If someone *were* to ask what happened, I'll tell them I got it after being knocked off a cliff. If they aren't impressed by that, I don't want to associate with them, anyway." I propped up my foot on the wall of the tub and dried my leg. Dale shut off the faucet.

"It's a wonder you didn't break your neck. This was an attempted murder, Bird. You don't shove someone off a cliff for fun, but for specific violent goals. Cartoons taught me that."

"Very educational, cartoons. Can you pass me that Neosporin from the counter?"

He did, and I smeared it along my largest wound. He readied a row of large bandages and placed them on my leg in fast sequence. We managed to get the cut covered before it dripped more blood on the floor.

"Are there other injuries that you can't reach well?" Dale asked. This man had earned the best-ever cheese plate for lunch tomorrow.

"I think I can take care of the rest once I'm home." I knew I had scratches around my bra straps on my back, but that level of intimacy with Dale needed to wait. "I owe you a lot of supplies."

"Don't concern yourself with that. They were probably on the brink of the best-used-by date. You saved me from wasting the whole lot, but that said, *please* don't provide me with more reasons to use these items. I'm serious, Bird. You need to contact that detective about what happened. Your trespassing is minor in contrast to what happened to you."

I tugged down my shredded pant leg. "I don't know if there's a point, Dale. I don't know if he'll believe me." Dale started to protest. I interjected before he could argue with me. "You need to understand, he called me into the station for questioning, but it wasn't about Chase. He'd found out that the guy who killed my parents in a drunk driving accident and got off scot-free had also died around Christmas. I have a solid alibi for that time period – I was working intense overtime, and Merrick knew that – but that didn't stop him from scrutinizing me. He even brought up how Grandma's presumed death is suspicious. I can't disagree with him on that, but even so, he was looking at *me*." I took a deep breath to get my bearings. "So yeah, I don't think it's that big of a stretch for him to doubt what I'm saying or even wonder if I hurt myself to throw him off my trail."

"Oh. Yes, I can see why you might feel that way." He considered me with a furrowed brow. "I'm very sorry to hear that you lost your parents, especially in such a horrible manner. And then to lose your grandmother as well…"

"Yeah. Last year sucked." I needed to change the subject. Immersing myself in that old grief atop the new trauma of today was not going to do kind things to my mental stability. "It probably goes without saying that my faith in the police was lacking before recent events in Foghorn, and it hasn't increased since. But anyway… I don't suppose you have some spare socks?" I considered my blood-crusted ones with a grimace.

"I do, actually, though they might be a tad big. Better than no socks at all." He left the bathroom, leaving the door open. Distant, faint mews rang from throughout the house. I heard the distinct thump of a dresser drawer. He returned, balled socks in hand. "You need to be especially careful when you return home. Your place is isolated. If whoever did this realizes that you're still alive, you could be in continued danger."

He tossed me the socks. I caught them with both hands.

"You're right." I considered my suspects. "I took my hike to look for clues, and I found different ones than I expected. Do me a big favor, Dale: don't tell anyone about what happened to me or that you even spoke to me this evening. I'm going to hope that no one is looking for my car as I drive home, and after that, I'm avoiding Foghorn for the next while." I pulled on the fresh socks. They were baggy, yes, but I'd make do.

"A low profile sounds wise. I won't tell anyone – but I will ring the detective if I don't hear from you a few times a day. I hope I don't sound like a controlling stalker when I say that."

"If someone else said that, maybe, but not you. My friend Mollie expects the same from me right now. I'm glad people are looking out for me." I needed to look out for myself more as well. A hike into the wilderness carried risks even if someone wasn't going around shoving people off cliffs. I should've let someone reliable know where I was going, murderer on the loose or not.

I took a few tentative steps with my boots on. "Well, how's that feel?" Dale asked.

"Painful, but I can drive."

"Where's your car? At the House?"

"Yes, the lower lot."

"By the shortest path, that's a solid half mile away." He smiled at my grimace. "I can drive you."

"You don't need to–"

"I want to. Be realistic, Bird. You're banged up. It's a hike on uneven terrain. Besides, if someone *is* monitoring the walking paths by the House, maybe they'll miss you along the roads."

"Okay," I said, somewhat grudgingly.

He quickly assembled a to-go emergency kit for me, which was good because I didn't think that I had any large bandages like he did. I followed him back through the house. The small living room held a sway-backed couch, glider rocker, and a TV. Everything looked old and worn except the sound system, which included speakers mounted on the walls. The kitchen kittens meowed in their cage, their frenzy increasing at the sight of Dale. They weren't alone, either. Two adult cats roamed around the kitchen linoleum, one a fluffy gray, the other a sleek calico.

"These two are Tacoma and Rainy," said Dale, gesturing to make proper introductions. "They are my permanent overlords. Their previous caretaker hailed from Seattle, hence the names."

"Nice to meet you both." I scratched their heads, earning instant purrs.

Dale watched the exchange with a proud smile. He'd passed a test at my house when Bowser immediately accepted him. I must have passed one here as well.

His little Hyundai was about as old as my car. The interior carried the distinct chemical-fresh odor of cat litter. I tried to hide my grimace as I leaned back in the seat. My back definitely had some cuts I needed to clean.

The setting sun cast clouds in a mottled purple-gray. "Beautiful evening," I said. "I should do more walks around here once I'm recovered."

We reached the end of the residential street. He cast me a sidelong glance. "Do give yourself generous time for that recovery, too. Tomorrow morning, you'll be in some additional discomfort."

I laughed. "Such a fine understatement. Yeah, my body will probably turn into one massive bruise overnight. But don't worry," I added, seeing he was about to speak up. "I do have pain medicine at the house, and tomorrow is my take-it-easy day. I'll get things done at my own pace. That includes lunch with you. Noon, right? My place?"

"Considering what I know of you, I'm curious about what your 'easy' day is like. Does that mean no dead bodies? No one in your vicinity is assaulted? No dramatic tests of gravity?"

"None of those things are on my to-do list, which is already pretty substantial." We reached the lower lot. My car was in sight. "So, cheese with me, right?"

He pulled onto the gravel beside my Kia and parked. "Yes. Maurice insists he can work, and Valerie will be on shift as well. You haven't met her yet. She mostly works weekends. She's a retired gal, rides a Harley, recites Star Trek scripts from memory. You'll like her."

I got out of the car, wincing. "She does sound like my kind of people."

"Bird." The softness in his voice caused me to turn to meet his blue eyes. "Be careful."

"I will," I said. "I'll text you at bedtime and again in the morning. Should we use a codeword so you know some stranger isn't holding me hostage and replying for me?"

The fondness in his smile made me smile in return. "Sure. What should we use?"

I thought for a moment. We couldn't use the same word every time or it would be obvious in our chat history. We needed a theme. "Places that make good cheddar, without mentioning the word cheddar. I'll avoid major brand names, too."

Dale laughed. "I'll need to hit a search engine for ideas after a few names, but you won't need to do that, will you?"

"Nope," I said, giving him a little wave as I shut his car door.

Chapter Seventeen

My body made sure my slow day was extra slow. Bowser had sprawled across my chest sometime during the night, his bulk like a hot furry weighted blanket, but even after nudging him off, I found I could barely move.

"Pain, pain, pain," I muttered, hobbling to the bathroom. I honest-to-goodness felt like I'd fallen off a cliff. I studied myself in the floor-length mirror on the closet door. Bruises marbled my pale skin. The big cut on my calf had bled more during the night but the bandages had contained the flow.

My next priority: security. My wounds were a very visceral reminder that someone had tried to kill me the previous day. I really should have inspected the property as soon as I returned after the attack, but I think my overwhelmed brain equated home with safety. That could have been a potentially lethal mistake. I needed to do better. I made a circuit of the house and the Kitchen, checking to make sure windows were latched shut and also had sticks in the sill tracks so that they couldn't slide open. At every door, I verified the knob locks and dead bolts were being used. I also made mental notes about what I needed for a new whole-house security system with cameras. Grandma had been leery of new technological advancements in monitoring systems. "Anything that uses a computer can get hacked or fail," she would say, insisting that her own two eyes and commonsense measures were adequate. Maybe that was true for Grandma, with her Bruce Lee-style skills, but not for me.

With a vow to remain vigilant and keep my phone on me at all times, I returned to the house to attempt a proper morning routine.

After I was clean, clothed, caffeinated, and had cheese for breakfast – the four proper C's to start any day – I settled into a cushioned chair, phone in hand, ready to do much-needed catch-up on the social side of my social media-powered business. I'd posted that I'd be mostly offline this week, and that had done little to prevent a massive backlog of emails and direct messages. Some people had even gotten snippy about a lack of an instantaneous reply, as if I was an auto-responder robot that happened to enjoy cheese a lot. As expected, a number of people had also reached out because they'd seen the news about the drama in Foghorn and wanted to make sure I was okay.

I dug into the digital pile, but after a few minutes, my mind went to Dale. I needed to message him.

"Wookey Hole," I typed.

I sent off a few email replies to potential customers, and then Dale responded: "HA! I KNEW THAT ONE."

I snorted. "Benefits of being British born," I tapped back. "Most people in America would think it was a Star Wars reference."

He replied right away. "And a select chosen few, here and abroad, would know the proper Star Wars reference should be spelled 'Wookiee.'"

Yes, we were meant to be friends. At minimum.

That reminded me, I needed to prepare our lunch cheese. I hobbled to my fridge to assess my personal stockpile. Dale had experience with good melters, so I needed to ignore those as I initiated his advanced cheese education. Cheeseducation? I'd need to submit that word for his approval.

I washed up and readied my workspace. A stack of boxes had been shoved near the wall, which I didn't remember doing, but I was glad it was done. I didn't have to dodge obstacles to get from the counter to the fridge.

Freedom of movement was something I needed to keep in mind, just in case someone did attack me at home.

I reached for a piece of Vella Dry Jack, one of the cheeses I'd also used in my grazing table arrangement. The savory-nutty-sweetness would blow his mind. I used my faithful Parm knife to create thin chunks of caramel-colored awesomeness.

I dug around more and found half of a large log of soft chevre. "He uses soft goat cheese on his sandwiches," I told Bowser as he sauntered through as if he owned the place after a day in residency. "I can't just slice this into a box. I need to make it special... Oh, I know! I'll give it the appetizer treatment. But sweet or savory, sweet or savory?" I closed the fridge to mull my other supplies for a moment. "I could do a bit of both, keep a nutty theme going. He had a box of walnuts and a nutcracker on his counter, so he can't be allergic to those."

I quartered the chevre and rolled it into balls. I tucked them into the almost-empty freezer on a piece of wax paper while I did other prep. A quick chop rendered a handful of candied black walnuts into pebbles. Kitchen shears reduced some juicy golden raisins to shreds. I tossed those two things together, then pulled out the chilled cheese. I rolled that in the nuts and raisin bits. I'd eyeballed the amounts just right. The cheese was perfectly coated. I tucked the cheesy balls into a lidded container in the fridge.

A good chevre isn't simply good because it's sweet and velvety on the tongue. It's also incredibly versatile. I could have used a different fruit and nut pairing, or gone super-savory with diced sun-dried tomatoes and fresh basil, or evoked spring by using a mix of edible dry flower petals, or rolled them in an everything-bagel seasoning. I'd ask Dale about other combinations he'd like to try in the future and have fun from there. This walnut and raisin mix happened to be one of my personal favorite combos, though, one of the few I liked to have prepared in advance; now I only hoped he enjoyed it as much as I did.

Those cheeses would do for the main board. I pulled on gloves and made some quick prosciutto roses and set them in a ramekin. I washed my last cluster of grapes and placed them, coiled up, on a saucer. I readied some of my favorite crackers in a plastic storage box on the counter. Hmm, maybe next time we did this, we could collaborate and he could bring bread.

"What about a simple dessert?" I asked Bowser. He yawned with a slight meow. My creative mania had provided a nice distraction, but the instant I started walking around again, I was reminded of my injuries and the danger that I might still be facing. "Some people would consider the chevre balls to be a dessert, but no. I need something with extra oomph. Ow. Ow. I hope that cut isn't bleeding again. It feels awfully warm." I knew I should probably sit and check on my bandages, but I wanted to stay oblivious for a while longer.

I poked around in cupboards for ideas. I didn't have time to bake anything for dessert. No way did I want to buy something from a store, either. I needed to show off my creativity. Pink Lady apples in a bowl caught my eye, probably because they were the only pretty things on the counter.

"I know!" I shrieked. Bowser's ears flared back, but he didn't scamper away. I returned to the fridge. "Gjetost!"

Gjetost was one of my favorite cheese names because of its pronunciation: *yay-toast*. The very name sounded celebratory! I had almost a full block of the square-shaped Norwegian cheese. It was a deep caramel color, and actually tasted like caramel or fudge. To be technical, gjetost wasn't even cheese, because it was made from whey *leftover* from cheesemaking, but hey, it was closer to real milk-derived cheese than vegan cheese, which I also considered a valid option for my platters and personal enjoyment.

I decided to hold off until our dessert time to use my hand-slicer to create thin, almost translucent leaves of cheese. The potently sweet slivers would be perfect atop slices of apple. That's how I had it for breakfast many mornings.

Did Dale like alcohol, I wondered? I had a few gifted bottles of wine from a Paso Robles wedding I catered in the fall, plus some hard cider. I could always pick up something like beer if that's where his preference went – but no, no, my thoughts were outracing the present yet again. I didn't need to go overkill on this lunch. Besides, he'd need to drive afterward to go to Quesoquick or do other business.

I needed to do some driving myself. "Taking it easy" didn't mean I lounged in bed all day, tempting as that might be. There were things to do, murders to solve. I couldn't deny that I needed to add an urgent care clinic to my list, too, because yeah, I probably should have a professional check my whole body and put some stitches in my leg. I needed to avoid Foghorn, but that was fine. I also needed to speak with the guy who had first told me about George days ago.

It was high time I paid another visit to Ray.

Driving hurt. I made a mental note that next time I fell off a hill, I needed to mess up my left leg, not my right, so at least I could move my foot between the gas pedal and brake without persistent stabs of pain.

As I left my house, I was ruminating what to say to Ray when a cloud of dust suspended in the air over Grizz's short driveway drew my attention to the two sheriff's department cars parking in front of the garden. I took a sharp left to pull in right beside them. Merrick was just emerging from one car as Johnson and another deputy came out of the other. Merrick looked at me in surprise, while I settled for a steady glare.

"What are you doing here?" I asked, my heart starting to pound fast. They couldn't be here to arrest Grizz, could they? Was there new evidence against him?

The screen door clattered as Grizz joined us, his eyes wide as he looked between the newcomers. He wore a faded Journey concert shirt featuring a large scarab. His dark jeans were worn white in spots. "Did you all come together?"

"Nope. I try to keep better company," I said in a forcefully perky tone. "I was driving by when I saw them."

"I talked to you yesterday," Grizz said to Merrick as the detective moved toward the bumper of his car. I drew closer, taking a defensive pose beside Grizz.

"You did. However, I spoke with a few witnesses yesterday evening who say they saw you with Chase right before he died, identifying you as a passenger in his car."

Grizz and I looked at each other, puzzled. "Sure, I was with Chase, in Lucille– in Bird's back-forty," Grizz said. "I never saw him after that."

"Then where were you that evening during the time frame in which Chase was killed?" Merrick asked. The other two deputies flanked him, attentive.

As much as I really wanted an answer to that question myself, no way could I let this conversation go further. "Okay, that's it." I shoved Grizz towards the door, almost knocking him over by accident. Sometimes I forgot I outweighed him. "Mr Ferreira here won't answer any more questions from you until he has his lawyer present."

"But you told me to talk to the detective after Ella May was attacked," Grizz muttered.

"Talk to him, yes. You say hi, affirm that you're still in the area. Not much more than that – unless you have your lawyer." I gave him a pointed look. "Did you get a lawyer?"

His gaze slipped away, slick as olive-oil-covered hands. That would be a no. I sighed. I couldn't gripe at him too much, though, as I'd been careless about this subject myself. I'd intended to look up the attorneys listed in the contacts on Grandma's phone, and promptly forgotten once I was home.

Grizz's steps were heavy as he proceeded up the two wooden steps to the trailer. I faced the officers. "Do you have a warrant to arrest him or to search his property?" I asked Merrick.

"I'm here to ascertain information, that's all, Miss Nichols." Merrick's expression was open, his tone frank.

"Good." I made a whisking motion to Grizz. He took the hint and entered his trailer. "Bye-bye, Detective Merrick, Deputy Johnson, and Deputy Whose-Name-I-Do-Not-Know." I gave them a wave and then followed Grizz, doing my utmost to move as normally as possible to avoid questions about my injuries. I decided I didn't like stairs anymore, because ow. I shut and locked the door behind me.

The living room was dark but for the sunbeams filtered through the blinds. Coffee perfumed the air. I took a deep breath, welcoming the cleansing scent even though I didn't like drinking the stuff. A tremble coursed through my hands. It felt like Merrick was getting closer and closer to arresting Grizz, and I couldn't let that happen, I couldn't.

Grizz turned on his old metal desk lamp and opened up a slim black leather-bound book. "I should've called a lawyer already, I know, I know."

"Why didn't you?" I said in exasperation.

"I don't know. The talk yesterday with that detective seemed fine. Didn't last five minutes. I thought... things were okay again. They can't really have evidence that I did it, after all."

Good grief. This man had only lived to this age because Grandma had coddled him for decades. "Grizz. The police had *absolute* evidence that the man who killed my parents had done it, and he still got off. You can't trust them, one way or another."

"I know." The words were mumbled, childlike.

I took another deep breath. "Is there any truth to the witness statements that Merrick mentioned?"

He braced himself on the desk to look up at me. "No. I didn't see Chase again after we booted him off your property, and that's the truth. I didn't kill him, either. I wouldn't be so stupid as to do that a half-mile from my own house, on a road that only the two of us travel on. Your grandma would have my hide if I did something as dense as that." His tone turned gruff as he focused on the book again, flipping pages.

His words rang true. A lump lodged in my throat.

"Someone is lying, then, saying that they saw you." I paused in thought. "Rita said she saw someone in Chase's car that night as he left Foghorn. She gave Merrick whatever security footage she had, too. I guess the cameras work at that end of the lot. Whoever left Foghorn with him was likely the murderer, so Merrick isn't stupid, following that lead – but you're not helping matters with your lack of alibi."

"The murderer needed a way to get home." Grizz looked between pages, frowning. "If I killed Chase at that spot, at least it'd be an easy walk home for me. If someone from Foghorn killed him, it wouldn't be much farther, maybe two miles. Anyone else, though…"

"They could call a taxi or ride-share, though they'd probably have a wait. I suspect Merrick has already examined that angle. If the murderer called up a friend or family member for a ride, that'd be harder to track."

"Yeah. The news likes to go on and on about lone-wolf killers and all that, but most people got other people to look out for them. Here we go." He pointed at the page. I drew closer to look, reading sideways. I recognized Grandma's loopy handwriting first. Under the heading of lawyers, she'd written out subcategories. Criminal Defense Attorneys listed three, Marital Matters had two, Estates had four, and they continued onward to the next page. Not all of the area codes were local – and some had changed, old numbers scratched out and new ones added.

"She told me she had lawyers programmed into her phone. Are these the same ones?" I asked.

"Probably. This paper list has been around longer than any smart phone, though."

"So these years in the margins: what do they mean? When she met them?" My eyes skimmed the page. 1981, 1983, 1988, 1988 again, every year of the 1990s, fewer in the 2000s. "No, that can't be it. Most of these lawyers have several years listed."

"Those years are when Lucille worked with them," he said absently. His thick finger tapped a name. "Curtis. Decent guy. Even if he's kicked the bucket by now, his sons joined his firm and they were good sorts, so I'll–"

"Grandma *worked* with them? How?" I loomed over him, giving him my best double-arched eyebrow, channeling Grandma.

Grizz visibly swallowed as he seemed to belatedly realize he'd let something slip. "Your grandma knew lots of people. She… she *networked* before that was some big buzz word."

"Uh huh." I hadn't ceased my glare. "Grizz, I'm twenty-five. I'm not a kid anymore. I don't need to be protected from her antics. She's dead. Maybe. Or frolicking with the mermaids." I'd shared that wistful hope with him before.

"Bird." He looked miserable. "I *can't*."

No, he *wouldn't* tell me the truth about Grandma's old intrigues. There was a distinction between those terms – a big one.

"Okay. I'll have to conclude that Grandma was some kind of super-spy on behalf of the U.S. government and that if you say anything, you'll self-destruct or something. Sure. Whatever. Yeah." I think Grizz knew I was at explosion point when I started using single-word sentences in sequence.

He backed away from the desk. "You won't tell me about Grandma's past – or your own, really. You won't say where you were when Chase died, but I assume it's the same place out in the mountains where you were when Ella May was attacked. Way to be consistent there. Since you won't tell me anything, I hope you can tell your lawyer. They'll need to know everything they can so that they can defend you to their fullest, which you need, because you look suspicious as all get out. Call a relevant lawyer. Now. I'm watching."

Grizz's Adam's apple bobbed as he swallowed. He edged forward to grab his phone from the desk, regarding me with the wariness of a coiled, sunning snake. "Okay, I'm calling." He peered down his nose at the numbers and dialed. "It's ringing." He brought it to his ear.

The voice on the other side was loud enough that we had immediate confirmation that he had reached an office – and he was asked to wait on hold. Horrible elevator music wailed out of the speaker, causing Grizz to cringe and hold it away.

"You can go," he told me. "Attorney-client privilege."

He was kicking me out. Okay, then. "You *will* stay on the line. You *will* get an appointment. If I need to help you set up a video call or something later, I can do that and still give you privacy, got it?"

"Okay." He cleared his throat. "Thanks, Bird. Thanks for looking after me."

"Someone has to," I muttered, and left.

In internet parlance, my departure was a flounce, a dramatic exit for show. My stiff, angry walk, made stiffer by my injuries, was completed with a slam of both the door and the screen. I was relieved to see both law enforcement cars were gone – and then my right leg gave way beneath me as I stepped down. I caught myself on the rail before I splatted on my backside. After a few seconds, I pushed myself upright again and continued downward under my own power.

I blinked back tears as I slid into my car. I hurt. My heart hurt. Even more, I knew Grizz hurt. He wanted to tell me the truth, but Grandma apparently had his tongue knotted by some kind of vow. He'd never break his word to her, never.

I drove slowly without worrying about traffic. Therefore, it was easy for me to pull off the road when I saw the sheriff's car parked on the grass near the broken guard rail. No one was inside the vehicle, but I recognized whose car it was. Merrick had to be down at the crime scene. I knew I probably shouldn't talk to him without a lawyer of my own, but I was all about doing daft things of late.

The trip down the slope reminded me of other poor choices I had recently made. Even so, I kept on going. Merrick had heard my car door slam and had turned to watch my approach.

Chase's car was gone, of course. Deep tire tracks furrowed the earth along the slope, evidence of the tow truck and extraction process, the surrounding grass trampled by feet. A gap in the foliage made clear where trees and bushes had caught the car, jagged broken branches stabbing outward as if to fend off further attacks.

"Finding anything?" I asked, stopping about ten feet from Merrick.

He seemed to consider the wisdom of sharing information with me, and then he shook his head. "I don't expect to. Our team was thorough. Sometimes I like to return to a scene, though, to think things through. As if being where it happened brings me closer to the solution." The man was frustrated, and not by me – at least, not at this moment.

"That makes sense to me. I've gone to the beach where my grandma vanished more than once, as if I could summon up some kind of closure. I'm waiting for a mermaid to toss her back on the shore and say, 'Oops, sorry, we started talking, and before we knew it, months had gone by.'" Merrick snorted. "I should apologize for being snappish with you. Grizz is the only close family I have left. I need to look out for him."

"I know you do, and he has every right to have counsel with him as he's questioned. I'm not intending to bully either of you, Miss Nichols. I want answers. I want to help Mrs Perkins find closure that many other families do not get. My department receives information and we follow up on these leads. That doesn't mean that we believe what we were told, but we must investigate."

"I respect that. I do. But this is personal for me, in many ways." I turned away, ready to go back uphill.

"Now, what happened to you? Why the limp?" Merrick called after me.

I hadn't hidden it as well as I thought I had. "I fell off a cliff," I said, relaxing my posture. No point in making an effort to hide the limp now.

"Ah. I see." Merrick sounded like he didn't know what to believe. Good. I smiled to myself even as I grimaced. I'd told him the truth, zany as it was. My conscience was clear.

Chapter Eighteen

My brain couldn't stop replaying my conversations with Grizz and Detective Merrick as I drove south. I peeled each line of dialogue apart like a college English assignment: How could this sentence be interpreted? What is meant by this gesture? What is the subtext here? By the time I reached Morro Bay, my analyses extended to Jessie, Belinda, Ella May, Rita, and even Mr Singh – no one had anything nice to say about Chase but Ray, but not even Ray was without motive, really. Three hundred thousand bucks was a lot of money.

But where was it? Had George already found that chunk of change? Or was someone else on the hunt for it? Or had these attacks been about something else entirely?

By some small miracle, the urgent care clinic in north Morro Bay was empty and I was promptly with a nurse. He clicked his teeth in disapproval when I said I'd tumbled down a cliff when hiking, and stared at me with a furrowed brow as I tried to make a joke about how my injuries would've been a source of pride if I'd acquired them in the famous Cooper's Hill Cheese Roll in England. I started to explain that the maybe-six-hundred-year-old annual event involved people racing down a steep hill after a wheel of Double Gloucester cheese, and stopped babbling when I recognized the blankness in his eyes. He didn't know what I was talking about and he didn't care.

I provided only basic answers to his questions from then on.

I departed with seven stitches in my leg and left behind two toothpick-sized wood chunks and a pebble that had been embedded in my backside. I can't deny that it creeped me out that I'd been walking around with debris inside my body, but I knew that it could've been a lot worse.

I could be dead.

Frustrated and flummoxed anew, I detoured toward Morro Rock. The morning sky was bright and blue, seagulls screeching and swirling about. Fishing vessels and tour boats were afloat on the bay, with two tankers visible way far out on the Pacific. The drive up to the Rock always impressed me because the rocky face dominated my entire windshield. Fencing and DO NOT CLIMB signs surrounded the base. I rolled down my window as I angled to park overlooking packed docks, the Rock behind me. A nearby van disgorged a family, a tiny, high-pitched voice announcing, "I want to climb it! Mom, Mom, can I climb it? You can post the video on the internet!" Seals barked from somewhere nearby.

Chaotic sea life noises didn't bother me as much as other sounds – though I'd feel differently if I tried to sleep near such a cacophony. I breathed in the salty, fishy air and pulled out my phone to glance at the whodunnit notes I'd made over the past few days. To complete the record, I added lines about the false reports about Grizz being sighted in Chase's car. That made me pause. Those accounts fundamentally didn't make sense. Grizz would have had to hold a gun to Chase's head for that guy to take him anywhere, and as Grizz had noted, he wouldn't obviously leave the body right near his house, even if it did give him an easy walk home.

Someone was lying to Merrick with intent. It could be a personal attack on Grizz – or a tactic to divert suspicion from another person.

A text message popped up with a chime. Dale. "How are you?"

"Vermont," I replied.

"Good." He added a smiley face. "Question remains."

I smiled and typed back. "Visited an urgent care. Brand new owner of seven stitches. With the limp I have today, I'm on my way to mastering a pirate cosplay for parties." I had a big hunch that he knew what cosplay was – costume wearing, for fan conventions and general enjoyment – and was pleased when his reply was, "You need a parrot."

With perfect timing, a seagull landed on my side mirror. I had to rear back in my seat to get a pic. I sent it along with the caption, "Central Coast substitute." His laughing emoji made me grin.

"I look forward to being schooled in cheese," he replied.

I guffawed so loudly that the seagull squawked and fluttered off. I typed back, "I look forward to schooling." I paused, studying our recent messages. Huh. I was pretty sure our exchange counted as flirting. Did that make our lunch meeting a date? I didn't think so. That hadn't been my intent when I invited him, at least. If we kept arranging these kinds of gatherings, however, I'd bluntly ask if he considered it a date. I didn't like things being left ambiguous.

I switched to check my email again. The backlog there remained dreadful. A new message had come in: someone querying about a St. Patrick's Day themed box for a party of ten. "Oh, awesome!" I bounced a little in excitement, then regretted the movement. I'd never done a full March 17th-themed box, and wow, did I love that idea. A plain Irish Cheddar was a must – oh, and I could also get two other cheddar variations that used Irish whiskey and Irish stout. The stout cheeses were especially pretty with dark brown marbling throughout. Ireland had some great blues, too. I'd used one for a corporate order last year, and it blew people away when they found out where it was from.

I really did love schooling people in cheese.

Feeling steadier, I drove back into town. More cars were starting to fill the lot near the volcanic plug. This was bound to be a busy tourist weekend. People from the interior San Joaquin Valley loved traveling to the coast a mere two hours away – I sure had when I was a kid. Back in those innocent days, I'd stay with Grandma while my parents grabbed a hotel room in San Simeon or points south. In hindsight, I understood that those weekends had been kid-free romantic escapes for them. The thought made me feel wistful. I was happy that they had those good times together. I wished they could've had more of them. My parents had truly doted on each other – and set an almost impossible standard for what a marriage could be, really.

I'd never given a marriage of my own much thought or really fixated on romantic relationships at all. I'd had plenty of other things keeping me busy in recent years. But now, well… I'd never hit things off with anyone the way I had with Dale. Maybe something more would come of it. Or maybe we'd just be giggly geeks and enjoy cheese together.

The one certainty that these past few days had proven: life was bound to bring surprises.

I parked outside the trailer park and walked onto the lot, paying special attention to the immaculate condition of the grounds. Ray had done great work. I traversed the first long street. As I looped back, I began to worry that I'd need to visit the office and ask for Ray – and hope that my inquiry didn't get him in trouble.

That's when I saw him working on a small median. Judging by the haphazard stack of plastic pots, he'd just finished planting flowers. He was in the midst of sweeping up remnants of leaves and potting soil when he glanced up and saw me.

"Hey there, Bird." His smile for me was soft and genuine. "How're you?" His gaze flicked down, taking in my stilted walk.

"I've been better, but I won't complain. The flowers look gorgeous."

Ray's smile made his whole face glow. "They really are. I love this early spring-like weather. I have cousins who are shoveling snow, but I get to do *this!*" He gestured to his work with genuine pride. For Ray's sake alone, I was glad Chase was gone. This guy was too good to be dragged down by his criminal distant cousin. "I talked to that detective. Mack, Merrick? Yeah, Merrick. I met him at the office in Los Osos. It went okay."

"He wasn't too harsh on you?" I still felt like I needed to be protective of Ray.

"Nah. I mean, the talk was unpleasant, but he didn't do the mean routine like you see on TV shows, you know?"

"I heard Belinda was working on funeral plans," I asked softly. "Is anything set yet?"

Ray's face crumpled, tears filling his eyes. "Almost. Wednesday's what I last heard. It's still weird, right? I'm getting texts from people, and I keep expecting one from him, but I guess it's good I haven't, huh? Though Chase would find it cool to be a zombie. Eating brains and everything." His laugh sounded forced as he set down the broom and began to gather his other tools.

If only Chase had had more brains when he was alive! "I wanted to ask you, Ray: have you seen George around?"

Ray stilled. "Nah. I don't even know if he knows where I live. God, I hope not. I tried not to be around when he was, but even then, I played invisible as much as I could."

"Can you tell me what George looks like?"

"Um, white guy. Tall. Like, super-tall. He probably gets asked a lot if he plays basketball. Sometimes he has a mustache."

The figure I saw from the trail at Slocombe House had looked to be of average height. With the distance and the shade, I hadn't been able to make out their skin tone, much less the presence of facial hair. "Do you remember if–"

Ray was leaning over his broomstick to grab a trowel when he lost his balance. He fell forward, right over the three grimy trowel prongs. A screech escaped his throat as he fell flat.

"Ray! Ray! Did it impale you?" I reached toward him, terrified, envisioning the blood, gore, and bacteria.

"Oh, God," he whimpered, lifting up his arm. The trowel stayed on the ground, thank goodness, but he had a long bloody scrape along the tender flesh of his bare forearm.

"How bad is it?" I asked.

"I wasn't stabbed." He examined his arm, the broomstick rattling as his other hand bumped it. "One of the prongs scraped me bad, though. Man, does that sting."

"You need to wash that out right away. Where's the best place to go?"

Ray stared at his arm a few seconds before answering. "Um, not the office; she'd freak out and think I was going to sue or something. My house. My mom's there." His voice rattled with checked tears.

"Okay." I quickly gathered his other tools together into the median, trowel included, but took extra care because I knew my own balance was considerably off. I wondered if I should ask him if he was up to date on his tetanus shots, but I didn't need to freak him out more. "Do you want me to bring your things?"

"No, no, they'll be fine there for a bit. Wow, this hurts." Blood formed a long line down his arm.

"Lead the way," I said. "Let me know how I can help."

I ended up using his key to unlock a door at the top of a steep access ramp that took up half of the narrow driveway beside the trailer. I was glad to avoid more stairs, but the ramp wasn't much easier to climb.

"Mom, hey Mom!" Ray called as he entered the mostly dark trailer. We passed through a galley-style kitchen. A microwave and a dish-drying rack took up almost the entire counter. "I have someone here with me, helping out. You dressed?"

"Yes. Who's here? Why do you need help?" called a raspy voice. We rounded the corner into a living room. A heavyset woman in a purple top sat in a recliner, a walker with a storage pouch in front of her. She was using the walker's lid as a table to hold a plate with a frosted toaster pastry on it. By the smell, it was strawberry-flavored. She took in Ray's injury, her eyes widening. "Oh, dear. What caused that?"

"A dirty garden tool. I know, I know, I gotta wash my arm right away."

"I told you that you should've worn a jacket today." She wrung her hands together. "That mighta protected you a little bit more. Who's this?"

Ray gestured to me with his head. "This is Bird. She's a friend." I appreciated that he readily described me that way. I considered him a friend now, too. We could ignore the whole awkward reality of his past trespasses on my property.

His mom's face puckered in worry. "You need the bandages from under the sink, and that antibacterial stuff – here, I should get up." She made to move, gripping the handles of her walker. That single motion told me that the effort to stand would be a major exertion.

Ray waved her down. "Mom, no. Bird can help me get supplies out."

His mom looked even more worried. "But it's not clean in there!"

"Please, don't worry about that." I tried to comfort her with a smile. Ray motioned me to follow him.

The bathroom was cramped. A full shoe box of prescription pills took up most of the counter space. I had to nudge a few things over to make room for the medical supplies from under the sink. Once everything was out, Ray said he could handle things from there. I went to join his mother. She looked impossibly more worried.

"Did you find everything? Was it–"

"He has what he needs. And please, don't worry about how it looks. My bathroom gets like that, too. My kitchen is the only space I manage to keep consistently clean." Only as I said that did I realize their kitchen was in rough shape, too. Oops. Fortunately, she wasn't as attentive as me, and didn't take my errant comment as a slight. She visibly relaxed in her chair.

"Does his cut look deep?" she asked.

"I don't think so. More of a scrape." I self-consciously moved my own injured leg, trying not to cringe. "Um, what's your name? I don't want to call you 'Ray's mom.'"

She laughed at that, leaning back. The recliner squawked. "Oh, I've been addressed by that name plenty of times, it's just been a while. You can call me Mrs Green." Her voice lowered. "Now tell me, how do you know my son? Please don't take this wrong, but you don't seem like his usual circle, because the usual circle is…" She grimaced.

"Chase?" I added, to which she nodded, relief in her eyes. Time for me to be honest yet tactful. "That's how I know him, actually. Chase was… well, using a back portion of my rural property for his party zone. Ray left something there by accident, and I tracked him down to return it. He's a nice guy." I tried to make clear there was no ill will.

"The opposite of Chase. That punk," she hissed. Her tan skin flushed. "God help me, but I'm glad he's gone, and I know Belinda feels the same." I nodded but felt weird doing so. Here was someone else with motive – but not the physical capability. "My boy, he's a gentle soul. He never really had friends other than Chase, and Chase wasn't a friend, truly. Ray was more like his sidekick. His minion. You don't know how many times I was afraid I'd get a call that Chase robbed a bank and Ray carried the loot for him."

I had a feeling she'd had these emotions bottled up for ages and hadn't gotten to vent them in person to anyone.

"I've talked to a lot of people around Foghorn the past few days," I said. "You're not the only one who disliked Chase. Ray is among the few who mourn him."

Sadness curved her eyebrows. "That's the truth of it. The tragedy. It breaks my heart that my boy's heart is hurting right now, but at the same time, I say, 'Thank God!'" She gestured gratitude to the heavens. The white ceiling squares had brown rippled stains from dried water leaks.

I felt self-conscious for her sake and looked away. Little porcelain birds decorated several tables around the room, squeezed in between piles of papers and magazines. An older model thick television sat on an entertainment center, plastic video game cases forming a skyscraper cityscape beneath it. I recognized the glow of a black game system in idle mode, the slim box almost invisible in a niche below the TV. I couldn't contain my curiosity.

"Can I take a look at Ray's games?" I asked. "I'm a gamer too."

"Sure, by all means," Mrs Green said. "I don't care if you want to play something. It's fun to watch."

"I won't have time for that," I said. I slowly, carefully, lowered myself to sit on the floor. I skimmed through the stack, smiling. He had some racing games, both serious and whimsical. A dancing game. A couple of re-released side-scroller classics. A few space shoot-em-up games. A nice variety overall.

"Hey." Ray came in.

"How does your arm look? How are you feeling?" Mrs Green edged out on her seat, clearly tempted to grapple him for a thorough inspection.

"I'm okay, Mom." Exasperation seeped into his voice. "It's a long scratch, that's all. Stung something awful when I washed it off, but it wasn't even bleeding bad at that point." He turned toward me. "Found my games, huh?"

"I had to look," I confessed. "Are these yours or Chase's, or a mix?"

"Those are all mine. Chase's collection is pure vintage."

I perked up with interest, even as Mrs Green guffawed. "'Vintage.' Everything before the year 2000 is considered 'vintage' these days! Just makes me feel so old."

Cheese had totally different standards for what was classified as vintage, but I resisted the urge to burst out with dairy facts. Instead, I stayed on topic with my other obsession. "My gaming interests are more 'vintage' too. 1980s and 1990s." I laughed at Mrs Green's groan. "I'm all about 8-bit and 16-bit systems. I don't play much myself these days, but I follow streamers who do replays. I listen to that as I work instead of the radio."

"'Streamers,'" Mrs Green mused. "I feel like I need a dictionary to understand what's being said now, but then my own parents went through the same thing when I was young."

I shrugged. "Not like I can keep up with everything, either. It's impossible."

"Would you like to see Chase's games?" Ray asked with a hopeful note. When I nodded, he scampered off.

"That boy." Mrs Green sighed. "He's sweet on you, and you don't even see it, do you?"

I blinked, taken aback. "What?"

"Yep. I thought so." Her smile was sad. "If you keep coming around, he'll attach to you like he did to Chase. A little lonesome puppy dog, that's my boy."

Well, this went extra-awkward really fast. "I don't know quite how to handle that. I'm not trying to– I don't want to–"

"Child, you're fine. You've already been nicer to Raymond than you had to be."

"He already has a hurt heart. I don't want to add to that."

"Sometimes, that pain is necessary," she said with

weary bluntness. "Let me guess, you're already in a relationship?"

Wow, the increasing awkwardness of this moment was sucking me down like quicksand. "Not really, no? Life has been pretty busy. Relationships are… a lot." Even as I said that, Dale's face flashed in my mind. If we could simply be cheese-loving geeky friends, I'd be happy with that. If we could be more than that, based on a foundation of aged Cheddar and delicious crusty bread… that might not be such a bad thing, either.

"They are," she said wistfully. "Oh, my poor boy."

"Ray needs to find another person, a good someone, to help him along." I didn't want to be Ray's fixation, but I didn't want to leave him bereft, either. Ugh, why did people have to be so complicated? From the far side of the trailer, I heard the distinct click-clunk of a folding closet door.

Mrs Green smiled. "You seem to be a good person yourself. I don't know what you do, of course. Clever as you are, you may be up to worse than Chase."

I felt like I needed a witty rejoinder, but lacking inspiration, I stuck with the truth. "I run a cheese board business."

"Do you, now? That sounds… dangerously delicious. I love good cheese. My grandmother used to make it at home, using old pillowcases. It's how she learned to do it as a girl during the Great Depression."

"Mom, are you telling her about the pillowcase cheese?" Ray returned carrying a cardboard box. "That's gross."

"The pillowcases were perfectly clean. She knew what she was doing!"

These two had such a wonderful relationship – quite a contrast to Chase and Belinda.

"Anyway. Sorry that took so long. He told me to hide it,

so I had it buried under a bunch of stuff. Can we clear the table?" Ray asked.

At Mrs Green's nod of permission, I moved several stacks of magazines and newspapers to the floor, then shuffled the fragile bird figurines to the far edge. Ray set the box down and pressed back the open cardboard flaps. I leaned forward. Half the box had video game systems in a careful stack, while the other had loose cartridges on top with visible boxes in neat rows below. Chase had taken more care with his game collection than he had his clothes.

I picked up several cartridges. "Are they all 16-bit games?" I tilted some items so I could look further into the box. "Are those game boxes complete? Oh my gosh, you've got to be kidding me – is that one *shrink-wrapped?*"

"Ray's told me that this stuff is worth a lot. I can't believe it," said Mrs Green.

"Mom, you still have a box of those bean-bag animals from the late 1990s that were supposed to be worth tons of money. Don't you even start," said Ray.

"At least they are cute," Mrs Green muttered.

I picked up a Super Nintendo system. The plastic casing was in great condition. Two controllers were unplugged and tidily wrapped up with their own cords. Below that was a Nintendo. I frowned. "He has an old Nintendo? Everything else here is 16-bit." It was also worth very little compared to everything else I'd seen. They had been heavily mass marketed. A shame he didn't have the original Japanese system by Nintendo, a Famicom – that would be something special to find here in America.

"Yeah, he's had that a few months, I think. It used to sit by his bed."

I picked up the Nintendo. "Wait, what?" I hefted it up and down.

"What? What is it?" Ray asked.

"This thing is way too heavy. Nintendos only have a few computer cards inside. Otherwise, they're mostly empty space. My dad used to refurbish dead systems and replace the old game batteries for fun," I added, seeing Ray's baffled expression. "There's a big online hobbyist community around that kind of thing. Do you have a long Phillips screwdriver?"

Ray squinted at the Nintendo. "Sure. Gimme a sec." He scampered off.

"What do you think is in there?" Mrs Green whispered.

"Something someone's looking for," was all I had time to say as Ray rushed back. He held several screwdrivers in his fist. I picked the one that looked right then flipped over the gray rectangular box. My heart raced, but my hands stayed steady as I worked loose the sequence of screws and set them aside. I lifted the hatch. The three of us leaned over the Nintendo and gasped.

Thick wads of cash, bound with rubber bands, filled the entire interior.

"Dear God!" cried Mrs Green. "How much money is that?"

Ray and I shared a look of grim horror. "I'm guessing it's $300,000 or a significant portion of that," I said, feeling excited and vaguely ill.

Chapter Nineteen

When I was a kid, I always wanted to find hidden treasure. I actually made some treasure maps one time, marking spots around the neighborhood where I knew, just knew, I would find good stuff, as if my act of creation meant treasure troves would spontaneously appear.

I never had the chance to test the accuracy of my treasure-finding powers. My mom caught me headed down the street with a shovel and a fistful of computer paper, and my treasure-hunting ways came to an abrupt end.

Now I held a legit trove featuring a ludicrous amount of cash, and I felt like I was about to vomit.

"I've never seen that much cash in all my life." Ray's whisper was hoarse. "Mom, think of what we could do with this! We could get out of here, buy a house!"

"Oh, child of mine," Mrs Green said, likewise hoarse but not the slightest bit dreamy. "This money wouldn't even buy a closet in California these days."

I angled the box toward the lamp light. "There's something at the bottom." The idea of touching money dirtied by misdeeds and murder repulsed me, but after a second of hesitation, I tipped the money onto the floor. The top of the Nintendo – the bottom, with the base open – held a different sort of wad, numerous triple-folded sheets of paper. Rough photocopies, I could tell at a glance.

"What are they?" Ray asked, his gaze still on the money.

"Medical receipts." I flipped through the papers. "Assessments of visits. These go back a few months." I looked at Mrs Green. "What's known in the family about Belinda's health?"

Surprised, her jaw flapped for a few seconds before she managed words. "Well, I... not much. We've all seen how she's lost weight, but we also know she's been working two jobs, largely because of Chase. She needs the money and could barely tolerate being home between him and his cat. Why? Those forms–"

"She's dying. Well, I shouldn't say that. The prognosis is poor." I waved the papers. "Late-diagnosed breast cancer, spread throughout the body."

Ray was wide-eyed. "Chase never said anything about that to me."

"Oh, no." Mrs Green began to cry. "Does it say– Does it say how long she has?"

"There's nothing like that here." I trailed my finger down a page. "None of these were mailed to their house in Foghorn. Belinda has a post office box in Morro Bay. Huh. Of course she did. Chase stole things from the house and pawned them. He couldn't have been trusted with the mail, either."

"That's the truth of it," said Mrs Green. "A private mailbox would have been necessary for her to intercept checks."

"But Chase found out somehow. Or found these papers in the house and made copies. Look here." I went back to the first sheet. "There's a column of handwritten numbers. Is this Chase's writing?" I held it out to Ray.

He squinted at it. "Yeah, for sure. His eights were always crooked like that."

"You said Chase said he had the right amount of money and didn't need to risk gambling it away now." I held up the papers. "He tabulated numbers here – and there's another column that's crossed out, too. Maybe that's money he previously won and gambled away?"

"Yeah, yeah. That would've been a few weeks ago. Oh, man." Ray swayed back, rattled.

"You think," Mrs Green whispered, "Chase stole this cash to pay his mother's medical bills?"

"Yes." I took a deep breath. "Chase might have been murdered over this money. A woman in Foghorn was also beaten two days ago. I think she might've been mistaken for Belinda." I really hoped that deputies were keeping an eye on her.

"You're saying this money puts us in a lot of danger." Mrs Green looked drawn and pale.

"But Mom, no one knows we even have this loot. No one has any idea!" Ray said, a note of desperation in his voice. "It might not be enough for a house, but we could do *something* with it."

"Ray, no one knows you have it – yet. Think about it. George wants this back," I said. "He's going to cast a wider and wider net. You've met him. He knows you hang around Chase. You're not going to be hard to find. I mean, I found you."

"Ray," Mrs Green said. "Who is this George?"

He shrugged off her question as he avoided her gaze. "But this… Is there any way we could…?" He sounded on the brink of tears.

"Ray," I said softly. "Call Detective Merrick right now.

Seriously. You're in danger. George has no qualms about attacking women."

The threat to his mom made the danger finally sink in. He nodded, pulling his phone from his back pocket. "Put it on speaker," Mrs Green said, to which he nodded again. She would make sure he did the right thing, just as I had with Grizz.

I left the game system on the floor beside the money as I stood. "I'm sorry that this had to be found here. Your house is going to be invaded by investigators."

Mrs Green sighed. "The place is already a mess. Maybe they can leave things a bit tidier as they go. Even if they don't, well. At least we're not scrubbing out blood."

I appreciated her realism. "I can try to check with you next week. Maybe help out some." My own house was a wreck, but whatever. I could take my time with my things. If her house was a mess, her limited mobility would make her life a hundred times harder.

"Thank you," she mouthed. Ray had dialed Merrick's number and it was ringing.

"Hey," Ray said to me hurriedly. "Will you get in trouble if I say you were here? Because I don't want that."

I moved toward the door. "Tell him the truth. My fingerprints are all over everything." Mental note: I needed to start carrying disposable gloves in my purse. "I'm not going to stay, though. Merrick knows where to find me."

As I let myself out, I heard the ringing stop. Detective Merrick's voice came on the line. "Hello?"

"Hi, detective. This is, uh, Ray Green. I found something. We found something. And, uh, we need you here right away. Please."

I closed the door softly behind me.

* * *

I'd gone to Ray for more information on George. I'd sure found out more than I bargained for. The whole drive back to Foghorn, I wondered if Detective Merrick was about to call me up and rail on me for interfering in a major way. He probably wouldn't even bother with a, "Thank you, Bird, for finding this load of cash. We should have searched Ray's place or asked him if he had anything from Chase. You did our job for us!"

Even if deputies *had* seen the game systems, would they have known what they were looking at? What a game system should weigh? Maybe, maybe not. Surely there were geeks among their crew, but Merrick hadn't shown evidence of those kinds of interests.

Grizz's truck was gone from his drive. I hoped that meant that he'd gone to talk to his lawyer.

I parked at my house and went inside. I had about thirty minutes until Dale arrived. That meant this was the ideal time to bring out my cheese and let it come to room temperature.

Only when I had the cheese on the counter did I realize I had two issues: First of all, I usually kept some of my small to-go boxes and dividers in my personal kitchen for my own use, but because of the move, everything was out in the Kitchen. Secondly, I had a big ginger cat rubbing my legs and purring. I couldn't even leave the cheese on the counter while I went to get a box. Bowser had already proven he could jump like a spear-fighting knight from some of my favorite old video games. I didn't need him to sample our lunch.

I debated unpacking my cheese dome collection, but in

dismay understood they wouldn't be safe from Bowser, either. With his size and strength, if he wanted whatever was underneath a glass cloche, he could shove it over.

What to do, what to do. I was more flummoxed by my cheese and cat safety issue than I'd been by the discovery of Chase's money hoard. After literally spinning in circles a few times, I stuck the cheese in the microwave. It just needed to be there for a few minutes while I dashed out to the Kitchen. If Bowser could figure out how to open the microwave door... Well, then I'd have a bigger safety issue to contend with.

I went out the back, locking the door behind me. The door to the Kitchen lay ten feet ahead along the covered brick walkway. I suddenly heard heavy panting behind me. Panic flared, my experience on the cliff flashing in my memory. I whirled around to find a strange man lunging at me, arms extended. I yelled and ducked, lurching to one side. The guy was unusually tall, near seven feet, and because of that, his reach was incredible. His fingertips scraped across my skin as I stumbled away, still free.

The house was closest. I had to make it inside. My keys still in my hand, I scrambled for the door. The man came at me again. By some miracle, I landed a kick to his thigh that propelled him away.

I grabbed the doorknob and fumbled for the right key.

"I don't think so." He gripped my left forearm with fingers so spider-like gangly they almost touched at the tips. My first thought was to pull back again, but that's when I remembered Grandma's advice: surprise your opponent, go directions they don't expect.

I flung myself into the flat of his chest. He grunted at the impact, bowling over, but he kept his grip on me as we smacked the ground, dried leaves crackling beneath us.

"Who are you? What do you want?" I yelled, but even as I asked, I knew.

This was George.

"Stop fighting, damn it." He had a deep rumbly baritone. "Be a good girl and come with me."

Be a good girl. Oh, I knew all about this kind of guy. If I hadn't already known him for a jerk, I'd know for sure now. Even though he still had my arm, I tried to regain my feet.

George gripped me by my shirt and yanked me close. His flailing leg struck the long cut on the outside of my calf. Pain dappled my eyesight in black as a scream tore from my throat. I couldn't move. He had me.

He hauled me upright, maintaining a strong grip on my left wrist. My thoughts raced to how I could escape. I'd dropped my keys somewhere. I realized that I didn't feel the weight of my phone in my back pocket anymore, either. I slyly gazed around, trying to conceal my search. There! I could just make out the custom cheese-print backside of my phone case partially buried amid the leaves. There was no active landline in the house. I'd need to get back here, get my keys and phone, and get inside.

"Now," he said, drawing back far enough for me to see the gun that he held. Oh. That changed things in a very bad way. "I been wanting to talk to you about Chase."

"What about Chase?" I asked. "I only met him once. Hey!" George yanked me by the left arm and dragged me across the yard, toward the back-forty.

"He's been coming here for weeks," he snarled, still panting heavily. He had run to attack me; where had he been? He hadn't parked by my house.

"He had, and my neighbor kept running him off for me. I only moved in a few days ago. This was my grandma's house." George's grip would have hurt even without my existing bruises and cuts. We'd made it to the partially paved road that led back to Chase's old party zone among the trees.

"You're in cahoots with him," George said with slow patience. "Tell me where my money is."

My immediate honest urge to say "in the custody of the sheriff's office" was significantly tempered by the presence of the gun.

"I don't know what you're talking about." My lie sounded blatant even to me, but maybe my shrill tone would throw him off. If his vigilance decreased for a moment, I could attempt to call for help through my watch. I was amazed he hadn't taken it away from me. His lapse gave me an advantage. "Why are you taking me back here?"

"He liked this place."

I blinked at his lack of logic. If I really had been in "cahoots" with Chase, the house or Kitchen would be a much better place to stash a wad of cash that could be destroyed by a bad storm if it was hidden outside. I wasn't about to suggest that he begin tearing apart my house, though.

That's when I remembered what Jessie told me.

"You often hide things outside, huh?" I asked.

His cold gaze flicked to me, his strides relentless. I thought it had hurt when I walked earlier, but wow, it hurt a lot more now. Heat bloomed against my bandages along the deep cut down my calf. Our tussle must have torn my brand-new stitches.

"Chase said he was going to hide it in his favorite place." George smiled, clearly pleased that he'd solved the riddle. "So that's where we're going to look."

I was again amazed by Chase's tendency to blab about so-called secrets to everyone who would listen. What George didn't realize was that Chase's favorite place had been in his vintage game collection.

We walked over a slight rise. A newer SUV was parked at the edge of the trees. I wouldn't have been able to see it from the house unless I'd been on the roof. "Stand there," he said, pointing with his gun. I wish I knew more about guns to identify what kind it was and how many bullets it might have. My fear of their noise and feel had made me ignorant to an extreme.

I did as George ordered. He opened the door behind the driver's seat. I heard a muffled noise, and as George moved aside, I recognized Belinda on the black carpet floor, bound and gagged. Her head angled up, her terrified eyes meeting mine.

"You kidnapped Chase's mom?" I said, horrified. Had a deputy been guarding her? Had they been disabled or killed?

"I planned to make her do the work for me, but she's useless, weak and crying. But you – you're thick and strong, the way a woman should be. I saw you going in your house and yeah, I knew you needed to do this."

"Do what, exactly?" I said, bristling.

"Dig." His smile was lazy, his teeth an even pristine white that denoted dentures or pricey dental work. "Shovel's already leaning against that tree over there. You dig up any and every soft spot in the dirt to find where Chase hid my money, and you give it to me. Easy, eh?"

I stared at him. "You do know that police fully searched this area, right? With dogs and all? They bagged some cigarette butts, aluminum cans, things like that. No major finds."

"Cops." George sneered. "They can't find nothing." My literal mind wanted to correct his grammar, but I kept my mouth shut. "You're going to find what they couldn't."

"What if I can't?" I asked, sincerely doubting that Chase had buried another stash here, though it could be possible. Not like I'd counted the wad of money at Ray's house.

"First of all." George pointed the gun at Belinda. A muffled cry escaped her gag as she bent her head into the base of the car seat. "If you don't dig, I shoot her, and I shoot where it'll hurt. Not to kill her or nothin'. Not yet. You need to stay motivated to keep working real good, right?" He smiled.

"Second?" I asked. I had to.

"We'll talk about that later. But come closer right now. You have one of them smart watches on, don't you? Here, I gotta take that." With that gun aimed at me, I had to obey, even as I shook in fear. Proximity only invited a different kind of assault, but thankfully, that didn't seem to be on his mind. His long, gangly fingers slipped beneath the watch band and popped it off. He tossed it onto the backseat above Belinda. So much for trying to dial 9-1-1 through my watch. I staggered away from him.

"Uh uh uh," he said. "You don't go too far. I still got this." He held up the gun.

He used Belinda's jacket hood to drag her out of the car. She had zip-ties around her wrists at her back. I knew how to escape zip-ties! Grandma taught me with the help of YouTube. The ties needed to be tight in order to break free. I could tell Belinda how to do it.

Part of her blue jacket sleeve had been ripped off to form her gag. George motioned me deeper into the grove. After lurching to stand, Belinda then staggered along with us as if she was drunk. He shoved her down where Chase had once had a fire pit, rocks still forming a semicircle, the center black with ash. She trembled as if she was freezing, though the temperature was mild even for a Central California January.

"Shovel's right there," George said to me. "Stop gawking. Get to it."

George stayed back about fifteen feet – far enough that I couldn't smack him, close enough that he could shoot me with some degree of accuracy. I stuck the shovel blade anywhere that didn't look too rooted or rocky. I formed a one-foot-deep hole, then another. George hummed as he watched. My breaths came fast, sweat beading my skin. Where was Belinda's phone? That might be in his SUV, too.

"Why don't you try over here?" George said, pointing between two oaks.

"It's covered with thick leaves. The ground there doesn't look touched."

"Well, check there. Check everywhere! I need that money *now*." The desperation in his voice chilled me.

I'd bet that the money hadn't been his to lose. He was one link in a chain – a chain that his lackey Chase had broken in Oakland.

I started a new hole, my movement slower. "If it was here, the sheriff's department would have found it. They searched for hours and they–"

"Secondly," George said. As terrified as I was about what he'd say, I was relieved that he was counting onward at last. "You're going to die today. Both of you. But if you find my money, that determines how you die, right? You find the cash, I make sure you're killed nice and quick. Merciful. Head shot. Boom. If you don't, well. I make it slow and painful. I got a lot of bullets, and we're way out here in the middle of nowhere."

Belinda sobbed again. She sat up, slumped. The light through the bare branches revealed her face was red and bruised. She'd been beaten, much as Ella May had been.

"Nobody's going to find your bodies, either," George continued with practiced zeal. He'd made this speech before. "I know how to get things done. I'll weigh you down, sink you in the ocean. Fish'll eat you, become bigger and tastier." He laughed at his imagery.

"You didn't kill Chase," I said. "You would have made him hand over the money. There wouldn't be any guessing game. You wouldn't have left him in his car, either."

George's lip curled back in a sneer as he paced. Twigs and acorns crunched underfoot. "That's right. None of this mess would've happened if I'd done it. Kid had it coming, though. Someone did good, but they offed him too soon."

"You did beat up Ella May, though," I said, and at his blank look I continued, "The woman at the salon who was attacked while she took out the trash."

"Oh, yeah. Her." He motioned toward Belinda. The sleeve in her mouth muffled her agonized wail. "These women, looking too much alike. Like sisters or clones or something. She didn't know nothing, though; that became clear real fast. This gal." He gazed thoughtfully at Belinda. "I dunno. You didn't know much about what that boy of yours was up to, did you? He had all kinds of secrets, huh?" George laughed.

That's when the bullet sliced through his skull with a spray of blood. His eyes widened as if with belated surprise, and he tumbled forward onto his face.

He'd been shot? He'd been shot! The blood– The matter– The smell! My stomach boiled in horror.

I didn't yell like Belinda did, but I did clench my shovel

and drop low, not sure what was happening or if a bullet was coming for me next. Leaves crunched and then a figure in jeans and a sparkly kitten sweatshirt emerged: Jessie. She held a gun. Her gaze went from George to me to Belinda. Her eyes filled with tears as she rushed into the grove.

"Oh, Belinda! Did he hurt you badly? Are you okay?" Jessie dropped to her knees, setting the gun to one side as she yanked out Belinda's gag.

"Oh, Jessie. Jessie." Belinda collapsed forward against the younger woman, shoulders heaving.

"Belinda, here. Wait. Let me get you free first." She extracted herself to pull Belinda's arms out behind her. Jessie used a long-handled hunting knife to snap through the ties.

Belinda wrapped her arms around Jessie to cry more, bloody rings visible around her wrists. Under other circumstances, the scene might be quite touching, but Jessie's arrival hadn't relieved me. Not one bit. Shovel still in hand, I eased myself up and began to back away, but Jessie wasn't as distracted as I'd hoped she'd be.

"Stop right there, Bird," she said, rising with the gun aimed toward me.

Chapter Twenty

Tears streamed down Jessie's cheeks. "You couldn't leave things alone, could you? Asking more questions than those cops, getting into everything, trying to find George." Her laugh verged on hysterical. "I guess he found you first, huh? Belinda, tell me... Belinda, how badly did he hurt you?" She glanced down.

Belinda rubbed her bloodied wrists. "He beat me. He threw me around once he had me tied. He didn't hurt me as badly as he did Ella May, though. He, he, admitted... he thought she was *me*." Her thin shoulders shuddered as she sobbed, her jacket still crookedly bunched from George's manhandling. "I should've accepted the detective's offer for a deputy to watch me, but I just couldn't, I didn't–"

"I found you. You're okay," Jessie soothed. They truly were like daughter and mother.

"Belinda's phone. Your phone. You can track each other," I said. My parents and I used to do that, too. We would joke that we were 'lovingly stalking each other.' "George probably left her phone in his car. You knew right where to find her when she went missing." Judging by the development of Belinda's bruises, he must have nabbed her an hour or two ago.

"That's right," Jessie said. "You're still nosy, even now. God, why can't you learn?"

"My skull is so thick, it didn't even break after you shoved me over a cliff." I shrugged.

"See, you even figured *that* out." Jessie rolled her eyes. She'd stopped crying.

"You told me to go there, and I trusted you enough that I mentioned when I'd make the hike. You hid and waited for me. George really has used it as a hiding stash in the past, though; you weren't lying about that." She'd actually told me the truth throughout our conversation.

Now that her guilt in that incident had been confirmed, the bigger picture was clearer as well.

"Jess?" Belinda's voice trembled. "What are you both talking about?" Between us, George lay limp. His soulless eyes stared at me. Crimson traced a line around his jaw and pooled beneath his neck. I shuddered again in revulsion.

"Belinda doesn't know that you attempted to kill me yesterday?" I asked. "Does she even know you killed Chase?"

I'd hoped that the big reveal would create a schism between them. Instead, Belinda only sighed, her frail form deflating impossibly more. "I know about Chase. She told me, right after. She had to. She was shaken up, hurting. He'd tried to kill her."

"You were the one in the car with him that day after you left work," I said to Jessie, who nodded.

"He needed help getting his stuff off your property. He came to me, and I just wanted to get him to shut up and go away, so I said I'd go with him. Then he started bragging that he was going to make things right with his mom, and I laughed at him. I couldn't stop." Wow. True to form, Chase had tried to boast about the money he'd stolen from George, but Jessie hadn't believed him. "That guy, he didn't know what 'right' was. I told him that, and he got mad. He tried to choke me." She touched the black scarf at her neck. No wonder she'd worn pretty scarves the past few days. I'd even complimented her on one. "I opened the door, and as I jumped out, he went off the curve." That's why she'd been limping the next day. She'd hit the asphalt hard, maybe rolled part way down the slope. "God, when I heard his car crunch, I hoped he was dead. I was *sure* he was dead."

"He wasn't," I said.

"No. Chase was like a cockroach. He wouldn't die!" Her gun arm trembled. "He was a wannabe crook, a punk. He'd wrecked Belinda's finances, her life, and now with his injuries, he'd hurt her even more. And me. He'd come after me, too. Hurt me, kill me, sue me. Maybe if I'd held back and hadn't cut his throat, George would have gotten him, but that's all hindsight. Chase had said George was a violent, horrible man, but I didn't understand how bad he was." Her voice hardened as she stared at his body.

"George was going to kill both of us and dump us in the ocean," Belinda murmured.

"Yeah, well, that's still going to happen to Bird. And George." Jessie's smile was grim.

"Jessie, don't." Belinda's soft, firm tone surprised me. "Bird has been a comfort these past few days. She only asked questions everywhere because she wanted to save Grizz."

"We *need* the detective to focus on Grizz, not us," snapped Jessie.

"That's why you both reported to Merrick yesterday that you'd witnessed Grizz in the car with Chase," I said.

Jessie shrugged. "I like Grizz. I've known him forever. But yeah, I'll throw him under the bus to keep us free. Toss the shovel over there, Bird. Right now." She pointed the gun at me again and used the barrel to gesture to one side.

I did as she asked, the shovel crunching on leaves as it landed behind a bush. Even though I'd suspected that Jessie had attacked me the previous day, I felt a new sting of betrayal. "You gave me a free sandwich. You love cheese. But now you're ready to kill me."

I needed to keep her talking. The longer this dragged out, the more likely that Belinda could plead for my life – and that Dale would arrive. The time had to be about noon. Dale would knock on my door. He'd text me. He'd get no answer. If he went around to the Kitchen, maybe he'd find my keys and phone on the ground. Where had Jessie parked? She couldn't be that close to the grove, as we hadn't heard a motor or car door. If she'd parked even a short distance up the dirt drive, Dale would see her car from the house. He'd recognize it.

But he would also come here, unaware of what his employee had done. He didn't need to be a third body in the ocean. Fourth, if I counted Grandma from months ago.

"You think I *want* to kill you? I mean, him," Jessie motioned to George, "he was scum. He's everything Chase wanted to be. But you, Bird, you got a good thing going. It's adorable, the way you connected with Dale. I hate that this will hurt him." Grief flashed over her face.

"Then don't do anything to Bird!" said Belinda. "You already tried to… what, push her off a cliff? Wasn't that enough?"

"She quite successfully shoved me off a cliff," I added.

"Belinda." Jessie's tone was soft, kind. "She's not going to keep her mouth shut, not about Chase, not about George, not about what I've done. We've known her all of three days, but her character is pretty clear."

"She *is* a lot like her grandmother," Belinda murmured, conceding the point in a way I found awfully disturbing.

"Did Chase brag to you that he stole money from George?"
I wanted that clarified.

"Yeah." Grief shadowed her eyes. "When Ella May was
attacked, that's when I knew he had been telling the truth
for once."

"Did he tell you what he planned to do with the money?"
I asked.

"No," said Jessie. "He kept playing up the whole secrecy
around that, trying to make himself into some big hero."
She absent-mindedly touched her throat. I wondered how
many times Chase had attacked her over the years, and yet
she had stayed close to him to support his mother.

I looked Belinda in the eye. "He knew about your cancer
and how pervasive it is."

Her jaw fell slack. "No, he couldn't– I didn't–"

"He knew about your PO Box. He had photocopies of
some of your medical receipts."

Belinda became pale, as if devoid of blood. If she hadn't
been sitting on the ground, she probably would have
collapsed as she had when she heard about Ella May. "How
did he – Oh, no. What was it? What was he going to do?"

"He had that paperwork hidden along with George's cash.
Judging by the numbers he'd crunched, my guess is that he
intended to cover a lot of your medical expenses."

"No!" The denial exploded from Jessie. "Chase didn't
care. He wouldn't care. He put her through hell. She's lost
almost everything, worked herself to the bone for him, and
he couldn't even say 'thank you' for the simplest things."

I shook my head. "He's a contradiction, I know. So are
you."

"Chase... wanted to help me? I can't... no. He never
could." Belinda shook her head.

Jessie dropped to a knee, lowering the gun as she faced Belinda. "No, he couldn't. He might have told himself that for a few days, but you know that within the week, someone would've offered him a sweet, sure deal, and the money would've been gone."

Belinda stared outward, dreamy. "He gambled with such... seriousness this past month, treating it as if he had a job. He even set up this place here." She gestured around us. "He had gambled for ages, sure, but never... never with that kind of gravity." Sobs choked her, and she seemed to melt into the ground, her back heaving.

Jessie shot me a look of sheer loathing. "Belinda, get up. Can you walk? Come on." Jessie helped Belinda to stand upright. "I want you to go to my car and wait there. It's just a bit past George's SUV. Can you do that? Wait there for me?"

Belinda was mentally and physically done. She gave me a look that could only be considered a regretful farewell. "I think so. I need your keys–"

"It's unlocked. Wait there. We'll talk in a bit." We both watched Belinda teeter away. Only when she was out of sight did Jessie speak up. "She doesn't have much time left. She didn't need to spend it worrying about Chase – or you, either." My brow furrowed. Was she jealous that Belinda had befriended me? "You've gotten yourself into deep trouble, Bird. God knows, your grandma used to be like that, too, but I idolized her for it. I feel like... I'm following in her footsteps right now. Being a tough woman against a harsh world."

"Oh, no. You are not going to try to justify your actions like that," I snapped. "Grandma was not like you." My heart threatened to pound out of my chest as I edged away from her.

Jessie stalked closer, gun steady on me. We circled around George. "She used to talk about you plenty, know that? But you were barely here. You grew up near Fresno, right? Like two and a half hours away?"

I shook my head, recognizing the manipulative meanness of her ploy. "What are you trying to do, prove you knew Grandma better than me? That doesn't even matter now." I looked around me for anything that might work as a makeshift weapon now that the shovel was out of easy reach. Too bad the police had taken the rest of Chase's furniture as evidence. I could use a folding chair about now, bust out some TV-style wrestling moves. "If you think there've been a lot of deputies around here the past few days, Jessie, watch what happens after I vanish. Detective Merrick is well aware of my investigation. He'll know I didn't go anywhere on my own, not with loads of cheese left in my fridges."

"You think I don't know that?" Her pitch verged on frantic. "But I have to do something, I have to!"

She was going to shoot me, I knew she was. I dropped down, grabbing a thin lichen-scaled branch as I rolled toward her. I must've taken her off guard, as she didn't fire. I thwacked the branch into her calves, feeling a sense of Hammurabi-style rightness for making her legs hurt even a tiny bit like mine were aching right now. Jessie fell, hitting the ground with a surprised gasp. The gun dropped into the leaves. I dove for it, but she knew right where I was going. She swung a leg around in a move reminiscent of an arcade fighting game, landing a foot in my gut.

I flopped backward, air shoved from my lungs. Blue sky and the upward-stretching canopy blurred as I forced myself to move, fast. I had to get to that gun before she did. I bounded up in time to see a figure loom behind her, bringing a branch much sturdier than mine in a baseball-bat-like swing against Jessie's head. The thud of impact resounded, grotesque and hollow. The sheer physics made Jessie spin in place before dropping limp beside George.

Giving me a full view of the very living, breathing figure of my grandma.

Chapter Twenty-One

Grandma had saved me from Jessie.

Grandma was alive. She was alive, alive, alive. The word tolled through my consciousness like a church bell. I felt woozy, and not just from pain. Grandma was here. She was real.

"You really did go frolicking with mermaids," I blurted.

Grandma furrowed her brow, an expression of annoyance, and pressed a finger to her lips. She wore clothes I'd never seen her in before, a black tracksuit like joggers used in cold weather – or joggers who sidelined as ninjas. Her usually curled, permed hair was cropped short and covered by a black hair net. I swallowed the urge to cry out to her as I drew closer, dragging my right foot. The bandages had ripped free. Blood soaked my pants leg.

She motioned to George with gloved hands. I peered close enough to see a handful of unused zip-ties sticking out of his flared jacket pocket. I nodded to show I understood – well, I comprehended what she wanted me to do with the ties, anyway. Everything else was a big spinning question mark.

How was she here? Where had she been for months? *Why hadn't she told me she was alive?*

Jessie was still unconscious. I bound her hands behind

her back. I fastened them with enough slackness so that she would have to go through extra effort to tighten them if she knew how to snap them off on her own. I repeated that with her ankles.

When that was done, Grandma motioned me away, deeper into the trees. She trod with precision. I noted she was stepping in the footprints left by police officers – and I was pretty sure she was wearing the same kind of black shoes worn by cops.

She'd come here prepared. But for what?

The shock of everything from the past hour seemed to strike me at once. Being attacked, kidnapped, watching a man die, facing death myself, Grandma's spontaneous resurrection. I bent over and retched. Grandma hovered close but she didn't touch me.

"That's good," she murmured when I was done. "Get it out. You've been through a lot today."

"That's *good?*" I echoed, incredulous. "How's it feel to come back from the dead, Grandma?"

Her smile was tight. She'd always worn a full face of makeup when she left the house. It was weird to see her bare faced. A lot of people probably wouldn't recognize her for that reason. "Not as wonderful as advertised, actually."

"You faked your death."

"Yes."

"How?"

"I've been swimming in the ocean my entire life." She sounded insulted that I'd asked. "I made sure that people witnessed me in distress, and then I swam underwater to a point farther away. I exited the water, went to the rental car I'd staged nearby, and carried on with my mission." There'd been no rental car charge on any of her accounts. She'd paid for that vehicle by some other means, some other identity. That fit with so many of her other antics: the car chases, the martial arts moves, the interference with law enforcement.

"Your *mission?*" I choked out. I wiped my sleeve over my mouth. I wanted to scream at her, demand to know why she'd done this, but the reason was suddenly clear. "Duvall Harmonson."

Grief flickered over her face and was gone like the shadow of a bird in flight. "Duvall Harmonson murdered my daughter," she snarled. "He murdered my only child. He murdered her husband, one of the kindest, gentlest men in this world. He devastated you. He did all that, and he was going to continue living his life of parties and privilege. I couldn't let that happen."

"Yeah, he devastated me, but you know what almost entirely obliterated me? Losing you. You let me think you were dead. Do you know how hard it's been?" My voice shook as I struggled to keep my volume down. Jessie wasn't dead. She could awaken at any time. She knew Grandma. Been inspired by her. Grandma, the murderer, inspiring another murderer.

Duvall Harmonson couldn't be the only person she killed, not with her interests. Merrick had even said she'd been considered a suspect more than once. She had known all of those lawyers for a reason – not simply as resources, but as her own private counsel. Rita had wondered how Grandma had acquired her property from Mr Slocombe years ago – land now worth millions. My bank account was plush, too, since I now owned everything. Where had those riches come from? Did I really want to know?

My parents had understood something nefarious was going on. Not the full truth, but enough to worry. They saw how Grandma wanted to train me. That's why they had tried to save me by keeping us apart for so much of my childhood.

"I'm sorry," Grandma said. "It was necessary. You needed to be innocent. I even made sure you had an alibi for the night Duvall was going to supposedly overdose."

I stared at her, thinking back to what Merrick had told me about the timing of Duvall Harmonson's death. "My coworkers came down sick. Food poisoning. I had to work overtime. You poisoned them, didn't you? You poisoned Duvall Harmonson, too. Fatally, in his case." I shook my head. Had those poisons been stored in that hidden nook in the Kitchen? "Where have you been since your 'drowning'? Oh, my gosh. These past few days. Grizz. He was with you, meeting somewhere out in the mountains. That's why he couldn't give Merrick an alibi."

Grandma's eyes glittered with both pride and sadness. "That's my girl. Yes, Grizz and I met up, with some unfortunate alignment in timing with the other attacks around here. I've made a point of staying far from Foghorn, but I took the risk now so that I could see how you were settling in. That new cat is a fine beast, by the way, even if he *is* mauling my curtains."

I rocked in place. "You unpacked some boxes for me. I thought my mind was being weirder than usual, that I was blanking out from stress and tiredness, but it was *you*."

"I wanted to help in some small ways."

"Help?" The word was strangled. I ached to vent my grief, my rage, the profound sense of betrayal that I felt. "Did Grizz know the whole time?" She nodded, and the horrible heat in my throat and head threatened to explode.

"Please, try to forgive him," she said softly. "It's broken his heart, keeping the truth from you."

"He's not the only one with a broken heart." I wiped my tears away with my sleeve.

"I love you, and I'm sorry." She looked past me, to where Jessie lay. "I need to go. You need to contact the authorities. I'm proud of you, Birdie."

I shook my head. Those words would have once made me beam, but now, what did her praise mean? So many people had told me that I was like her. Now, that felt like something gross stuck to my skin that I needed to scrub off.

My feelings showed on my face. I had never been able to mask with her. Grandma sighed. "I did what I had to do, Bird."

"What's going to keep me from saying you were here, that you are alive?" I asked. "You've obviously made an extreme effort to conceal your presence here today, but Merrick and other deputies know you. If I said you were really alive, they'd believe me."

"Ah, Merrick. He was such a green thing when he joined the department. Good on him for making detective." Grandma cocked her head, and I recognized the shift in her mannerisms. She didn't look at me as her granddaughter at the moment but as someone to outwit, to dismantle. "They would believe you when you said I was still alive, yes, but would they believe that you had been ignorant all this while? The house, the financial security you now experience – what would come of that? You never accepted my help with your college tuition. You were too proud. But now you have the stability to fully invest your time and energy into your cheese board business."

She outlined a nightmare with horrid plausibility. "Grandma–"

She wasn't done. "Would law enforcement here and in Fresno County truly believe that you weren't complicit in Duvall Harmonson's death? Grizz's role would be analyzed, too, as he *was* a true accomplice in my plot. You've worked hard these past few days, Bird, to prove his innocence and keep him from jail. At his age, how would he handle imprisonment? How would you handle it, knowing that it was your fault?"

Grandma had thought through everything. She always did.

"Now you've made me complicit too," I said hoarsely.

She shrugged, no regret in her eyes. "*That* wasn't in the plan, but I wasn't going to watch you die today."

I stepped away. "I love you, Grandma, but it was easier to grieve for you when I thought you were dead. Now I have to grieve for who I thought you were, too."

I stalked away, not with calm dignity, but with a dragging foot and throbbing pain across my body, the worst of it within my heart.

Jessie was still limp. I waited by her long enough to ascertain she still breathed, then thought to pick up the stick that Grandma had wielded against her. I gripped it all over, infuriated that I was contaminating evidence to protect Grandma. I was actually surprised she hadn't passed the stick to me right away – that was an unusual lapse on her part – but she was dealing with a lot of emotions right now, too. I used the stick for balance as I hobbled out of the grove.

I heard a familiar voice calling my name in the distance. I moved faster. "Dale!" I shouted, hoarse.

He was crouching by Belinda, who sat in the grass by George's SUV. She hadn't even made it to Jessie's car. At my voice, Dale jerked upright, relief painted boldly on his features.

"Bird!" He lurched like he wanted to run to me, but I waved for him to wait there. He needed to guard Belinda. "My God – are you okay?"

I blubbered out a laugh. "Not really, but I'm alive. Can you get a phone signal?" He held up his phone. I could now see that he'd parked behind George. By the dust still hovering in the air, he had just arrived. I could make out Jessie's car a little farther up the road.

"Is she dead? Is Jessie dead?" Belinda blurted, trembling all over.

"She's unconscious. Ready to be arrested, right along with you," I said. No point in being nice anymore.

"I get a signal here," Dale said. "I'm calling 9-1-1, but I'm not sure what to say."

"I do," I said, my stomach already sour with the lies I was about to tell.

Chapter Twenty-Two

Bowser yowled a welcome as I staggered through the front door of my house. Dale had an arm around my waist to help me limp along. Deputy Johnson was right with us, too.

Closing the door only dimmed the chaos of sirens outside. It seemed like the entire San Luis Obispo Sheriff's Department, with assistance from surrounding counties, had descended on my property, with the exception of Detective Merrick. He was being held up elsewhere – and I knew exactly where – and would be here as soon as possible.

"How can I help, Bird?" Dale asked.

"Help me to my bedroom. That way." I motioned with my head. I noted how Johnson was taking in the sight of my towers of boxes. Grandma had taught me to never let law enforcement into my living quarters because they could then search at will, but I figured it was safe to assume that my entire property was now going to be subject to a search warrant. I wasn't inclined to heed Grandma's advice at the moment, anyway.

"Hi, you," Deputy Johnson crooned, pausing to scratch Bowser under the chin. He didn't growl or swat her away, but he didn't deign to purr, either. He was perched on his usual favorite box in the living room. "Wait. I recognize this cat. Is this–"

"Yes, it's Chase Perkin's cat." I continued to trudge down the hallway. "Belinda was going to dump him. He's mine now."

"Does Detective Merrick know?" she called as she followed us.

"He knows I have a new orange cat." I couldn't see her face, but I could imagine the pursed lip look of criticism she was giving me. "When deputies search my house, can you please make sure that Bowser doesn't get outside or end up locked someplace away from his litter box, food, and water? You can see where those are." I vaguely waved behind me.

"I wish I could take him in for you for a day or two," Dale said.

"Don't feel bad about that, please. You're already juggling a lot of cats."

"We can cage Bowser while we search, and we'll make sure he has what he needs," Johnson said.

"If it looks like you'll be in hospital for longer than a day, I can come by to check on him as well, if you're fine with leaving me a key," Dale added.

I came to a stop near the foot of my bed and gazed around, overwhelmed. My stuff was partially unpacked and everywhere. My brain was likewise in disarray.

"My condition isn't anything dire," I said. But I still hurt. A lot.

An ambulance had been among the first emergency response vehicles to arrive on scene. With Belinda's tremendous medical debt on my mind, I'd refused treatment. I only had a modest medical insurance plan. No way did I want to pay the possibly $10,000-plus bill for an ambulance ride that wasn't necessary to save my life. Yeah, I had access to the wealth that Grandma had left me. Some other person might feel inclined to go on a spending spree, in light of recent revelations, but I had the sudden, profound urge to ignore that inheritance as much as I possibly could. I didn't know where that money had come from, but I had a strong hunch that the funds were dirty. I didn't like touching dirty things.

I was still going to the nearest hospital in San Luis Obispo, though. Dale had volunteered to be my ride.

He politely waited near the entrance to my room as I hobbled around, grabbing items to pack. It was weird to have him there. I was suddenly glad that I'd made the bed. I was glad that I was still alive and walking around, even if that movement pained me.

Grandma was alive, too. Alive, and a murderer. Alive, and forcing me to be complicit in her crimes. Horrible images fluttered through my brain. I had seen a man get shot in the head. I had been kidnapped. My hands shook as I grabbed pajamas from a drawer.

"Focus, Bird," I muttered beneath my breath, and kept moving.

"Detective Merrick is almost to Foghorn," Deputy Johnson called to me, relaying an update from dispatch.

"Good. If he's not quite here, we have time for one more thing." I emerged from the bathroom to stuff toiletries into my suitcase, then zipped it shut.

I led Dale and Deputy Johnson to the kitchen, where I pulled the cheese from its safe spot in the microwave.

"Miss Nichols, really?" Deputy Johnson asked, incredulous.

"Yes, really." I gave her an even look. "This isn't me being obsessive, but practical. I'm incredibly shaky right now, and getting some food in my belly will help alleviate that.

Plus, I know how hospitals are. It may take me hours to get checked in, and who knows when or if I'll get food." Johnson conceded my point with a grimace and nod. "Dale, please join in, if you want. You have some long hours ahead of you, too. Deputy Johnson, please feel free to partake."

"No, thank you, ma'am," she said, ever the consummate professional even as she eyed the platter with blatant interest.

When I'd put everything together hours before, I'd imagined how I'd present the cheeses to Dale, highlighting the origins, the different uses for the cheeses, and just generally geeking out. None of that was appropriate now, but I still felt a profound sense of sober appreciation. Dale joined me, small sounds of enjoyment escaping his throat as he ate the Vella and the coated goat cheese. I pulled the prosciutto roses from the fridge, too, but resolved to save the gjetost for later.

"This snack doesn't count toward the lunch debt I owe you," I said to Dale as we finished up.

"Understood." He cringed as he watched me slowly rise. "I really need to get you to the hosp–"

Loud, clipped knocks thudded through the front door. The knock sounded like it was that of a cop.

I looked to Deputy Johnson. "That'll be Detective Merrick," she said.

She opened the door to admit not only Merrick in his usual black coat, but Grizz, looking more haggard than usual. He almost shoved the detective aside to gaze at me up and down.

"You– Are you hurt? How are you?"

How was I? Not well, really, not that I could confess the whole how and why of that at the moment. I felt a spike of pain that went way deeper than my leg. Grizz had lied to me for months even as he comforted me through my grief. He'd known all along that Grandma was alive. He'd probably been in on the whole faked-death plot from the get-go.

And now I had to add more lies to the pile.

"I'm okay, all considered, but I'm going to get checked out at the hospital. Dale's taking me." Even on a good day, Grizz drove like a Hollywood stunt man with abrupt stops and careening corners. He did not need to get behind the wheel in his current emotional state. He looked like he'd been literally ripping his hair out, and he didn't have much more to lose.

Really, Grizz was accurate when he commented a few days ago that Ray was a lot like him. Ray had been Chase's minion. Grizz was the same way with Grandma. He adored her. He'd do anything for her. He had. But he adored and loved me, too, and the secrets he'd been forced into had probably been eating him up like acid.

I couldn't stay angry at Grizz, I couldn't. He was, as far as I was concerned, the family that I had left.

"Mr Ferreira here was about to get arrested as he demanded access to the crime scene to find you," Merrick said.

"I tried calling you! I even *texted* you!" Grizz said, and I felt such a swell of pride and dismay all at the same time.

"You used your phone the one time I couldn't reply," I said. "The deputies have my phone and watch for the time being. I'm so sorry that you were worried." I opened my arms wide, and he rushed into my grip. Off to one side, Merrick and Johnson were conferring, while Dale and Bowser were likewise engaged in deep conversation. Bowser had a perturbed yet tolerant expression that reminded me of an irate customer mentally composing a complaint letter to a manager.

"She saved me," I whispered near Grizz's ear. No need to clarify who "she" was.

"You know the truth," he said in a soft breath, slumping against me. "I'm sorry. I'm sorry. I wish–"

I gave him a warning squeeze. Merrick was keeping an eye on us.

"Yeah. I wish a lot of things had gone differently." I pulled back, but still leaned on him to keep my balance. Merrick and Johnson faced me.

"Deputy Johnson will follow you to the hospital and stay with you there," said Merrick. "We're not releasing names to the media at this time, but reporters will probably be watching the hospital. She and the other deputies will ensure you're not pestered as you get care, Miss Nichols. I'll be there soon to talk with you." Merrick eyed Bowser with a grimace. Bowser responded to the recognition with a toothy yawn. "We have a lot to discuss."

"We unfortunately do. Dale, can I ask you to get some things for me?" He gave me a nod. "There's the suitcase, of course, and my purse is hanging from the back of the dining room chair. Detective, should I get permission from you before I ask him to pull something from a drawer?"

"What do you need?" Merrick asked.

"Grandma's old cell phone and chargers. The sheriff's department already went through her phone months ago. She left it in her car the day she..." I let my sentence trail off, unsure of how to continue. "I need to call some friends to let them know what happened."

That was part of the reason. Most of all, I needed access to the list of lawyers in Grandma's contacts, but I wasn't going to tell Merrick that. He'd find out when we had new company during my interrogation at the hospital.

If I was going to spend Grandma's money on anything today, I was going to splurge on legal protection.

Merrick himself pulled out the sandwich bag that held the phone and chargers, gave it all a once-over, then let Dale put everything in my purse.

We were ready to go, then. I turned to address Bowser. He was in a bread-loaf pose, his paws tucked beneath his body and almost invisible.

"You keep on guarding the house, just as you have been," I said, testing my balance to give him a brief scratch between the ears. His eyes narrowed to happy slits, and I was incredibly pleased to hear and feel a rumbly purr. I leaned close to him to whisper, "Feel free to shred the curtains, too. They were Grandma's style. They aren't mine."

Chapter Twenty-Three

As Mollie drove me home on a sunny Saturday late morning, she'd offered to stop off at any store so I could get whatever I needed and avoid driving for a while. I told her I didn't need anything, which was a kinda-sorta lie. Really, I just wanted to get home as soon as possible. A new home for me, yeah, but a place I'd known my entire life.

Once there, I promptly had a good chat with Bowser about the questions that had been bubbling in my head throughout my hours away, things I couldn't ask anyone else. Where was Grandma now? What was she up to? What else had she done?

Bowser listened to me with perked ears, rolled over atop my feet, then briskly led me to his food bowl. It was still about 2/3 full but had a quarter-sized spot at the bottom where the base was visible.

"You poor starving baby," I said, shaking the bowl to even out the food. His glower made clear his profound disappointment in me, then he lowered himself to eat.

I walked through the house and Kitchen. The deputies' search had barely shuffled things around, but then, Merrick had told me that the intent of checking indoors was to see if George had encroached there. I was glad they hadn't taken an opportunity to trash everything, just because. Though

I'm sure Bowser would offer vehement disagreement if he could, I thought the food and water amounts in his bowls were strangely high; I had a hunch that was Deputy Johnson's doing.

I did a quick check on my kitchen and cat supplies, then I drove into Foghorn. Slowly. Carefully. My doctor hadn't forbidden me from driving but had advised me to limit any physical activity that used my legs. Fresh stitches extended down my right calf like a clumsy seam. They felt weird, too. Like my skin was on too tight.

I parked halfway between Quesoquick and the grocery store.

At the counter window, Dale's expression flickered between joy and frustration as I joined a long line at Quesoquick. I had seven groups ahead of me. He looked to be working alone, so there was no way for us to talk right away. I was okay with that. I was just... glad to be there. Alive. Breathing in the refreshing scent of ocean saltiness mixed with baked bread and hot cheese.

Finally, I reached the front. No one stood behind me.

"Bird! I'm so relieved to see you!" Dale vanished within the small building, and two seconds later, I heard the heavy metallic bang of a door. He rounded the corner to stand there, staring at me with a big grin. "Can I hug you? Is that all right?"

"That's fine. Just be gentle. I ended up getting some stitches on a shoulder blade, too, and some swathes of skin look like how a stormy sky is described during a tornado. It'd be cool if it didn't hurt so much."

"Pain is something of a bummer." His hug was warm and perfectly gentle. My cheek ended up pressed right against his chest and the embroidered logo for Quesoquick. I could actually feel his fast-fluttering heartbeat, which made my heart flutter a few extra beats, too. He stepped back. "Thank you for the texts a while ago. I was glad to know you didn't have to stay overnight at hospital."

"So was I. I got to my friend Mollie's place about midnight. I didn't want to text you right then and wake you up."

"You likely wouldn't have awakened me. I didn't sleep well." His smile was tight.

I only nodded. My efforts to sleep on Mollie's couch had been haunted by the sound, the percussive violent feel, of gunshots in close proximity. I didn't know how many times I'd jolted upright, gasping.

"Did your new lawyer work out?" Dale asked. He knew about that plan because I'd started calling lawyers as he drove me to S-L-O. I still regarded it as a minor miracle that the car charger for Grandma's phone was compatible with his Hyundai.

"Yes. I had about an hour to talk with Mrs Higgy before the detective arrived. I felt better with her there, too." I didn't want to bring up that two FBI agents had also come by and asked a lot of questions about Chase and George. They didn't offer me much info in turn, but I inferred that they'd been after George for some time.

I'd had a lot of experience with lawyers in the past year between my parents' death case and Grandma setting me up as her successor. Those lawyers had worn suits and shrewd expressions. Mrs Higgy had shown up at eight o'clock on a Friday night wearing a sweatshirt with a front graphic of an adorable smiling piglet. Her hair was pulled back into two long, silver braids.

"I was gardening with my grandkids for half the day," she'd said after shaking my hand, then motioned to her shirt. "My eldest grandchild realized at a young age that Higgy rhymes with 'piggy,' and now I get new shirts like this every Christmas. I do dress up a bit more for court. Now, it sounds like you and your grandmother have some common bonds, too. You both get into barrels of mischief. Tell me the whole story from the top."

I did, of course omitting the fact that Grandma was still alive.

"Dale." I hesitated. "Have you heard about Jessie?"

Dale turned a deeper shade of pale. "No. The radio news this morning simply said the suspect was unconscious. Has she– Did she–"

I leaned on the building to take weight off of my bad leg. "She's not dead, no, but it seems unlikely she'll wake up. No brain activity is being detected." My throat was so tight I could barely squeeze out the words.

"Oh," he said softly, deflating.

Grandma had struck Jessie with all the strength of a Major League Baseball player at bat. The brain damage was apparently catastrophic. Of course, Merrick had informed me and my lawyer of Jessie's condition because I was supposedly the cause. Mrs Higgy had assured me that I had a clear case for self-defense, but that didn't comfort me a whole lot.

I hadn't struck the blow, but Jessie's life was effectively over because of me. Grandma had known what she was doing when she jumped to my defense. She made sure that Jessie would never be able to testify that Lucille Franklin was still alive.

I'd liked Jessie. She'd been nice to me, up to a point. She'd made awesome grilled cheese sandwiches! I wanted to think that we'd been friends. I understood that whatever sense of betrayal I felt, though, was nothing compared to what Dale, Maurice, and others who knew her were experiencing.

How many people had Grandma killed over the years? How many had she poisoned, how many had she made certain to silence? I knew I wouldn't like those answers, but I also knew I wouldn't feel any kind of peace until I understood who and what Grandma truly was.

"This is all hard to take in," Dale murmured. "I've known Jessie for years. She began working for me before our grand opening. I don't suppose the detective mentioned how Belinda is doing?"

"He said she was in the hospital, but he didn't offer anything else. I haven't heard any updates this morning." It wasn't hard to imagine Belinda experiencing a complete mental and physical breakdown after what had happened, especially if she knew about Jessie's condition.

"A tragedy all around." As Dale shook his head, he stared back at the restaurant. "By the way, I have something for you. I almost called up the sheriff's department this morning, but I wanted to ask you about it first."

Dread came over me with a chill. "What is it?"

"A card was left tucked in the shop window overnight, addressed to you. Would you like me to get it?"

"Yes, please. Didn't you say before that you had a security camera at your window? Did it catch anyone?"

"Funny, that. I checked the footage. No one directly approached during the night. All I can guess is that whoever placed the card did so by leaning over from the building's corner. I hadn't realized that there was a blind spot there."

A minute later, he handed me a plain white card. My name was printed in block letters on the front, the penmanship unfamiliar. A dove sticker acted as the envelope's seal. I pried the flap open to find a card with Christian religious iconography: a wooden cross, sunset clouds, silhouetted mountains. "TAKE COMFORT!" read the text. I opened the card.

There was no preprinted text, and the loopy handwriting here looked different from what was on the envelope: "Remember when times are tough that you are being watched over from above." There was no signature. None was needed.

I stroked the letters, remembering a lesson from Grandma when I was maybe six. I'd been so proud that I could write whole sentences in school. Grandma had then told me, "You can actually write using different penmanship, Bird, pretending that you're someone else. Let me show you."

She had then rewritten a simple sentence about fifty times over on the same sheet, each one in a different hand. I'd been awed and inspired, and tried to replicate her efforts myself. In hindsight, I had done a terrible job, especially with a cursive line, but she'd praised me nevertheless and told me to keep practicing.

I knew with horrible certainty that this card came from Grandma.

She was going to continue to watch over me from afar. She probably fancied herself as my guardian angel, but I didn't take any comfort in the notion. As far as I was concerned, she had fallen from heaven.

"This is super creepy," I said in all honesty, showing the card to Dale.

"Dear God, Bird. That looks like it's from a stalker. Why did they leave it here? Was it– Oh no, your last social media post was about your visit to Quesoquick. I haven't seen your name released in the news, though. I haven't seen

Quesoquick mentioned, either, but I suppose it's a matter of time until reporters show up. Everyone around here knows who was involved."

"I'm sorry, Dale." I hated to think that his livelihood would suffer because of what had happened.

"This isn't your fault," he admonished. Several car doors thudded in sequence nearby. "We'll get through this together, won't we? I must get back inside, but oh!" He stopped a few steps away. "Do you want a sandwich? I'll throw something together for you."

"Thank you! I'm starving. You pick the sandwich. I trust you."

He gave me a quick smile as he hurried away. I stuck the card in my purse.

A family passed by me, headed to Quesoquick. I spied another figure approaching, too: Rita. She marched toward me with a grimace, probably ready to berate me for bringing disgrace upon Foghorn.

If so, I couldn't be mad at her. She had been right about Grandma, after all, not that I could admit that outright. I needed to say something affirmative to her, though. She needed to know I didn't hold a grudge.

"Bird." She eyed me warily. "I heard you were in the hospital. How are you?"

Huh. I hadn't expected an inquiry after my wellbeing. "Pretty banged up but happy to be alive." I extended my hand toward her. She gawked at me as if I held a rattlesnake. "When we spoke recently, I accused you of having a good motive to kill Chase. I said that more out of anger than anything, and it was wrong of me. I'm sorry."

She still looked at me askance. "Your grandmother never apologized for anything."

"I," I said hotly, "am not my grandma."

Rita absorbed that statement with a pensive expression, then accepted my handshake. Her grip was firm, businesslike, and after a few seconds, we let go. "I see that. Yes. But strange things have still happened around Foghorn since you showed up. Oh, Chase had caused trouble for ages, but then everything..." She paused, seeming to struggle for a word. "Culminated. After you moved in."

"I don't understand why everything happened as it did, either. Or why so many things happened here over decades, with Grandma meddling all the time. I'm left with a lot of questions about her, actually. I don't even know how she acquired her property from Mr Slocombe. I'd really like to understand the history between them since the land is now mine. Maybe we can talk sometime?"

"I don't have clear answers about that matter, either, but I might be able to find something. Maybe." She was no longer scrutinizing me as if I gripped a rattlesnake but as if I held something weird, like a hot dog without a bun. "I'm glad to see you're out of the hospital, in any case. I thought–" Rita shook her head. "Get well soon." With that, she strode away, heels clip-clopping on the asphalt.

I stared after her. That sure ended abruptly. What had she stopped herself from saying? At least she was no longer regarding me with outright animosity. Progress!

A child skipped past me singing, "French fries, French fries, I'm gonna eat all the French fries!"

"No you're not. You're sharing!" said a woman about my age as she trudged past, carrying a paper bag freckled with large grease spots.

"Hey, Bird!" I glanced back at Quesoquick. Dale waved to me from the side door. He hoisted up a bag. It didn't have grease spots, at least, not yet. He continued to talk as I hobbled closer. "I made you one of my favorites, our San Joaquin Style Chicken Sandwich. It has white cheddar cheese, mozzarella, finely shredded grilled chicken, and crumbled bacon, served with a side of ranch dressing."

I gasped in delight. "I don't even remember telling you that I'm from the San Joaquin Valley!"

Dale blushed. "You are? I promise, I didn't know! One of our former employees was from Lemoore and created the combination. I thought he was jesting when he first told me that it's popular to dip pizza slices in ranch there."

"It's no joke. When I was in school, pizza was never served without ranch, though I didn't even give it a try until I was a teenager. I was too sensitive to textures to try dipping any foods when I was young. This sandwich combination sounds fantastic, thank you."

"You'll need to try our pepperoni pizza version of the sandwich sometime, too. I put our flash-fried green beans in the bag just now. I like them even more than our fries, but those are also delicious. No need to pay me today. Please, just accept the meal."

"Well, I won't argue with you, but I will still reciprocate with a personal cheeseboard. I owe you several at this point."

"I'm fine with continuing a meal trade." We grinned at each other as I accepted the bag.

"Thanks for the food. And the ride to the hospital. And everything." I waved my free hand to encompass the chaos of recent days.

"I'm glad you haven't been scared away from Foghorn. It's a sleepy place, usually."

Would Foghorn become sleepy again, or was the

weirdness going to continue? If Grandma was lurking around, I felt like the latter was the better bet. Maybe it was unfair to blame Grandma entirely, though. I had every intention of rummaging for answers in the next while, and I had a hunch I'd disturb some cockroaches.

"I'm not going anywhere. All my cheese is here!" I said, managing a little laugh. Dale laughed, too. I kept a forced smile on my face as a car slowly rolled by Quesoquick. The driver was wearing a hood and I had a two-second view of their face.

I recognized Grandma. She was smiling.

She'd taken a big risk coming where she was most likely to be recognized. She probably intended to comfort me, but I felt her presence like a slap.

"Is something the matter, Bird?" Dale asked. I apparently hadn't hidden my reaction well.

"I should get off my feet and enjoy this food." I would enjoy it, too, despite the dismal circumstances around us and the difficult questions that were to come. I was alive. I had an ooey-gooey cheese combination in my hand, a super-nice guy looking out for me, and an orange cat making my home extra homey. All considered, I was pretty darn lucky.

Recipe for
Nutty and Fruity Chevre Balls

These easy goat cheese rounds are great on a cheese board alongside other cheeses, or as an appetizer, or can be part of a simple meal for one or two people.

> *4 ounces plain goat cheese log*
> *3 tablespoons candied walnuts or other nuts*
> *3 tablespoons golden raisins or other dried fruit*

1. Divide the cheese log into quarters. Compress and roll each into a small ball. Place them on a piece of waxed paper and set them in the freezer while the next ingredients are prepared.

2. Use a cutting board and knife to chop the walnuts into small pieces. Place them in a bowl. Use kitchen shears to shred the raisins into smaller pieces. Add them to the walnuts, and mix.

3. Bring out the cheese balls. Roll each in the bowl, using fingertips to press in the nut and fruit bits to fill in empty spots.

4. Store the cheese in the fridge until near serving time. Cheese is at its best when brought to room temperature after sitting out at least thirty minutes. If the cheese is softer, it will also be easier to slice or press onto bread or hearty crackers for serving. A drizzle of honey atop these cheese balls can add sweetness and a pleasant textural contrast. Or, the cheese balls can be halved then wrapped in half a slice of bacon (or a pig meat alternative) to use as a yummy appetizer. Or, eat the cheese straight. Whatever brings you joy.

Store any leftover (it can happen!) chevre balls covered in the fridge. They'll keep for at least two days – and who knows, maybe they can last for a week, but a person will need fortitude to resist the cheese for such a long stretch.

Acknowledgments

Foremost, I extend my gratitude to a whole lot of people. This book wouldn't be here without the help of my agent, Rebecca Strauss at DeFiore & Company. My husband, Jason, enables my cheese habit by driving me to many gourmet markets and grocery stores that I otherwise could not access; I do love him more than cheese, as the sign on our fireplace mantle attests. The team here at Datura has been wonderful. Big thanks to my editor Gemma Creffield, developmental editor April Northall, and everyone else who made my book a reality.

Readers, thank you for visiting the fictional village of Foghorn. I envision it as a small pocket universe tucked between San Simeon and Piedras Blancas Light Station along Highway 1. Many of the major locations I mention in the area, such as Morro Rock, are quite real, and I highly suggest a visit. The Central Coast is less glamorous than other parts of the California shore. More rustic, more homey, a great place to get a sourdough bread bowl full of clam chowder followed by a slice of olallieberry pie for dessert. It's where the people from the San Joaquin Valley go for vacation; that was the case for my protagonist Bird as she grew up, and that was also true for me as a kid in nearby Hanford.

As a child, I was precocious, imaginative, and immersed in books from age two. I was also often told I was "weird." I was clueless about social cues, overwhelmed in many settings, and obsessive about horses, food, and many other subjects in turn. By the time I was in 3rd grade, I was quite certain I was a time traveler or an alien, or perhaps both. What was certain was that I didn't belong in this time or place. As a girl, of course, I was told I was oversensitive, that I needed to develop a thicker skin, that something was wrong with me, that a prescription or two would make things all better (spoiler alert: they didn't).

I'm in my forties now, and I know I'm not a time traveler or an alien, but for a few years now, I've been diagnosed as autistic, and the world makes more sense. My understanding of myself was helped immensely through my experiences as the mom of an autistic child (now in college!) who happens to have a very different personality and interests, but oh boy, we still have an awful lot in common. The DNA runs true and strong.

If you see some of yourself in Bird Nichols, consider getting tested for autism and neurodiversity – but also go into that process with the awareness that official testing can be expensive and difficult to access. There are online tests for diagnosing yourself, too. Whatever your path, I hope you find self-validation and peace.

The cheeses I vividly describe in this book are real, glorious, and out there, waiting to be consumed. The artisanal cheese business is hard, people, and these last few years have been especially difficult for the industry. Wherever you are in the world, please, support your local cheesemakers and mongers whenever and however you can. They are modern purveyors of an art of preservation that has truly kept humanity alive across time. As Bird might well say, cheese makes a house a home, but it also makes us happy. We all need more happiness these days, right?

Go forth and be cheesy, my friends.